AN ISLE

FOR THE

AGES

Gary D. Henry

Whimsical Publications, LLC

Florida

An Isle for the Ages is a work of fiction. Names, characters, and incidents are the products of the author's imagination and are either fictitious or are used fictitiously. Any resemblance to actual events or persons, living or dead, is entirely coincidental.

To purchase the authorized electronic edition of *An Isle for the Ages*, visit www.whimsicalpublications.com

Cover art by Traci Markou
Editing by Brieanna Robertson

ISBN-13: 978-1-940707-90-7

Published by
Whimsical Publications, LLC
Florida

She pointed the boat in a certain direction and playfully commanded Bronson to do her bidding as the captain of the boat. Amazed that she found humor in their dire state, Bronson laughed as she joyfully mocked him at the helm. However, one time, she pointed to the horizon and yelled, "Land!"

Bronson looked to where she pointed and his smile turned to horror as he walked to the wheel and removed her from her lofty perch.

"I'm sorry, sweetheart, but that's not land. It's another storm and it's approaching us fast."

"A storm? Oh dear God! Steer toward the island, Bronson, I don't want to go through that again," she said as she gladly returned control to her husband.

"There is no island, Catherine!" he stated firmly. "We can't outrun this storm. We have no sails and we have no engines. It's coming in too fast. Go down below and strap yourself in!"

"No, not this time! I will stay here with you," she stated as she started to buckle herself in on deck.

"Please, Cathy, I don't have time to argue. The waves will break your tether and I don't want to lose you. Please do as I ask. If it goes bad, I will come and get you. Our rescue boat is stocked and ready should the old girl not be able to stand up to this storm."

Catherine complied because she knew he had a lot on his mind and she did not want to be another problem.

The storm came upon them quickly and felt like a head-on collision. It hit the boat broadside, nearly capsizing the huge vessel. The boat survived the first salvo, but surely weakened further. Bronson struggled to turn against the might of the sudden storm's surges.

The storm did not have the voracity of the previous one, but without the controls or sails in place, it worried him greatly.

The rudder had no hydraulic system, which made steering very taxing to Bronson despite his strength. He could not direct the boat into the swells. The waves crashed against its side, causing it to change direction on a dime. For the first time, Bronson had serious thoughts of giving up the battle. Struggle as he might, he could not gather control. The waves poured over the deck and the rain stung his face relentlessly.

In the valley of the swells, he noticed the boat list to the right. He tied the wheel, hoping the newly repaired rudder held against the mighty pressures of the undersea forces pushing against it.

Bronson dangerously unhooked his tether and walked across the deck, but a wave caught him in the back and sent him flailing over the rail. Holding on for dear life, he thought about his helpless wife in the lower deck's chamber and gathered enough strength to pull himself back on board. His injured arm gave way, but his other arm held strong.

The violently rocking boat tossed Catherine around below deck, but her tether held her firmly in her seat. The boat took on a lot of water again, now in danger of sinking. The storm subsided as quickly as it came about. The seas slowly returned to normal after an hour of taking a beating. The boat listed badly to the right, and about to sink into the abyss.

Bronson went below to check on Catherine. She'd avoided the larger objects jettisoned toward her, but a laptop computer slammed against her head, rendering her unconscious. Wet and bleeding slightly, he gathered her up in his arms, carried her to the waiting lifeboat, and gently placed her on a small mattress in the large rescue craft that floated on its own, tethered to the sinking boat. He found some dry blankets and lovingly placed them over his wife. He returned many times to the cabin to gather last-minute supplies for their new journey on a decidedly smaller craft. The yacht took on more water, beyond repair.

It stayed afloat long enough for him to gather things too important not to take. Catherine's plastic-encased photo albums made their way onto the boat. Finally, he had everything he needed. He released the Sea-Doo from his lifeboat because it had sustained irreversible damage. It sank immediately. He cut the rope from his majestic boat, and they floated away.

Catherine did not witness the sorrowful event of seeing their wonderful boat silently sink below the water's surface. He bid farewell to his friend of forty-eight years and actually believed that it treaded water just long enough to supply him with sufficient time to gather as much as he could in order to continue his fight for survival.

Dedication

This book is dedicated to my sister and editor, Belinda Bell, who left us too soon.

Live your life to the fullest. Create a wealth of memories in your lifetime and relive them as often as you can, because memories will be your riches when your allotted time on this Earth has been expended.

Reflection will be your last greatest moment.

PART 1

Chapter One

The Plan

It all started innocently enough for young Bronson Pre-minger as he looked out over the Pacific Ocean with his beautiful twenty-five-year-old wife, Catherine, both yearning to travel the high seas again. All adventures end in death, but their adventure endured for a century and a half with minds full of memories of their time together. They talked about their miracle often, but Catherine loved to listen to it repeatedly through Bronson's soft, melodious voice. They thought it was funny that their new life together had started when Bronson turned seventy years old and Catherine sixty-eight, and the only plan they'd had for the future was a sui-cide pact that they wanted to implement because of Cathe-rine's mind-destroying illness. There have been many stories told about the famed couple; most were outrageously false, but Bronson and others remembered it like this...

Murray and Brooke Parsons sat in the harbor restaurant overlooking the marina waiting for Brooke's parents to join them. Looking out through the large window, they saw many expensive boats bobbing in the water, moored at the long, wide, weathered-planked pier. Murray asked, "Which is your father's boat?"

She looked out, trying to find a distinguishing attribute; they all looked similar. She finally pointed. "It's the one at the end of the pier. The big one."

"Honey, they're all big ones. I can't see the one on the

end. I tell you what, your dad won't be here for another hour. Let's go take a look at it." He got up from the table and reached for Brooke's hand.

She rose from her seat, grabbed his hand, and they strolled outside as the last of the mist on the water dissipated in the morning sun. "They seldom have taken me sailing since my brother died. However, that was not all their fault considering my hectic life. I haven't seen the boat since our wedding," she said as she guided Murray to the gate access to the pier.

Murray closed the gate behind them and they walked toward the docks as the bright early morning sun peeked out from behind a cloud, causing a glimmer on the water all the way to the breakwater barrier. With Catherine still lovingly holding Bronson's hand, they walked to the end of the pier, passing many multimillion-dollar yachts. Arriving at the boat, the sheer size of the old but luxurious vessel amazed Murray.

Seeing the storied boat again with its folded white sails and clean lines made her nostalgic for a time gone by. The huge yacht bobbed gently as another boat sailed by, creating a small wake that licked its hull. The boat brought back fond memories for Brooke of a time when the whole family sailed together. Remembering the many times she excitedly stepped aboard, wondering what memorable adventures lay ahead of her; she mostly remembered her older brother, Bradley, who died at twenty-two fighting in the first Gulf War, when Iraq invaded Kuwait in 1990.

She mentioned Bradley often to Murray, and he knew that the memory both hurt her and made her smile, but he never stopped her from recalling her times with her big brother.

Murray eyed the length of the boat and shaded his eyes with his hands to peer up to the massive naked mast. "He's able to sail this alone? This must be a hundred-footer!"

Walking toward the gangplank, she explained, "It's a hundred and fifty feet. My dad has sailed this boat for forty-eight years. He and my mother were married on it and both have sailed on this yearly ever since." Stepping onto the boat, she continued, "He bought it new in 1965, but has renovated it a few times over the years. They nearly sailed around the world ten years ago before they experienced engine trouble and had to curtail their trip. My father may be seventy years old, but he's in great shape. I've seen him take the boat out and return weeks later, countless times." She pointed at a new, stylistic name painted on the back of the boat and muttered, "Murray! He changed the name of the boat! Why did he do that?"

Seeing that the new moniker appeared to upset her, Murray asked, "What does it mean when the boat's name is changed? Why does changing the name of the boat frighten you?"

"He named it *The Atlantic Eagle* just after he bought it. Now he's changed it to *Sailing Into Our Sunset.* This is not good!"

Murray asked, "Why?"

Brooke explained, "A captain never changes the name of his boat. It's considered bad luck. He told me that a hundred times. Superstition has it that they change the name of their boat when they intentionally sink it after it falls into disrepair. It supposedly protects the original name from being associated with a boat that has sunk."

Spying the boat's caretaker polishing the chrome on a much smaller boat, she walked over to him, leaving Murray to look over the massive yacht on his own.

Jose Rodriguez, with his wrinkled face and weathered look, worked on her father's yacht. Bronson had the largest boat in the marina and its upkeep took up too much of his time, so he hired Jose to do most of the work.

"Jose, when did dad change the name of his boat?" Brooke asked as Jose stopped polishing, wiped his hands, and greeted her with a broad smile.

"Is that little Brooke? I haven't seen you in two years." He climbed out of the boat and hugged her. "He had me change it just a few days ago. Do you like it?"

They both looked at the stylishly written words.

"Why did he do it?"

"I don't know, he just came up to me and told me to change it. It's a great old boat. Gassed up and ready to go."

"Go where? Is he going to take it out?"

"Yep, tomorrow, I think. He told me that he wanted to take your mother out for their anniversary. First time he's going out without a crew."

"He's seventy! Can he handle it alone?"

"I've known your father for going on forty years. He's a tough old bird. With or without a crew, he can handle it. You should know better after that storm they hit seven years ago." Jose paused as tears welled up in Brooke's eyes. "He'll be fine. He may be seventy, but his mind is as sharp as ever; besides, you tell him that he's too old to sail and see what kind of response you get." He smiled broadly.

"Not me! But I'll find out why he changed the name." She waved goodbye to Jose and hurriedly walked back over to Murray, who awaited her return. They stepped aboard to see the living quarters, having already walked around one side of the boat's exterior.

"He changed it a few days ago. There's something he's not telling me," Brooke muttered.

Bewildered, Murray noticed Brooke's determined gaze and faster pace. "Why are you so concerned?"

"Murray, he's planning something. I just know it!"

"Well, ask him when he arrives. Can we see inside?"

Brooke held out her hand. Murray helped her onto the boat.

He noticed the pained look on Brooke's face as she walked around the boat's main deck, which indicated to him that she had strong feelings about being aboard again. They walked to the bridge where her father once allowed her to steer the massive boat when she barely stood taller than the wheel. She pointed to a tarnished plaque above it. It read: *Dedicated in 1967 to my wonderful and beautiful new wife, Catherine Preminger, and to my son Bradley, born to us in 1968, and to my beautiful daughter Brooke, born to us in 1979. I am a blessed and profoundly proud father.*

Brooke ran her trembling fingers over the words. "He added me and Bradley as we were born."

She grabbed Murray's hand and led him to the living quarters of the boat, looking back at the plaque one last time.

The sea air wafted through the enormous cabin from an open window and mixed with the finely polished cedar and teak, creating an aromatic scent that made a sensual and relaxing setting. There was a complete kitchen equipped with the finest stainless steel appliances all neatly tucked away within the windowed cabinets under finely polished granite countertops. There was a spacious, plush living area with comfortable chairs, and a full bar. They toured the six huge and perfectly adorned bedrooms, as well as the three massive full bathrooms.

A collage of travel photos from over the years, and of people Brooke's parents met in many ports of calls around the world, adorned three walls in the living area.

Murray sat down on a fine leather chair to gather it all in. "This is amazing! How much did all this cost?"

"In 1965, I think he paid one hundred and fifty thousand dollars. It's worth well over ten million now. Well, we'd better get back. Dad should be arriving at the restaurant soon."

Reluctant to leave the relaxing atmosphere of the boat, he finally relented, held out his hand, and walked with Brooke back to the gangplank. He helped Brooke out of the boat and tears welled up in her eyes as she gazed back at the name emblazoned on the back of the boat.

Murray asked, "Why are you getting emotional?"

"I don't know!" Her face tensed up and she turned her back on him.

Walking back to the restaurant, he implored her to open up, but she could not find words adequate to explain her fluctuating emotions. She feared her intuition. She knew her parents well and how much they depended on and loved each other. Her tears dried up in the early morning sun as they reentered the restaurant and sat down, awaiting her parents' arrival.

Her father, Bronson Preminger, walked toward them. His face, lined by years of responsibility, still possessed the shadow of the chiseled features he proudly presented as a younger man. Brooke loved the man who traveled across the globe just to attend a simple birthday party, a special event, or any time she needed a loving shoulder to cry on. As a toddler, she did not understand why his job took him away as much as it did, but later she realized the importance of his many secretive missions for the Navy.

The nearer her father, the safer she felt, because his happy nature made her smile even though there were times when she did not want to be happy.

She had difficulty holding a scowl with him around; he went out of his way to pull a smile out of her before he left the house for any reason, but especially when the Navy planned another six-month absence.

Her father had had many nicknames over the years. During his naval days, he captained one of the largest aircraft carriers in the fleet. His superiors called him "The Sea Warrior," but the men he led called him "The Saint of the Sea," and both factions adored him as a seaman and a commander. His knowledge of warfare and the sea carried him to unparalleled heights in the annals of naval lore and his ships' logs stood as teaching tools for up-and-coming leaders of the sea. Around the docks, mariners called him "The Gray Captain," but the name he liked most was when Brooke called him "Dad," the only moniker reserved for him and him only.

Tall in stature, Bronson had a mane of long, thick white hair and a youthful gait that belied his seventy years. He wore an old sailor's cap embroidered with the names of the last of three naval ships he had captained during his career, proudly presented beginning with the first destroyer, the *U.S.S. Warrior*, he commanded. He never replaced the old, worn hat because he considered it his good luck charm.

Always happy around boats and the water, he wore a perpetual smile on his face at the marina. Looking out at the boats and water as a child, seeing his first swimming pool, or experiencing his first fishing adventure, he reveled in the experience. Thoughts of wars and past responsibilities vanished, replaced with a childlike demeanor that Brooke loved. She saw right away how her mother had fallen deeply and instantly in love with the man. He garnered accolades from ships' cooks to presidents, but he gathered the most awards as a loving father and husband.

The marine world respected him as a captain, but he stood much taller to Brooke.

Many a night, she went to bed while Murray read from her father's journal on his wartime heroics by night light. There were many sleepless nights when he nudged her awake to relay an exciting passage. She knew her father's past intimidated Murray, but only with regard to all things military. She noticed that he tried hard to gather favor, regardless of Brooke's insistence that her father already liked him because he was the man who his daughter had chosen. He'd treated him as his own son ever since.

Bronson greeted his daughter with a tight hug, then firmly shook Murray's hand and sat down. Instantly, Bronson knew something troubled Brooke. He knew how to pry the deepest fears out of her, regardless of her desires to hold them in.

"Okay, what's wrong? I know that look. There's something that's bothering you," he questioned with a smile.

She stared intently at him. "Dad, are you and Mom taking the boat out soon?"

"Your mother requested that we go out. You know how much she enjoys sailing. You also know that whatever your mother wants, she gets," he explained.

"Where is Mom anyway?"

He ordered his and his wife's breakfast, then returned the menu to the waiter.

"She's getting ready; she'll be here in a few minutes."

"How's she doing, Dad, and don't sugar-coat it," she asked as the waiter left.

He expressed a worried look and replied, "She's fine. I mean, at times she forgets things, but she has a very serious condition, so we adapt."

Brooke had a fearful look on her face, but nothing scared Bronson. However, a diagnosis of Alzheimer's disease two years earlier had chopped the stoic man down to a trembling, sad, and worried elderly man. The blow took much of the life out of him, but he tried not to relay his sorrow to his daughter. He stood strong for Catherine and he allowed no one to alter his new and painful mission.

He noticed a single tear fall from her face and instantly knew that his stoic facade betrayed him. He saw pain and confusion in his daughter's demeanor and felt sorrow that he was not able to confess his plans for their upcoming voyage. Bronson hated to deceive her, as she was obviously distraught, and realized that he'd miscalculated her uncanny ability to see through him.

She slammed her fist on the table. "Dad, you changed the name of your boat. It's stocked with enough provisions to last months. What are you and Mom planning? I'm your daughter and I demand to know what is going on!"

"Easy, Brooke," Murray pleaded as he attempted to calm her down.

She fixed her stare on Bronson, awaiting an answer. "Murray, I know my parents. I know how devoted they are to each other and I have to know." She continued to stare accusingly at him. "Dad, are you and Mom planning on sinking your boat at sea because of her illness?"

"You think your mother and I are contemplating suicide?" he asked with great concern.

"Well, all the signs are there. I know how much Mom likes being out on the water. Besides, every time you two went out, you invited us regardless of whether we went or not, but this time, you didn't ask." Her voice broke into a more sympathetic tone.

"I'm sorry, sweetheart, but next Saturday is our forty-sixth wedding anniversary, and we wanted to do what we both love. We want to take the boat out for a week or two. I'm also sorry that we didn't invite you and Murray, but we wanted to be alone. As far as the name on the boat goes, your mother wanted me to change it. We talked about it last week and she thought it fit for this time in our lives. It's true that a captain never changes the name on his boat, but as I've told you before, your mother's wishes supersede any superstition."

Brooke, obviously embarrassed at accusing him of such a heinous plan, relented. "I'm sorry, Daddy. I just remember what you told me a long time ago."

"It's okay, dear. I understand why you are concerned."

Seeing Brooke in her unsettled state troubled Bronson and Murray, but then she spilled some news that explained her unusual and uncharacteristic fears.

"Dad, Murray, I wanted to wait for Mom to get here, but I feel that I'm about to explode with emotion. Knowing how romantic my parents are, naturally I felt that they wanted the perfect end. You see, Murray, my father cannot function without my mother and vice versa, so I reacted to what I saw. Dad, the reason I feared that you and Mom were about to embark on a suicide voyage is because I need you here. Murray and I are about to become parents. I wanted to tell you earlier sweetheart, but wanted to find the perfect time. This, I feel, is that time."

Murray, stunned, fumbled his words to the point where he muttered incoherent sentences trying to relay his happiness, but his mind swirled with too many thoughts to settle on just a few. Bronson stood up, walked around the table to his tearfully elated daughter and hugged her tightly. Murray stood up proudly and embraced her, then kissed her gently on her quivering lips. His tears mingled with hers as he wiped hers dry, shook Bronson's hand, and again, hugged his wife. He yelled to the rest of the patrons in the restaurant, "I'm going to be a father!"

The crowd stood up and applauded the happy couple, as most of them knew Bronson and his family from many past encounters. The celebration took hold as Brooke's mother stepped into the room. Her startled expression made him think that she thought the applause was oddly for her. However, he quickly directed her attention to Brooke and Murray.

Catherine walked toward the table and clapped her hands as well. "What's going on, Bron?"

Brooke saw her beautiful mother and screamed, "Mom! I'm pregnant! You're going to be a grandmother!"

"What? You are? Oh, sweetheart, I've been waiting to hear you say those words. Did your father cry when you told him?" She hugged Brooke and her face beamed with pride.

Brooke smiled. "I don't think he did."

"I know he did when we had Bradley and you," Catherine said.

"No, I didn't, dear, but I'm about to!" Bronson confessed as he saw the restaurant's patrons leave their tables to congratulate the entire family.

One by one, they shook hands and hugged the happy couple. Bronson, still shaking congratulatory hands, saw Catherine sink down into a chair away from the celebration. Excusing himself, he walked over to her and removed her hand from her face. "What's wrong, sweetheart?"

"Oh, Bronson, I walked away because I'm so happy and wanted Brooke to enjoy her announcement." Her tears of apparent joy hid a deeper meaning.

Her hands shook and Bronson felt through his touch that something else caused her great pain. He had a penchant for extracting troubling thoughts. He liked to get them out in the open to be discussed and discarded.

"Cathy, what's really going on with you? I know you better than anyone on this planet; your daughter is over there and you are here alone. Tell me, dear. What are you think-ing?" He dabbed the tears from her face with a napkin.

She stood up and hugged Bronson, and with a gentle kiss on his cheek, confessed her fear. "I'm not going to be here to see her baby being born."

"Nonsense! Listen, Catherine Preminger, I hate it when you talk like that! We fight the good fight in this family. We do not give up! You will be here and so will I. By the way, your daughter knows about our plan. I am determined to die with you regardless. We planned everything out to the letter, and allowed for every contingency, except for this. It is the perfect end, but this news changes everything."

"I know it does. I'll fight, sweetheart. I'll try to last for Brooke's sake, but lately, it's been hard. My memory goes in and out. Do you realize how I feel when I wake up next to the man I've loved and adored for nearly fifty years and I don't know his name?" she tearfully explained.

"No, I don't, but I know your name and I'll remember for the both of us. That is enough for me! You have been my entire life. You've given me two wonderful children. You were my rock when we lost Bradley in Iraq. I intend to be with you through all of this nonsense and, when you die, I will die with you. It's our destiny, our fate! However, right now, our daughter needs us, so we will postpone our plan and be par-ents for a bit longer."

Catherine, seeing his resolve, agreed. "Hold my hand, Bron, and get me through this. I think I have more fight in me when you hold my hand."

"I don't intend to ever let go. I loved you when I first saw you walk past my ship. A year before I gathered up enough courage to introduce myself, I knew that I loved you."

"God, I love you, Bronson. How could a girl possibly get as lucky as I did?"

"That's simple, it's because I'm all that!" He laughed as he saw a smile break through the heartache that he knew she felt.

"Yes, you are all that, and it sickens me to see that you know I need you," she sarcastically stated as she mocked hitting him on his shoulder. "Let's get back to the party. I want to start planning for my grandchild's arrival."

He proudly placed her arm in his, led her to the party,

and whispered, "That's the woman I married."

"Where have you two been?" asked Brooke as she and Murray sat down.

"We've been having a discussion about the baby and wondering how much you two are going to allow us to interfere," Bronson stated with a smile.

"I want both of you to be involved as much as you want," Brooke confessed. "Mom, I need you to help me and tell me that it will be fine and painless." She placed her hand over her abdomen.

"Oh, I'll be here for you, JoAnne—I mean Brooke. Oh my God! I just called my daughter JoAnne! Please excuse me, sweetheart!" She abruptly walked away in tears.

Seeing her mom in distress, Brooke got up from the table, intending to follow Catherine, but Bronson stopped her. "Sweetheart, let me take care of this. She's embarrassed and hurting because of her illness."

"Dad, no! She's my mother and she has to know from me, that I understand what's going on with her and that I love her."

Bronson gave in and Brooke ran to the bathroom. Opening the door, she saw Catherine wiping her tears, walked up behind her, and hugged her. "Mom, I love you. I know you're having a tough time, but I love you and want you to come back to the table and allow us to show you that we need you regardless of your memory issues."

"I'm sorry, sweetheart. I try to fight and your father expects me to fight, but it's hard for me. I'm losing my mind."

"I'm about to be a mother and I'm depending on you to teach me how to be a good one. Because that's what you've been to me."

Catherine responded, "I will, sweetheart, to a point. You know I have trouble with seeing blood, so I won't be there in the delivery room unless you need me to be there."

"Oh, I know all about that. I remember your expressions when I scraped my knee or accidentally cut myself. Even with that fear, you cleaned me up. I love you, Mom."

"I know you love me, Brooke, and I adore you. You know that. My illness is changing me. I'm sixty-eight years old, married to the most wonderful man ever. When I look at you, I see me."

Emotionally spent, Brooke tried to keep it under control while her mother continued.

"I promised your father to try harder and I will. I will slip up on occasion, but I know your face. Let's get back to our guys. I'll be fine. Thank you, sweetheart."

Back at the table, no one mentioned Catherine's pain-filled exit; they finished their meals at a leisurely pace. The waiter cleared the table and brought coffee as Brooke again brought up their upcoming anniversary voyage.

Catherine and Bronson looked at each other as Catherine explained, "We planned to go because of my diagnosis. I want to go before I forget how much fun we had at sea."

The allure of the sea enamored her. She loved watching her husband take the wheel, fight the elements, and deliver them to calmer seas like a true champion.

Much more than a passenger, Catherine, in her younger years, steered the yacht with ease, to the great delight of her proud husband, but now she sat back as a shipmate who enjoyed the ride.

Having seen her father's expertise firsthand, Brooke also knew that he delivered them back safely. Many times, she and her brother saw the sea calm her parents' anxieties, also how raging and dangerous the waters were in a storm. During the sea's rage, or the lack thereof, her father weathered the wrath of Mother Nature and sailed his craft to safe harbors.

Regardless of her father's prowess as a sailor, Brooke still worried that their advancing age and her mother's illness marred his ability to fight the seas should a storm brew.

Murray assured her, "That old bird is in great shape. He's as tough as nails."

She knew what her husband tried to do and she loved him for it. Eventually, Murray made her see that all her fears were unjustified and they settled down and switched topics to talk about their future.

Morning broke and the sun shone brightly. They finished their breakfast. Brooke and Murray went back to their home. The Premingers strolled to their boat to make sure that Jose had done what they asked him to do. Catherine saw the new name and questioned why her husband changed it, not re-membering that she had requested it. Bronson, not wanting to reveal her forgetfulness, told her that the name needed to be changed, and Brooke had asked the same question.

Remembering why they were going on the voyage, she acknowledged the intellect of their daughter. "She's right. She knows exactly what we planned." That plan consisted of them spending a week or two on the water and then sinking their yacht in a grand gesture to the love they had for each other. Catherine had suffered with her illness for two years, and her memory and mind had faded. Neither of them want-ed to experience her eventual heinous end.

Setting sail, Bronson prepared to take the boat out for a short practice spin around the harbor. He looked up at the new sails and tried out his newly installed remote controlled actuators to raise and lower the massive sails, and they worked to perfection. The sails were up in a mere three minutes and returned to their covered box in less than a mi-nute. Bronson thought about his and Catherine's noble de-ception. He lived a great life, but could not see a life worth living without his devoted bride by his side.

They sailed for an hour and everything worked perfectly, so he navigated the huge yacht back into the harbor and carefully guided it back into its slip. They were prepared to venture out the next Saturday morning.

The week went by fast. Bronson and Catherine drove to the marina to prepare for Brooke, who customarily visited prior to each of their voyages. They looked forward to seeing her and Murray before they set sail.

Waiting in the boat, Bronson and Catherine walked to the living room and noticed Brooke and Murray walking the length of the pier to meet them. Murray helped Brooke aboard and she immediately noticed breakfast service laid out in the kitchen, compliments of their favorite marina res-taurant. They had a leisurely meal and talked for hours. Their departure time came and went as the two couples enjoyed talking and remembering all the past voyages and the people they'd befriended. Murray did not offer any because he had

never been on one of their cruises, but the stories still en-
thralled him and he wanted to be included in future voyages.

Soon, the time came and Bronson wanted to set sail, so
he kissed his daughter goodbye and thanked them for stopping by. A long journey lay ahead of them and they wanted
to get started, but Catherine stepped in and asserted, "No,
I'm not done talking to my daughter. We have time, Bron!
Besides, I'd rather leave early in the morning so we can see
the sun come up over the water."

He raised his glass. "Bring out the wine. We're partying
tonight."

Brooke emerged from the kitchen with two bottles of
wine and a diet soda for herself. She handed the bottles of
wine to Murray, who popped the corks, poured drinks, and
toasted their individual journeys.

For the rest of the night, they laughed, reminisced, and
made plans for the future. Catherine felt at ease on the boat;
the gentle rocking relaxed her, and for the rest of the night,
she remembered everything. For Catherine, her illness appeared to wane when she was on the boat, but Bronson
thought that the wine also played a large part in the way she
felt.

The party ended at ten o'clock, and Murray and Brooke
left. The Premingers immediately went to bed, as they intended to leave at dawn.

They decided to sail to Bermuda, which had made Brooke
a little more comfortable since, prior to her pregnancy announcement, Bronson had no destination planned. Now, he
and Catherine planned to spend the next week sailing to
Bermuda, and then relaxing on a beautiful sun-drenched
beach for two more weeks before finally returning home.

At five o'clock in the morning, the lights of the pictur-
esque marina dimmed and the waves gently licked the many
boats there. A full moon appeared to be dipping into the water and supplying all the light they needed. Many people lived
on their boats, but they slept soundly. The generous moonlight engulfed the marina and created the perfect setting during the warm, dark morning.

Looking out over the harbor, Bronson noticed his lovely wife silhouetted against the bright moon and saw her stunning features as he had fifty years earlier.

Brief gusts of wind bounced off the water, supplying a crisp breeze. She held her jacket tight as she turned toward Bronson and smiled, not knowing what the future held for them. She assisted him in stowing the mooring ropes, then they motored away from the dock. With sails partially hoisted, the vessel turned toward the open sea. Trying not to create a wake and awaken the other boaters, they glided through the eerily calm water of the marina. The boat, equipped with silent trolling motors, maneuvered out of the harbor and toward the open water.

They quietly set the sails, which immediately snapped tight and full as they caught a breeze and hastened their pace toward Bermuda. They did not know or care how long it would take to get there but just like in past voyages, time mattered little to either of them.

Bronson recited his favorite saying, "Our wake is our past, our sails are full, and the horizon awaits." He stated that at the onset of all their adventures together, and he did not disappoint now.

Chapter Two

The Voyage

Five miles out, they anchored. The sun appeared ready to crest on the horizon. On their previous adventures, they had stopped and gathered in as much of the scenery as they could, and sunsets and sunrises were always high on their list. Holding each other in their arms, they watched as night turned into day. They welcomed the new day and were thankful that the skies were clear to capture the full effect of the rising sun.

They ate breakfast; afterward, Bronson went into sailor mode and steered his boat east. Fifteen hours later, on calm seas, another of Catherine's favorite views came to her. Bronson allowed the boat to glide on its own. They watched the billions of stars above them unobstructed by clouds. Some moved, most did not, and a few far-off planets flickered. The celestial show never disappointed them and made time stand still as they each pointed to any peculiarity they could find. They hadn't had sex for many years due to their age and her debilitating illness, but the spark was still there just beneath the surface, waiting for the moment where the desire overtook the pain. Neither of them rushed the other. A shooting star hurtled across the moonlit sky, and they kissed because of a made-up old sailors' yarn Bronson told her requiring lovers at sea to kiss when a star scorched across the night sky. Catherine knew that he made up the story, but she never questioned him about it. She had hoped for some streaking stars and, that night, the stars did not disappoint.

The quietness of the setting calmed Catherine, and that elated Bronson. Aside from the waves periodically splashing against the hull, the seas supplied no sound. To Bronson, the silence and the gentle rocking of the boat arrested the onslaught of Catherine's disease. They enjoyed those times the most and were thankful that the sun took its sweet time to complete its cycle.

The sun rose, and they noticed the coastline of Florida in the distance behind them. Catherine made a breakfast of bacon and eggs as they talked about what lay ahead of them and what they wanted to do. Despite their years, they moved around like a much younger couple, but they knew that age had caught up to them.

With breakfast over, Bronson happily set the huge sails east. Motorizing the sails prior to his journey proved valuable because cranking them up by hand taxed his strength and speed. With the sails full of wind, Bronson donned his favorite sailor's cap and steered the boat toward Bermuda.

Catherine stayed below and cleaned up the morning dishes, but she could tell that the boat's sails were full because they were moving very fast. Peering out the door, she saw him steering the wheel, singing all the old pirate songs and moving his legs, which he called dancing. She laughed uncontrollably. The sea transformed him into a child, and that attribute, among many others, endeared her to him.

She closed the door, but he knew she still watched and listened to his antics through the window.

Hours went by as they sailed to the tunes of Dean Martin, Led Zeppelin, and her favorite, "Brandy," by Looking Glass, because he loved to sing it to her.

On their second day out, they encountered minor mishaps. Bronson, wanting to set a different course, started up the motors as the wind stopped. One of the engines failed, so he decided to keep their same course and wait for the wind to return. She didn't mind the delay. Catherine loved being out on the sea in her floating house; the longer it took to get to Bermuda, the better. After hours of trying, she finally got a signal from a television station; she watched the local weather and noted that a major storm lay a few miles ahead.

"Bronson, come down here and look at this," she said as she homed in on the weak signal.

Bronson tied the wheel off, climbed down into the cabin, and saw what Catherine observed. "That's a big storm. I think we're going to have to turn back."

She pointed to the screen. "No, we can get through. See, there's a path around it."

"Honey, we lost an engine, but we've been through worse. I'll get the sails up. Maybe we can ride through it quickly. Besides, it's a little more than a day away. Okay, we'll move on. How are you doing?"

"My hip is bothering me a little, but I'll be fine. It's one o'clock. Can we anchor and at least have one more calm night before this storm hits?"

"That sounds like a great idea, but I want to get underway at about ten o'clock tomorrow morning. I want to get ahead of that storm. What's for dinner?"

"I've got a roast in the oven and it should be done in a few minutes. You know what I want, though, don't you?" she stated with a smile.

"Yellow fin tuna steak? I'm thinking the same thing. After we get through the storm, we fish. How's the food holding up?"

"We have plenty of food. My God, Jose must have emptied the grocery store! However, I am looking forward to a nice tuna steak with lemon pepper."

No clouds existed that night. The seas were eerily calm for being so far out to sea. Catherine, feeling no sway on the boat, brought a bottle of wine up on the deck and Bronson followed. Sitting down on one of the spacious chairs handmade for two, they drank as the stars twinkled above. An errant meteor streaked across the sky, disrupting the tranquil beauty.

"Look! There's another falling star. Wow, they're really flying tonight," he said, pointing to the dazzle of light.

"I love nights like this. It's funny. I forget a lot of what's happened in my life, but I remember all of our adventures at sea."

"I guess you're relaxed and tend not to think about life so much. I remember every one of our voyages as well. Catherine, I'm worried about what tomorrow night will bring. In my younger days, I embraced the storm and enjoyed the fight against nature, but I'm old now. My arms aren't as strong as they used to be."

"You're strong enough, sweetheart. I have complete faith in you. I've seen you handle many storms and you will handle this one as well. Do you remember how we felt when you beat that last storm?"

"Yes, it scared me shitless. I always remember the bad ones, but thankfully, the swells didn't cause any damage and I steered out of it pretty quickly, but we did have a fight. Afterward, we had quite a laugh about it."

"Because of my illness, I'm not as afraid as I used to be. I hope I last long enough to see my grandchild."

"You will. I've noticed that you seem better when on the boat. Maybe we should sail more often."

They retired to the plush lower deck as the boat steered itself. The gentle rocking, caused by small swells licking the boat's hull coupled with, lilting melodies of Cole Porter, Irving Berlin, and the brothers Gershwin accidentally lullabied them to sleep.

Four hours later, both were thrown from the leather chair and flung across the carpeted floor.

Bronson took a bit of time to check on Catherine; however, both of them realized that during their romantic embrace and eventual slumber, the tremendous storm on the horizon had picked up speed and rocked the boat into a frenzied, uncontrolled state.

They got to their feet, but were unsteady due to the out-of-control yacht pitching.

"Catherine, tether yourself! I have to get to the wheel!" Bronson screamed as he ran amid debris flying all around him.

"The sails! I need to help you with the sails! We have to take them down!" Catherine reminded him.

"Okay, but you tether yourself when we get on deck, then when the sails are down, get your butt back down here and strap yourself in!"

"Wait, here's your slicker!" Catherine handed him the orange slicker.

They opened the door and it flew off the hinges and into the depths. He walked out to pitch-blackness. The stars were gone, covered by thick black clouds.

The wind took his favorite cap, never to be seen again. Bronson walked out to a torrent of seawater splashing across the bow, stinging his face and blinding him temporarily. The seawater cleared the deck, covered with white foam, of everything unattached away to the depths; the storm pitched the boat violently and threw him across the deck, injuring his arm. Getting to his feet and fighting the gale-force winds, he struggled to get to the large wooden wheel, held firmly by a rope. He climbed up the stairs to the captain's deck and the stinging rain pained his face like a thousand needles penetrating his skin. The wheel violently shook, trying to free itself from its bindings.

Catherine saw Bronson struggle to gain his balance, and crawled out of the cabin, but the relentless wind and the wall of water stilled her ascent toward her husband. She lost her balance and fell, but her tether held strong and she pulled herself back into the cabin.

"Get back in there, Catherine!" he bellowed through the loud howls of the unforgiving wind. "I'm fine! The sails are shredded! Send a mayday now!"

Fighting the wind and water, Bronson struggled and took one step at a time, but finally reached the wheel, removed the rope, and smashed his hand as the wheel ferociously whipped side to side. He grabbed his hand, dropped to his knees, and screamed in pain. His left arm and hand were useless.

Waiting until the wheel ceased its motion, he grabbed it with his right arm and got back to his feet. He lashed himself in front of it. He pushed the button to retrieve the shredded sails from the mast. The billowing sails slowly came down, but not without destroying everything as the wind caught them and bullwhipped everything on deck. He spied Catherine trying to get his attention.

She screamed, "The radio isn't working! I've tried every channel!"

"Go back inside! I'll get this under control!" Bronson demanded as he struggled to hold the wheel and spin it into the wind.

The ship listed to its side as it glided sideways up the twenty-foot swell and nearly capsized as it slammed down the other side. The sudden dramatic action sent Catherine airborne, but again, her tether held her firmly and prevented her from being tossed across the room. However, pots, pans, and everything else in the cabin were thrown about the room and hurled toward her, then clanged against the far wall. Some of the deadly projectiles missed her, but many did not. She protected herself as much as she could with seat cushions, but cooking pots eventually found their mark. A frying pan grazed her head; she fell backward, rendered temporarily unconscious.

Bronson steered the boat perpendicular to the huge swells and crashed into the first one. The front submerged as it sliced through the top of the swell. The boat creaked badly when it crested the swells, half of it soaring over the swell in midair. Bronson muttered to himself, "Please, you old boat. Don't break in half!"

The yacht pierced the swell and sank its bow deep into the valley just to tackle another large swell that rolled ominously toward the boat. The boat climbed and again blasted through the top. The huge mast broke off from the deck and harpooned the rising swell as all lights went dark. In the dead of night, Bronson steered blind, not being able to see if it still tacked toward the massive swells or parallel to them.

Catherine woke from her unconscious state, gathered her senses, and remembered where she was. She screamed as the lights doused. She could no longer see what catapulted toward her. Bronson fought hard and even used his injured arm to attempt to hold the wheel steady. The pain seared through his brain as the wind remained strong and constant.

The merciless blowing seawater stung his face and hands, but he held a strong grip on the wheel and masterfully guided the ship into each swell to keep it upright and going forward. Throughout his fight with the elements and the pain he felt, he thought of Catherine in the cabin and hoped that she fared better.

After an hour of fighting Mother Nature, he felt his resolve weakening. The monstrous storm and the large rolling swells seemed to be never-ending as the creaks and ominous noises the boat made increased in frequency and volume, twisted out of shape but still buoyant. He mustered the strength to fight Mother Nature's wrath.

The boat rocked sideways with wild swings until his last

vestige of control left. The damaged rudder made it harder to control the boat's path. The storm destroyed his beloved sea craft. He looked down at his feet and saw his crawling wife inching toward him, then pulling on his pant leg.

"What the hell are you doing? Get back to the cabin!" he said forcefully.

"Bron, come with me," she yelled through the crashing waves and wind.

"No, get out of this wind! I'll get it through! I know I can get it through. I have to get through it."

"No, Bron, I'll not go back to the cabin without you. The storm has won this time. Allow it its victory and be with me. Let fate have its way."

Bronson, still fighting at the helm, knew what Catherine meant, and what she wanted him to do. A sense of calm came over him as he saw his beautiful wife bleeding from her head, so he decided to let her have the end she desired. He'd survived his fight with the storm, but his wife's desires were more important. He tied up the wheel again, gathered her to her feet, and guided her back to the cabin.

Thankfully, the cabin blocked the stinging wind and seawater from blasting his face. The boat still rocked badly, but they sat on the floor and held each other. His strength completely spent, he mustered a smile as they waited for the heavens to take them together.

Amazingly, they took comfort amid the torrent of movement and wind squeaking through the cracks. Things flew around the room at great speed and the boat took on water, but their arms intertwined around each other stilled their rapid heartbeats. Content, happy, and grateful for the life they had, they looked forward to the next step because they were confident one existed.

Their energy to fight expended, they closed their eyes amid the terror and Bronson gently sang "Brandy (You're a Fine Girl)" to her. They were seriously injured, but their resolve cut through the pain. They managed to close their eyes after a final kiss and a promise to find each other, if separated, in the afterlife.

Bronson felt the violently swaying vessel, but there were no thoughts of hindering its fate, and he allowed it to destroy itself. Captainless, the boat fought the swells for hours after the loving couple relaxed, unconcerned that their home on the water eventually succumbed to the forces of nature. They slept soundly that night.

The next day, they woke up still holding each other's hands. The bright sunshine shone through the multiple missing roof panels ripped from boat. Bronson blocked the sun with his hand and squinted, not yet realizing that they had made it through the night. It surprised him that he lived, but Catherine did not move. He removed all the clutter from her and nudged her gently as she woke up.

"Am I dead?" she asked as she gazed into Bronson's eyes.

"Nope, it looks like we made it through the storm and we're still floating. We're alive, babe!"

She grabbed her husband and embraced him. "We are? Oh, Bronson, I knew you could do it! I love you so much!"

He helped her to her feet. "Are you all right?"

"I think so. Yes, I'm fine. A few scratches, that's all. How about you?"

"I think I may have a fractured arm and broken hand, but I can still move both. Other than that, I'm fine. Let's go see the damage."

They walked out to see calm water, nothing other than a few small waves licking the hull, and the tinkling of a pulley clanging against the lone mast still upright. One of the tie bands that held the Sea-Doos in place snapped, causing one of the two recreational vessels to drift away.

The tie band on other one held it solidly on the deck, and it was undamaged by the storm. The yacht's main mast and sails were gone and the steering mechanism destroyed; to make matters worse, all the electronics had burned beyond repair. Bronson thought an unobserved lightning strike likely destroyed the electrical system. However, they were safe for the moment and, fortunately, their large lifeboat still hung in its davits. Most of Bronson's beautiful boat had been destroyed, but it still floated. Without a working motor and a broken rudder, the once-proud yacht aimlessly drifted with the tide with no possible way of stopping or controlling its direction. But they had plenty food, water, and a shelter from the elements.

They drifted hopelessly in the Atlantic Ocean for a few days. The boat took on water. With no power to start the pumps and, convinced that the storm had not breached the hull, they bailed water out of the boat and, soon, the water level receded.

Periodically grabbing the radio microphone, he tried to make a call, but the radio didn't work due to power loss; the batteries were under water below the deck. Looking out over the horizon, neither he nor Catherine saw boats or land.

They traveled on a very expensive raft with its direction determined by the currents. Throughout the day, they removed water and straightened out the interior of the boat to make it livable. Bronson loaded the lifeboat with his survival trunk, a large, solid waterproof teakwood crate filled with a large tent, disposable lighters, canned and dried food, four cases of bottled water, pots and pans, clothes, boots, knives, and guns. The trunk took up much of the space in the lifeboat, but still allowed for two to three passengers. He had it specially made to fit with the weight dispersed evenly, and had loaded it years earlier in case the boat sank suddenly.

Bronson thought that he had better prepare the lifeboat, himself, and Catherine for a larger catastrophe. Just in case, he added the photo album to the watertight chest because looking at the photos instantly brought Catherine back to reality.

The sunlight waned as one of their favorite times of the day on the water presented itself, except, this time it didn't hold the same meaning. Despite their desperate situation, they still paused to observe the sunset's splendor. They slept soundly for the next four nights, but stayed ever alert for a horn from a passing barge or pleasure craft, to be rescued.

Catherine and Bronson loved each other deeply, but being confined on the boat for twenty-four hours a day created a small amount of boredom. The many books on board occupied Catherine's time, but Bronson hated reading. He entertained himself by trying to catch that tuna that he wanted to prior to the storm. He caught many of them, but without the means to cook them, he could not see any reason for keeping them.

The largest one he carried to Catherine and joked, "Hey,

can we lemon pepper this one?"

"Great, I have no stove and no way to cook him. Throw him back. You get what I get. Canned food."

"Dammit! He's a big fellow. I guess you're right. Okay, big guy, the wife gave you a reprieve. Off you go."

Bronson took the fish outside and released it. Walking back inside, he gathered up his scuba gear and began putting it on. Catherine, seeing this, asked, "What are you doing?"

"I'm bored. I'm going to see if I can fix the rudder, or at least try. This drifting about is killing me."

"The hydraulic system is not working. Why bother?"

"If I can fix it mechanically, I can still steer the boat. It will be harder, but I can steer it if another storm crops up."

"Okay, I'll prepare what I can. Sandwiches?"

"That's fine. I'll be back."

Bronson checked his air supply, carried the tanks outside, placed them on his back, and jumped in. He swam to the rear of the boat. He shone his solar-powered flashlight on the rudder and saw the damage to the linkage. Needing tools, he resurfaced, collected a small tool pouch, then reentered the water. Ten minutes later, he reemerged, climbed onto the boat, and tested his repair. Due to the lack of hydraulics, the ship's wheel did not turn easily, but enough to steer the boat. Excited, he called out to Catherine.

"Catherine, I want to show you something."

She didn't answer so, he yelled louder, "Catherine! Where are you?"

Still, she did not acknowledge his calls, and a sense of worry made his news less important.

Bronson dropped his scuba tanks and ran to the kitchen. He saw a sandwich on a plate next to a glass of tea, but no Catherine. Frantic, he ran to every room, including the water-filled rooms below deck.

Catherine had disappeared.

He screamed, "Catherine? Where are you?"

Then, he saw some movement skimming under the water's surface. He grabbed his binoculars and spied Catherine swimming away from the boat. Not hesitating, he immediately unhooked the remaining Sea-Doo without caring about setting the anchor.

Speeding off and kicking up water, he raced to his wife as he called out, "Catherine, I'm on my way! Hold on!"

Pulling up alongside his wife, he jumped in the water and grabbed her to help her onto the watercraft, but she resisted.

"What are you doing?" she asked as he struggled to get her to stop swimming. "I have to get to that island or I'll drown! Let go of me!"

"Honey, there is no island! Come with me!"

"There is an island, sir. I see it! I know what I'm doing and I can swim the distance. I am on a swim team and was a finalist for the Rome Olympics last year."

"Last year? Honey, you're having an episode. If you don't get onto this Sea-Doo, I'm going to lift you up and put you there!" he bellowed.

"What about the island?"

"There isn't any damn island! Look! There is no island! There's nothing but sea!"

Catherine, treading water, acknowledged that she saw no island, but she still did not recognize Bronson. She climbed up on the watercraft and Bronson climbed on behind her.

Catherine said nothing all the way back to the boat, which had drifted far from its position. He helped her onto it and tied the Sea-Doo to a mooring ring. She stood shivering on the deck, not seeming to know where to go. Bronson grabbed a large blanket, lovingly wrapped it around her, and led her into the living room, where he began undressing her.

"What are you doing, sir?"

"I'm getting you out of those wet clothes."

She stopped him and said, "I'm going to tell my father about you."

"Your father? Listen, dear, I don't know how to put this lightly, so I'm just going to blurt it out. Your father died ten years ago and I've been your husband for the last forty-six years. As far as the Olympics go, you were a finalist, but in 1960. It's 2013 now."

"No, you're lying!"

"Honey, you're not fifteen years old anymore. You're six-ty-eight and I love you very much."

"Stop it! Stop it! I don't believe you!" She screamed hys-terically as he grabbed her and hugged her.

She fought with him and struck him across his face. He

went down, not expecting the blow. He spied a broken mirror on the floor and handed a shard to her.

"Here. Look into it. Is that the face of a fifteen-year-old?"

"Oh my God! No! It can't be! I'm old!" She screamed, as she threw the mirror against the wall, shattering it into smaller pieces. Sitting down with her head in her hands, she started to cry profusely.

Bronson walked over to her and hugged her again; this time, she embraced him back.

"Why am I wet, Bron? What's going on?"

"Honey, you had an episode. You forgot who I am. What's the last thing you remember?"

"I remember making us sandwiches. Why am I wet?"

"I'll explain later. Let's get you into dry clothes."

Walking to the bedroom, she located and changed her clothes without a hint of confusion. The incident hurt Bronson because he could not help her as much as he wanted to. Sitting down in front of her, he brushed her hair, grabbed her battery-operated hair dryer, and dried it. When he was finished, he placed the hair dryer on the table and gently hugged her from behind. At that moment, he too forgot her age because he remembered the time he'd dried her hair forty-six years earlier. They'd married soon after.

She closed her eyes and wondered what she'd put her loving husband through with her latest episode. It hurt her greatly knowing what troubles he bore. She placed her hands on his, and said, "I'm sorry, sweetheart. I know that I'm putting you through hell, but you know that I'd never do that knowingly."

"I know that, Cathy, but you scared me. You jumped in and when I went to get you, you told me you were swimming toward some imaginary island."

"I remember seeing an island. I remember that part of it," she corrected.

"I didn't see one and I still don't see one. Do you?" he asked.

She looked out to the horizon and stated, "No, I don't see one. I think I'm losing my mind."

"Honey, you have an illness. The doctor told us what to expect and how this will end. I just want you to know that I will be with you every step of the way. It's our illness, not just yours."

"I know, dear. I'm sorry that you have to go through this."

"We've had a lifetime together. Think about that. We've had a wonderful life together. We've sailed around the world. We had two wonderful kids. We lost Bradley in Iraq, but we still have Brooke and she's having a baby, our grandchild, and we have to get back to them, for them."

"We will! We have to! You're right. What can we do now?"

Bronson looked around his broken boat and said, "Nothing. We have seven months to figure it out."

The seas were calm and the ship glided quietly. Catherine read a book and seemed content in the cabin, which provided an opportunity for Bronson to go on deck and write in his ship's log.

This is our second week at sea. The first few days were magical by seamen's standards. A brisk and solid wind took us out. I used the engines only once. We had amazingly calm seas and gentle winds at night with not a cloud in the sky. Cathy showed no symptoms of her disease, and for that, we are both thankful. Moonlight enhanced her beauty and reminded me of the first time we set sail, her eyes still wide at the majestic sights of schools of dolphins in the distance, welcoming us to their domain with cries that echoed in our ears. The uncountable stars that flickered over our heads seemingly appeared just for us those nights. I've been to sea most of my adult life, but never have the elements been so perfectly aligned for our benefit. We swam, we ate, we danced, and we stared with a younger couple's eyes at those nights. We still remember those times often.

The waters calmed my wife and allowed her mind to be well again. I'm convinced of this. However, the next day brought out the demons of the sea, because a ferocious storm hit us, the likes of which these eyes have never seen. I navigated us through it, but not without serious damage and loss. The main mast and sail ripped off the boat during gale-force winds. The boat, which had weathered many storms, tossed about like a toy in a bathtub and I expended all my strength to steer, but the sea's savage wrath beckoned us to the depths and seemed relentless in its attack.

I fought for eight hours, ripping sails and breaking beams with whole waves crashing about the bow and stern, but the boat stood its ground and won the battle with the thanks of a grateful captain. The seventh day of our voyage found us drifting toward the unknown. We've lost one of our Sea-Doos, the engine room is flooded, and all power is gone. The radio does not work due to a lightning strike and the sudden movement of the boat damaged the rudder, but I repaired it.

That storm took a lot from us, but mostly it removed the calm from my precious Cathy. She forgot my name twice this week, and jumped in the water and started swimming aimlessly to an unseen island. She still insists the island is there, although she does remember my name and I'm thankful for that.

I thought I lost her that day. I spied her swimming in the distance but recovered her, yet not without a surge of heartache. She didn't know me when I approached. I somehow convinced her to allow me to save her and she eventually came back to me. I'm unsettled by this new direction in her illness. I can take the memory loss, although it hurts me, but now she's seeing things that aren't there. We have enough food and supplies for another few weeks, but after that, I'm at a loss as to what to do. I just hope the current is in our favor because, although I can steer, I don't know where I'm steering to. I'm chronicling this adventure for Brooke, our daughter, in hopes that it finds her eyes one day. Should the current not take us to a port and we are unrecoverable, I will float this journal in hopes that it finds its way back home to Brooke. I'll sign off for now because Cathy is calling me.

Bronson closed the journal and walked below deck to see Catherine crying.

"What's wrong, babe?" he asked, sitting next to her.

"I can't remember my name. Please tell me my name!" she asked, still whimpering.

"Your name is Catherine Preminger," he said as he hugged her tightly.

"I'm Catherine. Oh, Bronson, I feel so useless. I'm losing my mind. I feel like my mind is being attacked and it's taking my most precious memories first. I have many more, but I don't want to lose them too."

"Honey, just remember that I love you and I'll always love you. I don't know how all this will end, but if it ends for you, it will end for me as well. I will not allow you to die alone. I will be with you. We will be holding hands as we leave here," he said as he gently cleared her hair from her face.

"I don't want you to die, Bronson. I need you to look after our daughter."

"You're wrong, Catherine. You see, if you die, then I will die inside anyway. The fact that I breathe and that my heart still beats won't bring me comfort. I will die when you die. Our daughter is a grown and married woman and we raised her to be strong. She will be fine."

"Brooke is married? Oh God! I can't remember the wedding!" she screamed.

"Relax, sweetheart, we still have the photos here. You see them and those memories will return. In fact, we have our whole history together here."

"How did I get so lucky to find a man like you?" she asked, feeling better about her situation and opening up one of their photo albums.

"Let's go on deck. It's a nice day and maybe those dolphins that were following us earlier will be there. They always make you feel better."

Carefully guiding her to the deck, they found a comfortable place to sit as the boat drifted. Looking at the horizon, they did not see another boat or signs of land. The ship's wheel navigated its own course as they talked and looked at photos, laughed, and remembered better times. Catherine saw the wheel moving at its whim and decided that she wanted to steer it.

"I always wanted to steer the boat. May I?" she asked.

"Of course, Captain. Let me help you up," he said, with a smile.

Catherine took control of the wheel and she instantly turned the boat in a certain direction.

Curious, Bronson asked, "Why are we going over there?"

"Because that's where the island is," she said with wide eyes.

He did not have the heart to question her decision, and

allowed her to go wherever made her happy.

It appeared to work because she had a broad smile on her face as she navigated what remained of the boat. He did not tell her that the boat traveled in circles. They had plenty of time and he enjoyed her antics behind the wheel. She pointed the boat in a certain direction and playfully commanded Bronson to do her bidding as the captain of the boat. Amazed that she found humor in their dire state, Bronson laughed as she joyfully mocked him at the helm. However, one time, she pointed to the horizon and yelled, "Land!"

Bronson looked to where she pointed and his smile turned to horror as he walked to the wheel and removed her from her lofty perch.

"I'm sorry, sweetheart, but that's not land. It's another storm and it's approaching us fast."

"A storm? Oh dear God! Steer toward the island, Bronson, I don't want to go through that again," she said as she gladly returned control to her husband.

"There is no island, Catherine!" he stated firmly. "We can't outrun this storm. We have no sails and we have no engines. It's coming in too fast. Go down below and strap yourself in!"

"No, not this time! I will stay here with you," she stated as she started to buckle herself in on deck.

"Please, Cathy, I don't have time to argue. The waves will break your tether and I don't want to lose you. Please do as I ask. If it goes bad, I will come and get you. Our rescue boat is stocked and ready should the old girl not be able to stand up to this storm."

Catherine complied because she knew he had a lot on his mind and she did not want to be another problem.

The storm came upon them quickly and felt like a head-on collision. It hit the boat broadside, nearly capsizing the huge vessel. The boat survived the first salvo, but surely weakened further. Bronson struggled to turn against the might of the sudden storm's surges.

The storm did not have the voracity of the previous one, but without the controls or sails in place, it worried him greatly.

The rudder had no hydraulic system, which made steering very taxing to Bronson despite his strength. He could not direct the boat into the swells. The waves crashed against its side, causing it to change direction on a dime. For the first time, Bronson had serious thoughts of giving up the battle. Struggle as he might, he could not gather control. The waves poured over the deck and the rain stung his face relentlessly. In the valley of the swells, he noticed the boat list to the right. He tied the wheel, hoping the newly repaired rudder held against the mighty pressures of the undersea forces pushing against it.

Bronson dangerously unhooked his tether and walked across the deck, but a wave caught him in the back and sent him flailing over the rail. Holding on for dear life, he thought about his helpless wife in the lower deck's chamber and gathered enough strength to pull himself back on board. His injured arm gave way, but his other arm held strong.

The violently rocking boat tossed Catherine around below deck, but her tether held her firmly in her seat. The boat took on a lot of water again, now in danger of sinking. The storm subsided as quickly as it came about. The seas slowly returned to normal after an hour of taking a beating. The boat listed badly to the right, and about to sink into the abyss.

Bronson went below to check on Catherine. She'd avoided the larger objects jettisoned toward her, but a laptop computer slammed against her head, rendering her unconscious. Wet and bleeding slightly, he gathered her up in his arms, carried her to the waiting lifeboat, and gently placed her on a small mattress in the large rescue craft that floated on its own, tethered to the sinking boat. He found some dry blankets and lovingly placed them over his wife. He returned many times to the cabin to gather last-minute supplies for their new journey on a decidedly smaller craft. The yacht took on more water, beyond repair.

It stayed afloat long enough for him to gather things too important not to take. Catherine's plastic-encased photo albums made their way onto the boat. Finally, he had everything he needed. He released the Sea-Doo from his lifeboat because it had sustained irreversible damage. It sank immediately. He cut the rope from his majestic boat, and they floated away.

Catherine did not witness the sorrowful event of seeing their wonderful boat silently sink below the water's surface.

He bid farewell to his friend of forty-eight years and actually believed that it treaded water just long enough to supply him with sufficient time to gather as much as he could in order to continue his fight for survival.

Still unconscious, Catherine appeared comfortable in the lifeboat. Bronson went back and forth to the sinking vessel, grabbing anything he saw that could possibly help them. Mostly he searched for food and water. Their cell phones, submerged in water, were of no use.

For the next day, he kept Catherine dry, monitored her temperature, and administered to her wounds using the large first aid kit he retrieved from the trunk. He took off his shirt and fashioned a shade for Catherine.

She awoke exactly two days later, when a slight wind blew Bronson's shirt to the side and the bright sunlight shone on her eyes. She awoke oblivious to her surroundings, but when she saw Bronson's sunburned chest, she felt safe. She sat up and calmly asked questions and he dutifully answered them for her. Bronson looked withered and worn, and that concerned her. He'd been awake for two days and accidentally nodded off while steering the boat with the manual rudder. He awoke suddenly to see his bride alert and talking to him. She begged him to take a break and sit with her, but he needed to be alert for other potential calamities.

He assured his wife that he needed no more sleep. But age and hard days of aimless drifting on the endless ocean at the helm of a doomed ship caught up to him and suddenly, he collapsed into Catherine's lap.

The seas were mildly rolling, but not enough that it prevented her from taking over at the rudder and allowed her exhausted husband to sleep.

Her delusions came back to her as she steered the vessel toward that imaginary island she'd seen numerous times.

For the next three days, they drifted. The boat had an outboard motor, but Bronson used it sparingly. They had a mere ten gallons of gas on board, and needed it should another storm threaten them, or they encounter land and need to get to it or to motor toward a distant boat. Nothing presented itself, though, so they drifted quietly for the next few days. Luckily, she showed no signs of her illness. Mostly, when Bronson thought that she began to allow her dementia to take hold, he showed the photos to her to quell the on-slaught, and he felt pride in her for fighting the good fight.

At nighttime on the fifth day, Catherine took over the watch. Her bearded and sunburned husband took his turn resting on the mattress. He slept, but not soundly, because he constantly worried about Catherine's moments of confusion. He listened to her sing to herself to while away the time, but sudden splashes alerted him because he thought that his wife might start swimming again and forget where they were.

Catherine spied the imaginary island again when the moonlight shone on the glistening rocks, and she steered toward it. She didn't awaken Bronson from his restless nap because she didn't want to argue about the existence of the island. She wanted and needed it to be there, so she went with her feelings and steered toward what she saw. They drifted for hours, but it never appeared close, so she walked to the back of the boat, sidestepping her sleeping husband, started the outboard motor, and gave life to the drifting boat as she motored full speed toward the her island.

Bronson woke up suddenly, sent backward with the force of the boat jetting toward nothing that he could see. "What are you doing, Cathy?"

"I saw it! There's an island there! I know it."

Bronson looked at the horizon, but saw no island or any-thing that looked like a land mass. He walked to the back of the boat and turned off the motor, much to the dismay of Catherine.

"It's out there, Bronson!" she screamed.

"Catherine, it's my turn, please go lie down. There is no island."

He turned the motor off and steered the boat westward. They drifted as the sun came up.

The morning sun shone brightly on Catherine and she woke up and said, "Good morning. Did you see anything?"

"Just a hell of a lot of water. Did you enjoy your sleep?"

"Yes, did you find the island yet?"

Bronson was obviously frustrated. "No, there is no island. How many times do I have to tell you that?"

Just as he said that, something abruptly stopped the boat; the collision sent them both crashing into the large rock protruding from the surf. He looked up, and to his astonishment, the boat had struck a reef off the coast of an island. The land mass instantly appeared one hundred yards in front of him. He knew no logical reason for it to be there, because not five minutes had passed since he had looked out over the horizon and seen only water. He could not explain the island's existence, but felt thankful that they had found it. He looked at his wife and felt ashamed that he had not believed her, but regardless of his mistake, he was happy that their lives might be prolonged. He reached over and kissed his wife, elated for the promise of rescue.

"I told you. There is the island. Look, sand and trees. That is an island! We're saved!"

The sight completely changed his attitude. "Yes, you did, sweetheart. I can't explain it, Cathy. It just appeared a minute ago! I apologize. Look at it! The mountain and all the trees. It's not that big, but it's there. I hope that what I'm seeing is real."

Catherine smiled broadly at seeing her suddenly exuberant husband focused and serious about getting there. She said, "Slow down, we'll get there."

He did not respond to her warning.

"Bronson, are you ignoring me? Bronson!"

Bronson said, "I'm sorry, dear, did you say something?"

"I asked you to slow down. These waves are throwing me all over the boat."

"I'm sorry, I did not hear you. There...is that better?"

"Maybe you're having a senior moment. Lord knows I know a lot about those."

However, he sped up again as they approached the land mass. He drove the boat to the beach so fast that when the boat's hull hit the beach and stopped suddenly, it caused him to tumble from it and land on the soft, white sand beach.

He sat up and smiled. "Nope, this is no senior moment."

"Oh, dear, are you all right?"

"I feel great, dear. In fact, other than marrying you and my kids being born, this is my next finest moment."

Catherine righted herself after being tossed a little. Bronson stood up and helped her out of the boat, and he moored it on the beach. The loaded boat was too heavy for him to pull it too far, but he pulled it far enough to prevent it from drifting away.

They stretched out some little-used muscles as they looked around, but saw no signs that natives of the island existed. Bronson and Catherine dragged the boat onto the beach as far as they could. He secured a rope and pulley from the trunk, wrapped it around a large palm tree at the tree line, then winched the boat the rest of the way onto the sand. He removed the contents of the trunk and began creating a temporary shelter.

Chapter Three

Happily Marooned

Bronson spread everything from the trunk on the beach and Catherine watched, amazed that he could get so much survival equipment in one trunk. He picked up a box and pulled out a large tent, unraveled it, and set it up in minutes. The soft sand made it easier to hammer in the long stakes. He placed the mattress from the boat in it, then pulled out four blankets, solar-powered lanterns and flashlights, a pistol, a rifle, and cases of canned foods and bottled water to store in the tent.

Placing the supplies inside, she asked, "Wow, how did you get all that in that trunk?"

"I know how to pack things. I got both of our suitcases. I'm sorry, but I didn't have much time to pack everything. I grabbed what I could."

"I know, and thank you. We haven't had a shower in weeks. You want to go for a swim? I feel great for some reason."

"Let's get this set up and get a fire going and then I will join you. Please don't go without me. I'm worried that you will not come back."

"Okay, let me help you. One thought, though—shouldn't we find out if this island is inhabited?"

"Good point. Perhaps we should take a walk before that swim. To be honest with you, I feel great, too. Even my bum knee doesn't hurt."

They started their walk at the water's edge, around the island. Talking about their grandchild made the walk seem less daunting. They went at a slow pace, but they had time and did not care how long it took.

Hours later, they began to run faster and childishly played with each other, and marveled that their energy level increased more than it had in years. A few times, they entered the jungle and spied banana trees as well as coconut palms dotting the interior of the island.

They determined that the small island had no inhabitants, but they needed to be sure.

After they circled the island, they ended up jogging the rest of the way back to their new camp. Winded but not tired, they approached their tent to see that a palm tree had fallen across it. The tree crushed the tent, but Bronson worried more about the tent's contents. He'd placed the five cases of bottled water inside to protect them, but noticed that some of the precious liquid leaked from the shelter. He walked back to the trunk, pulled out a saw, and cut the palm tree into manageable logs so he could remove the tent and set it up elsewhere. They needed wood for a fire anyway, so he cut it into one-foot sections. He moved the remnants of the tree off the tent and he saw that a third of the water bottles lay smashed and emptied.

He set up the camp farther away from the tree line and closer to the calming surf.

"Well, now we will have to find water somewhere. The tree didn't destroy all of it, but enough to worry me," he stated as he threw the smashed bottles aside.

Catherine, still invigorated by her walk, said, "Okay, set it up and let's go. I want to explore the island's interior. It's got a mountain, so the rainwater has to go somewhere."

"It's getting dark. Let's get the tent set up and sleep. There's no need to explore the island at night. We've got a lot of time."

"You're right. Do you need any help?"

"No, I got it."

Bronson removed the rest of the tree, straightened out a few bent tent poles, and set up the tent a few feet away. He and Catherine lay down on the mattress and slept for ten hours.

The ocean breezes blew against the canvas tent, waking them up the next day. They dressed, walked outside, and stretched their sore, seldom used muscles.

"I'm going to turn the boat upside down in case it rains. Wait a minute! Where did all those smashed bottles go? They were right here!" Bronson searched around the camp.

"I saw you throw them right there and now they're gone. Maybe the wind blew them away."

"Oh well, let's go exploring. Here, put your boots on. We may have to do some climbing. How do you feel?" asked Bronson

"I feel fantastic; in fact, I can't remember when I felt better," she said with a smile. "How's your knee holding up?"

"Funny thing. It hasn't hurt a bit, even during our walk around the island," he acknowledged.

Catherine put on her heavy boots, and they entered the jungle. Bronson hacked away at the brush with a machete and made a path, with Catherine following behind.

Encountering many banana plants, she picked a green one and tasted it. Sour and inedible. She spit it out. "They will be fine once they ripen a bit," she said.

They plowed on for many hours, making discoveries along the way, and in the center of the jungle, they found what they were looking for. A small brook ran through the forest and as Bronson took a drink, he nodded, acknowledging that they had found water, although it had a slightly brackish taste.

Two hours later, they made another discovery in the tangled thicket—a small plane, which appeared to have crashed many years earlier, but appeared reasonably intact. They cautiously moved toward it. They opened the side door and noticed four empty seats in the back. Entering, Bronson walked toward the cockpit and noted a bony hand to one side of the seat; he knew that the pilot and co-pilot were still there. "They died where they sat."

He did not see any benefit in removing them and giving them a proper burial.

Searching the plane's hull, Bronson found a journal. He opened it and recognized the name attached to it immediately.

"Catherine, this is C.K. Corker's plane. Remember the millionaire who disappeared back in 1977?" He turned the pages as he waited for her response.

"Yes, he vanished. I guess we know what happened to

him now. Do you think he's one of the skeletons up front?"

"No, he hated flying. I remember reading about his paranoia about flying. He always had two pilots. This is his plane! Maybe he ejected from the plane upon impact or, if he survived, lived out his life here. If he did survive the crash, he must have had a camp somewhere on the island," Bronson explained. "Well, let's get back to camp, it's getting dark. We'll come back here to investigate further."

As Bronson read the journal, Catherine opened the suitcases to see clothes from another era, which they needed badly. They grabbed the suitcase containing clothes, and the journal; however, little else seemed usable at the time.

They started their trek back to their camp. Catherine observed something that escaped Bronson's mind.

"It's too quiet. Do you notice it?"

"Now that you mention it, I don't hear any sounds, nor have I seen a single insect, bird, or any animals. Seems odd."

"It's sort of scary. The only sounds I hear are what we're creating. This isn't normal. We've been in jungles before and there's always something buzzing about."

They did not appear to tire. In fact, they seemed to be changing for the better, but they did not know where their newfound energy came from.

They slashed their way back to the beach, but their campsite had again, been disrupted. The tent no longer stood and it appeared that something had ransacked it. They cautiously walked toward it, but did not see anything except a mess. Bronson quickly re-erected the tent and gathered up the supplies strewn about. Luckily, his guns were untouched and the water supply intact. Bronson started a fire with the cut wood and Catherine made dinner, though their camp's disruption concerned him.

A feast of canned beans and soup sustained them that day. They had one pot and one pan and a few dishes, but they did not complain.

After dinner, Catherine sat on the sand, near the huge fire, while Bronson returned from the boat with a pack of cigarettes and promptly lit one up.

"Where did you get those? Bronson, we gave up smoking forty years ago," Catherine scolded.

"Hey, we're marooned on an uninhabited tropical island.

It's been a helluva few weeks. Navigated through two heinous storms, I've yet to see a boat on the horizon, and I'm
seventy. I don't think cigarettes are a concern anymore,"
Bronson explained. "They relax me, dear. I have four cartons
stashed in the trunk."

"Well, you're right. Let me have one." He gave her a cig-
arette and lit it for her.

An hour later, snuggling under a billion stars, they held
each other tightly in the chilly ocean air and remembered the
important aspects of their lives. They laughed most of that
hour, but eventually, the cold air got to them; they retired to
the warmth of the tent and their comfortable mattress.

Falling asleep right away, each of them had vivid dreams,
but their dreams did not include a rescue boat. The island
provided them with a sense of peace that they had not encountered in many years. The only sounds they heard were
the rhythmic crash of waves in the distance and the gentle
culmination of the weakened waves hitting the shore.

Suddenly, movement under their tent abruptly ended
their calming sleep. It moved with great speed under the
sand and burrowed beneath the tent, sending the couple airborne. The mattress softened the blow, but the impact still
caused pain to the elderly couple. Bronson grabbed his solar-
powered flashlight and ran from the tent, but saw no movement in the fine white sand. He saw a path of disturbed sand
heading toward and through the tent, and the path continued
as far as the light could shine.

"What did you see?" Catherine asked as she came out of
the tent wrapped in a blanket.

"Nothing, but look, there's a path in the sand where it
dug. It seems to be gone now. Let's go back to sleep."

Bronson did not want to worry his wife but he felt that an
animal stalked them. Waiting until Catherine fell asleep, he
ventured outside again except, this time he brought his pistol
as well as his flashlight to investigate their strange visitor. He
did not see anything. Then he sat on a log and wrote about
what had just happened in his journal by the light of his
flashlight. He also wrote that he and Catherine had solved
the mystery of the disappearance of the millionaire and explorer C.K. Corker. He gathered items they'd brought back
from the plane and placed them in the trunk in the boat

without even reading Corker's journal. He thought that Corker had written in his journal prior to the crash, and though they did not find his body, he assured Catherine that Corker had died somewhere on the island and the underbrush hid his remains.

He fell asleep outside the tent, lying in the sand.

Catherine came out and woke him. "Wake up, Bronson! Why did you do this?"

"Do what?" he asked as he wiped the sleep out of his eyes. He focused and saw the remaining wood stacked neatly around him. "What the hell? I didn't do this. Did you?"

"No, I didn't. I just stepped out of the tent and saw the wood surrounding you on the sand." Catherine helped Bronson to his feet. As they were walking back to the tent, they noticed violent movement within their tent.

Bronson, with his gun in his hand, approached the tent with great caution. Catherine slowly walked behind him. He thrust open the flap, but saw nothing inside.

"It has to be somewhere!" he muttered to himself.

"What? What has to be in there?"

Bronson removed the mattress and said, "Whatever ran around in here."

He took everything out of the tent but found no animal inside. Once cleared, he returned all the items to the tent, all the while baffled as to what had caused the violent movement.

The instance of the logs neatly stacked around him also played havoc on his thinking. Catherine suggested another walk around the island to take their mind off the strange occurrence.

Every day for the next month, they had a routine of filling water bottles at the stream and foraging for food to supplement what they had in the trunk and what Bronson could catch fishing. After daily chores, exploration of the jungle continued. Since they'd landed on the island, Bronson noticed subtle differences in the way Catherine looked. She walked faster and smiled easier despite their desperate situation. She had a playful outlook on their situation, and her hair appeared to be getting less gray. He speculated that being in the bright sunshine most of the day lightened her hair.

Later, Bronson wrote in his journal about the stark

changes in Catherine's appearance. She loved the island, but Bronson wanted to leave as fast as possible. Although most of the time he deferred to his wife's sudden reemergence to her previously healthy self, he reminded her that soon they had to search for edible plants. Banana trees were plentiful, as well as coconuts, but getting the coconuts proved difficult for a seventy-year-old man, and he did not want to use bullets on them. They marked a few of the banana plants to remind themselves to harvest the fruit once it ripened.

Their food supply dwindled, so he went to the marked plants, but he saw something odd. Not only were the bananas not ready for harvesting, they appeared to be regressing. The bananas were twice as small as they had been when he first marked them. They appeared to be growing backward, or younger. Searching for the other plants, he found one deeper in the jungle, picked a bag full of bananas, and brought them back to the camp.

Occasionally, he asked her if she really wanted to leave the island, but she offered no opinion. She loved the warm winds, the tropical setting, and the never-ending intuition that her salvation existed there.

Embarrassed to talk about her feelings, she knew that Bronson wanted to leave as fast as possible because he worried about the things happening around them. Catherine knew little of what Bronson experienced because he shielded her from the bizarre and unexplainable occurrences. He loved her newfound glow of happiness, and for the month and a few days they'd been on the island, she'd had no memory breakdowns or any indications that she suffered from a lethal illness. Her mind and body changed daily, but she attributed her improving health to her walks around the island.

After six months of living on the island, Catherine's former quick smile returned to her, which led to practical jokes on her loving husband. She hid things from him, and after he had spent hours looking for items, she proudly produced them and laughed at his frantic behavior. He laughed with her and he loved those times.

Her happy nature turned serious, however, because she sensed that she missed something. "Bronson, what do you think the date is? There's something I feel I should be remembering."

Bronson had been marking the days off in his journal and went to get it, then returned in five minutes. "It's early January, the tenth, I think."

Saddened, Catherine, said, "Oh dear God, we missed it!"

Bronson had no idea why Catherine had gone from being the happiest he had seen her in years to the saddest. "What did we miss? Christmas? New Year's?"

"Yes, we missed all the holidays, but we missed Brooke's due date. We missed the birth of our grandchild!"

"Oh shit! You're right! We're grandparents!"

"I hope she's okay. I promised her I'd be there to ease her fears. I feel so bad right now." Catherine began to cry.

Bronson consoled his grieving wife. "Easy, Cathy, we're stuck on an island. I'm sure she forgives you under the circumstances. We're alive and maybe we'll still get to see him or her one day."

"I hope so. I hope everything went well."

"I'm sure it did. I guess by now she thinks the sea swallowed us up. We have to stay alive. I'll figure a way to get us off this island."

Catherine grabbed his arm and wiped her eyes on his shirt. "I know you will, sweetheart."

Catherine did not know that the unknown entity burrowing under the sand had attacked many times and Bronson didn't tell her. He made up stories of skin cancer with hopes of convincing Catherine to stay off the sand.

Bronson was fishing from the beach on a beautiful warm morning when he saw something heading toward him from farther down the beach. The small mound of sand moved very fast. He ditched the fishing rod and jumped out of the way as it sped past. He got to his feet and saw his fishing rod pulled into the sea. He wanted to follow the mound, but their survival depended on him supplying fish for the dinner table, so he ran toward the surf, dove into the water, and collected the rod just in time.

He sloshed out of the water, and the mound barreled toward him once more. This time, it changed course to match his movements and once it passed him by, he ran toward the tree line and to the tent twenty feet further inland. He saw Catherine reading the same book she had read on the boat. She had read it many times, as it was the only one Bronson managed to save before his ship went down.

During their walks on the beach, Bronson's tormentor never appeared. He tried to explain to Catherine what he had seen, but he never could describe it adequately.

Catherine figured that he was trying to scare her into never walking off by herself. She had serious doubts about the monster under the sand, but listened intently to her husband's unbelievable stories.

Two weeks later, during one of their adventures far away from their camp, they walked hand-in-hand on the other side of the island; Bronson looked back and saw the mound barreling toward them at an incredible speed.

In the nick of time, he pushed Catherine out of the way into the jungle and jumped to the beach side as the mound passed by them. Catherine did not see it, and the sudden jarring of being thrown so far and hitting a tree caused an injury to her leg. She screamed in pain as Bronson ran toward her.

He kneeled and assessed the damage. "Oh dear God!"

Catherine angrily asked, "Why did you do that, Bronson?"

"The mound of sand stalked you! I had to push you aside!" he explained. "Let me see your leg, honey! Move your hands."

He took off his shirt and shredded it because she bled badly and he needed to make a tourniquet. She removed her hand; he saw the gaping slice in her flesh that oozed blood at a rapid rate. He frantically tried to get the blood to stop flowing out. He applied pressure and suddenly, without reason, the blood stopped before he applied the tourniquet. He removed her bandage and saw an incredible sight. The gaping wound healed itself right in front of him. The gash sealed itself in seconds and once he wiped away the excess blood, the wound had disappeared. There were no signs, no scars, nothing to indicate an injury of any kind.

Catherine could not see a wound and did not believe Bronson because she saw the amount of blood that soaked her husband's shredded shirt. Her pain subsided and she felt her leg, which was as smooth as ever. "What did you do?" she asked.

"I didn't do anything! Your leg healed itself in seconds! I saw the gash close up instantly. This is impossible. Honey, you were sliced to the bone and now there's no sign that you were ever cut! How do you feel?"

"I feel great! The pain is gone. There's just a small ache that I can't explain. It's a miracle!"

"I think it's this island. A lot of strange things are happening here. Your hair has a small brown streak in it."

Catherine responded, "Yours appears to be getting darker too."

Bronson replied, "I sort of liked my gray hair, but look at it now! And it's growing at an incredible rate."

"I like it like that. I say let it grow out. It's sort of sexy. I don't care how my leg healed, as long as it did. Let's get back to camp, I'm getting hungry. I'm sorry about your shirt. I know you have only one left," she said as she tried to piece it together to go over his shoulders.

Catherine had a slight limp in her step as they headed back to camp, and she leaned on Bronson the rest of the way. While the mystery of her leg healing so quickly still preyed on his mind, Bronson decided that the camp needed a few chairs to sit on.

He waited until Catherine fell asleep, then wandered into the jungle and cut small, low-hanging branches from trees, as there were not any dead branches on the jungle floor. He carried them back and piled them by the tent. He made three trips to collect enough to make two chair frames, and checked on Catherine each time. He skillfully cut notches in the legs with his machete to interlock with the side slats of the chairs to ensure strength, then tied them together tightly. He made the two chairs match as much as possible, for warm nights on the beach to watch the ocean side by side. He tied the branches together with strips of moist bark and interwove them to make the backs of the chairs. He sewed the seats from the canvas bag that once held the tent, which supplied plenty of material. He cut it in half and formed two pillows, sewn together crudely with thinner strips of bark on one end and stuffed with leaves and unusable clothing. When both were completed, he sat down and felt pride at what he constructed; it held his weight easily.

Sitting in one of chairs, then in the other, he could not wait any longer and woke Catherine. He kissed her lightly; she opened her eyes, smiled, and pulled him nearer. "I've got a surprise for you right here."

He saw that she was naked and apparently ready to seduce him. Given their age and her illness, Catherine never wanted to have sex, and Bronson never demanded it, but he could tell by her sly smile that she wanted it. Her newly rejuvenated sex drive enticed him, but he wanted to show her what he'd built first.

"Well, my surprise isn't as good as that one, but given our circumstances, mine ranks right up there. Come on, get up."

"Really, why can't you just lie next to me for a few more minutes?" she wantonly asked.

"I've been up for four hours. Come on. I want to show you something."

Catherine rose slowly because her leg still ached. Bronson led her out of the tent and showed her the chairs. "Oh, Bronson, they're beautiful. When did you do this?"

"I got up early this morning and made them. I thought that you were getting tired of sitting on the sand. I know I am. See how they feel."

Catherine sat and said, "They're perfect! I want them by the ocean."

"You got it, sweetheart!"

He took them to the beach and they relaxed for an hour, just watching the surf.

Bronson asked later, "Care to go for a stroll?"

"After all that work, aren't you tired? But yes, I think I can walk."

"I'll be fine. Feel like running?"

"I don't think I can," she explained, rubbing the sensation back into her leg.

They walked the length of a football field; then, Catherine took off running and a youthful Bronson kept pace, ever vigilant of moving mounds of sand both in front of them and behind. Three hours later, they arrived back at their tent exhausted and bent over, gasping for air.

"We need to take it easy on the running. We're not twenty-five anymore," he stated between deep breaths.

However, Catherine felt great, not as winded as Bronson. She went inside the tent and gathered some water for him as he sat, sweating profusely, on one of the new chairs.

"We only have a few cans of peas and corn left. After that, we're out of food," Catherine confessed.

"It lasted a long time, though. We'll never go hungry with an ocean of food swimming about. I'll get us some fish as soon as my heart rate goes down a bit."

After an hour of talking, Catherine reminded him about those fish he wanted to catch, so he got out of his comfortable chair, went to the boat, and gathered his deep sea fishing gear and a tackle box full of lures. No live bait existed anywhere on the island. Trudging toward the surf like a man on a mission, he cast the hooked lure out as far as he could. Catherine watched from her new chair.

He tossed the lure out many times, but caught nothing except clumps of seaweed and an occasional crab that he kept in case he did not land a substantial fish. Catherine loved seeing her tanned man fishing. Lately, she'd had many thoughts of sex as she watched her husband struggle to catch a fish. Thoughts that had long left her mind now returned to her instantly as she gazed at his muscles rippling with every cast. She did not know why the sexual thoughts manifested on the island, but given the fact that they had been non-existent for many years, she welcomed them back. Given the sparse amount of food, each of them had lost a considerable amount of weight; however, not so much as to appear unhealthy. Coupled with the exercise they were getting, they were actually healthier than when they first arrived.

Bronson could not explain it, but their energy level had rocketed up, which enabled them to jog, run, and walk for most of the day. The bottled water supply had long since run out, but the brook supplied them with what they needed, though it had a slight salty taste to it. They were just happy to have a seemingly never-ending water supply.

The sun rose high and bright that afternoon, and it bothered Catherine, so she walked a slight distance to the tent and entered to finish reading her much-read book. A half-hour later, an excited Bronson ran into the tent and informed her that he had caught a huge shark. She put the book down and walked with him to the edge of the tree line to see a two-hundred-pound tiger shark violently whipping its rear fin trying to get back to the water. Bronson ran to it and muscled it on the beach, where it finally gave up and died.

They were hungry; Catherine returned to the camp and set up everything she needed to fry up the catch once Bronson extracted the steaks. It seemed a shame to her that they did not have enough salt to make the fish last longer. However, drying some strips in the sun would preserve some of it. He returned to the camp and asked, "Where's my big knife?"

She said, "I think it's in the boat."

She followed him to the beach and stayed at the tree line as Bronson ran to the boat. However, beyond Bronson's view, something brewed underneath the white sand. Catherine saw an indescribable beast emerge from the sand to eat the massive shark in one bite. She let out a piercing scream.

Bronson ran to her, but she could only point toward where the shark once laid.

Ignoring her pointing, he asked, "Catherine? What's wrong?"

She could not speak. Scared, he did not look toward the surf; he knelt by her side, hoping to get a few words out of her. He had never seen that look on her face before.

Frightened, she again pointed toward the beach.

Bronson followed her gaze to see that the great fish he had just caught had vanished in mere seconds—save the rear fin.

"Where did it go?" he questioned her. "I saw it seconds ago. I just went to the boat! Catherine, what did you see?"

Still horrified many minutes later, she could not muster enough coherent words to express what she had witnessed. He begged her to take deep breaths to calm her heart rate.

Bronson walked over to where the shark used to be and Catherine screamed, "Get off the sand! Please! Get off the sand!"

He ran back to the tree line and again tried to calm her. He speculated that her old disease had returned because she cried openly and nonstop. Bronson understood every other word. He had never seen Catherine so frightened. Even the death of her son had not presented such horror. Shaking and stuttering, she mustered the words, "It came out of the sand! It came out of the sand!"

"It came out of the sand? *What* came out of the sand?"

"It's a monster! A great monster and it swallowed the shark in a split second."

"A monster? What did this monster look like?"

"It's huge. It's bright red with a head made up of teeth. Hundreds and hundreds of teeth, and then it went back under the sand in a second. It had the body of a snake but the head of a dragon. We need to move the camp to the jungle. We can't stay out here anymore. Come on, Bronson! Help me!"

Catherine tried to pick up everything and carry it to the jungle all in one trip, but she carried too much and she fell over.

"Easy, sweetheart. I'll help you."

He gathered her to her feet and put a more reasonable weight in her arms. She ran into the jungle, Bronson following close behind. "Cathy! Stop running! We'll make camp here in this clearing. I know you're scared, but if you keep going, you'll hit the beach on the other side of the island."

Catherine turned back toward him.

The clearing had very little underbrush, and the canopy allowed a slight bit of sunlight to penetrate it. They'd visited the site many times before, and it appeared to them that it had expanded. Bronson had no idea why nothing grew there, but he did not care. He quickly set up the tent and made many trips to pick up the rest of their possessions.

They were closer to their water supply, and after getting used to the new site, it equaled the ambiance of their surf-side campsite, though it lacked the soothing sounds of the rolling waves crashing on shore.

Catherine found a pool within the jungle where fresh water cleansed her body and rejuvenated her spirit.

The new location brought new fears because the wind and the plants surrounding their tent conspired to create sounds outside that mimicked footsteps and whispers of unknown and unseen beings.

Many nights, Catherine's fears that someone or something stalked them awakened Bronson. He went outside fully armed, but never found anything out of the ordinary.

Catherine held Bronson much closer after the beach incident. Her carefree romps on the beach were gone, as were their long walks around the island, and that saddened Bronson. They walked the interior, but when their walks ended at the beach, she recoiled and led him away quickly.

An invisible barrier existed that Catherine did not want breached again. She knew that their lives depended on Bronson's ability to catch fish. She followed him, but never ventured past the tree line. However, she had a full view of Bronson's angling adventure. He always caught fish, but only enough to last for a day or two. There were many times that he saw the mounds of sand roll toward him, but Catherine kept a wary eye out for dangers and she quickly warned him in plenty of time for him to evade the attack. Still, each time scared her terribly.

Four months later, Bronson had not yet seen what lurked beneath the sand, but he wanted to get yellow fin tuna for a special occasion. They celebrated their birthdays, but today marked their first anniversary on the island.

He caught one, carried the small tuna to the camp, and presented it to Catherine. "Look what I have."

"It's a yellow fin!"

"Yes, it is. It's our anniversary."

"We were married in May!"

Smiling, Bronson explained, "I know. This is for our first anniversary on the island."

"Has it been a year? My, it doesn't seem that long."

"It is according to my journal. I've been marking the days. Now let's filet this tuna and celebrate!"

They ate the fish and, with full stomachs, they did what they always did—watched the sunset and talked about their lives together. Catherine loved their new camp because it supplied them with ample shade as well as a sprinkling of the sun's rays. Their clearing got larger as time went by because the plants and trees around them were dying. Amazed, Bronson found no remnants of the dying plants. They just disappeared.

They stayed there for the next year with very little problems outside of the fact that they had not had a decent meal since their one-year anniversary, or a good shower for over a year. Both of them had dramatically changed. Bronson did not expect them to live as long as they did, but not only were they alive, they thrived. Catherine's illness had all but vanished, and both of them were in great health and getting better. Bronson attributed their appearance to hard work and the most exercise they had gotten in twenty years.

Eventually, Catherine braved the beach because she felt dirty and wanted to go for a swim. She could no longer resist the ocean's allure, so she ran to the surf and dove into an incoming wave. She instantly felt a surge of strength that she thought had left her years ago.

She swam effortlessly, and remembrances of training for the Olympics popped into her memory. Always a strong swimmer, Catherine's strength exploded so much that Bronson could no longer keep up with her. She playfully swam around him, taunting him, effortlessly circling him in the calm water.

"What's wrong, dear? If you can't keep up, I'll save you," Catherine said with a broad grin.

"How the hell can you do this? You're a seventy-year-old woman!" He smiled along with her.

"I feel young, Bronson. I can't explain it, nor do I care how it's happening. I feel like I'm in my twenties." She pointed toward the shore, signaling that she wanted to go back.

Wary of the animal underneath the sand, she waited for Bronson. As soon as he met her in the shallows, they both ran for the tree line as fast as they could. Once reached, they looked back, but saw no mounds of sand chasing after them.

Chapter Four

Unknown Attacker

The Premingers faced many storms during their first two years on the island, but none so strange as the one they suffered during a sleepless night in their now tattered tent as they lay with glorious visions of the sunset still percolating in their minds. The wind started to howl and the rain poured in from the many holes in the tent. It had suffered numerous rips and tears over many storms, but not catastrophically, due to the large trees and foliage around them, which blocked much of the gale force winds.

That night, the wind came in strong from the north as they were nestled inside, and hit hard. The tattered part of the tent whipped around with great force. Bronson quickly cut the strips of canvas off because they were attacking them on the inside. They felt as if they were in the middle of a hurricane as they listened to Mother Nature's wrath. The storm scared Catherine so much so that she clamped tightly to Bronson's arm and caused numbness from lack of blood flow.

"Shit! Catherine, I forgot to check on the boat! This wind could take it away. I have to go secure it!"

"You can't go out in this! I'm scared! I've never seen it like this," she yelled over the loud howls of the unrelenting wind. She pulled him closer and begged him not to leave her.

"I'm sorry, honey, but I have to protect the boat. If it's blown away, we will never get off this island! We need it if we ever see a barge or boat on the horizon. Don't worry, I'll be back soon."

Their elevated voices fought the intense sounds of the flapping of the tent's loose parts and the deafening, destructive wind. As they argued, part of the tent collapsed, which made the urgency to go outside much more important. Checking on the boat suddenly became secondary in his thoughts now that the tent needed repair with his scared wife inside.

He tried to re-prop the tent from the inside, but he was unsuccessful because of the compromised aluminum support poles.

Bronson braved the wind and rain, left the tent, and repaired the pole, and then walked around to assess the potential additional damage, but found none.

He reentered to see a frightened Catherine cowering under the blankets. She feared the flying debris, so he took a deep breath and bolted outside, but he saw something that appeared impossible to behold. No wind blew outside the tent. The tent's main support pole had fallen and he quickly reseated it. He saw no indications of wind damage anywhere else. The surrounding foliage was still, no loose branches had broken off, and there was nothing to indicate that gale force winds had just blown through their camp. In fact, he looked up and saw perfectly clear twinkling stars breaking through the darkness of the thick jungle. The wind had stopped as quickly as it started. The weather patterns on the island had always been unpredictable, but this shocked him.

The strange occurrence got eerier when he returned inside the tent to see that nothing had changed. The wind still howled and the tattered parts still whipped around. He stepped back outside and the wind ceased.

Bronson coaxed Catherine to come out, and though skeptical, she stepped outside to notice the same thing Bronson observed.

She looked around. "How is this possible? What is happening to us?"

"I don't know, but we're not going back in there! I guess we're going to have to build another shelter. Tonight, I think we should sleep outside. I hate that insects will be biting us, though."

"Insects? Bronson, I haven't seen one ant or insect since we've been here. Have you?" She pulled the mattress and blankets out.

"There have to be insects here somewhere, but you're right, I haven't seen any. I'll start building a new shelter tomorrow morning. That old tent is worn out anyway. Still, I feel like we're being watched. Someone or something is out there that doesn't want us here."

Catherine, too tired to think, said, "Come, let's try to get some sleep. We'll worry about it tomorrow."

They tried to sleep, but the events still weighed heavily on their minds; sleep remained an impossible task.

The morning sun broke through a few clouds, shining brightly in their eyes. Hungry, Bronson started with his usual routine of catching fish and collecting bananas and coconuts. They were tired of their daily fare. Then Bronson remembered something he had done five years prior to their voyage, when he packed his survival trunk, and wondered if he had actually done what he'd thought of at the time. Age had a way of making remembering such things difficult. At the time, he had wondered why people did not simply pack seeds, should they ever get lost on an island.

He reached the trunk. There were small pouches on the sides of the interior, and when he opened them up, the seeds were there. He thought of all the time he'd squandered worrying about gathering food and smacked his head. He had corn, tomatoes, cucumber seeds, and many other varieties of fruits and vegetables. He could not wait to tell Catherine of their good fortune.

Running back to their camp, he noticed that the path had changed dramatically. The thick foliage seemed sparse compared to his remembrance of the area. There were no dead branches or leaves scattered about to indicate what had happened, so he did not dwell on the mystery and continued toward the camp.

Arriving, he presented the seeds to her and placed all thoughts of building a new shelter on the back burner because they had to get a spot cleared to plant. Catherine beamed at the thought of growing her own food. They searched for the perfect spot by the stream, then cleared a small area where the sun did not bear down on their garden. Because of its sandy base, the questionable soil did not provide confidence that the plants would grow. They planted their rudimentary garden anyway and impatiently yearned for the day when they could eat something that they had not seen or tasted for two years. The fruits of the island sustained them, as did the fish that Bronson caught daily, but now, they looked forward to variety.

With the garden planted, Bronson and Catherine began the construction of their new, more permanent shelter. They were amazed that they both possessed the strength to carry out such an undertaking. The battered tent had served its purpose for nearly two years and protected them through too many storms. They also appeared to be getting younger physically, but they attributed that to all the exercise they were forced to do in order to survive, as well as the fact that they ate only healthy foods. They constructed the foundation of their new home, and dutifully watered and cared for their new garden. A week later, another mystery confronted them. Sound asleep in the tattered tent, Catherine awoke to hear noises, which caused her to nudge Bronson awake.

She placed her hand over his mouth and whispered, "I hear footsteps outside! Do you hear them? Someone's walking around the tent!"

"I hear it. It must be right outside," Bronson uttered in hushed words.

He slowly and quietly grabbed his loaded pistol, readying himself for a possible confrontation. Catherine did not let go of his arm, terrified because they had determined that they were the island's only inhabitants.

Bronson looked through some of the many holes in the tent to give him an idea of what lurked, but he saw nothing other than a strip of canvas that the wind had blown away. Bronson's bravado waned with the sounds of each creaking branch. The stalker made no other sounds. Then, suddenly, the footsteps stopped.

"Is he gone?" Catherine whispered.

"I don't know, but I'm going to have to find out. Here, you take the rifle. Do you know how to use this kind?" he asked as he checked his pistol once again.

"Yes, I've watched you long enough. Bronson, I'm scared! We've canvassed this entire island. There are no people here."

"Well, we haven't checked the mountain yet, so I guess there could be a cave or two. I'll be right back."

"We've walked there, but there were no openings and there is no way we can climb that to check for caves."

Bronson left with his pistol drawn. He looked around into

the darkness, then turned on his solar-powered flashlight and surveyed the area, but saw nothing.

"Come on out, Catherine. It's gone now. Dammit!"

"What's wrong?" Catherine asked, as she attentively walked out.

"Our shelter! It's destroyed!"

They went over to inspect it. Bronson's finely weaved walls made of vines and large leaves were missing. The rocks that he collected and carefully placed for the foundation had also magically disappeared.

"How did they do this without making a sound? It's as if we didn't do anything." Catherine asked.

"I don't know, but we'll start to rebuild it tomorrow."

He walked over to the pile of leaves that were once his walls and noticed something moving. He kneeled down, separated the clutter all the way down to sand, and noticed that the leaves and vines were being absorbed by the island's sandy floor. He pointed his flashlight downward. He grabbed the vines and felt something on the other end pulling. He struggled to retrieve the vines, but the pull was too strong. He let go and watched as they disappeared. Soon after, there was no trace of the semi-built structure.

"The island swallowed the entire thing!" Bronson bellowed.

Catherine asked, "How could that be? Quicksand?"

"No, it's solid all around. There is no quicksand here. It appears to be eating all the leaves and vines I picked."

Suddenly, a flying coconut grazed Catherine's head. She dropped to the jungle floor. She held her head as she attempted to stand up.

"Stay down, Catherine. I'll be right back!"

"Bronson, don't go in there! Please stay with me!"

"I'll be back in a few minutes. Just stay there until I get back. I have to see where it came from."

He'd seen the projectile hurled through the darkness and ran to the place where he thought it came from. He slowly moved leaves from his path, ready for an altercation. His pistol and flashlight pointed forward. His senses were alert for anything. A gentle wind brushed against his face as he trudged through the thick jungle. He heard no footsteps or whispered words.

He flashed his flashlight, searching for footprints or anything that marred the smooth, sandy floor, but he saw nothing. With every step, the surrounding jungle created an unnerving fear. Normal sounds created by the wind caused him to wave the gun wildly, ready to pull the trigger at the slightest sound.

He traveled far enough, and the thought of his injured wife overtook his desire in finding the culprit. He carefully backtracked to Catherine. He arrived to see her face covered in blood from a cut on her head. Bronson knelt beside her to determine her injuries. She fainted when she saw her hands bloodied. He grabbed her in his arms, carried her into the tent, and laid her gently on the ground. With his lantern supplying light, he dabbed a clean cloth with water and wiped away the blood to see the extent of her cut. The wound had stopped bleeding. After a few minutes, she opened her eyes.

"Bronson, what happened?" she asked as she attempted to sit up.

"It's the damnedest thing I ever saw. Someone threw a coconut and knocked you down."

"Thrown at me? You mean a coconut fell from one of the trees?"

"No, thrown! It came from out of the darkness. I searched for whoever threw it, but I found no one. I stopped because I had to tend to you. You fainted when you saw all the blood."

Catherine asked, "There's someone else on the island?"

"Possibly. I don't know how it was thrown at that angle. Oh, I don't know. It could be that the creepiness of the jungle is making us crazy. It was probably just a coconut that fell from a tree and the wind took it, making us believe that it was thrown."

"There isn't that much wind, Bronson."

"I know that, but perhaps a gust of wind above us that we can't feel made it appear it was thrown. We've searched this island and found no one here. After thinking about it, it's a logical reason."

Catherine accepted her husband's reasoning, but regardless of the logic behind his explanation, the structure that they had toiled over had mysteriously disappeared. That remained a mystery to them both.

The strange occurrences scared her, but she remained as calm as possible, thinking that another more plausible explanation could be determined in the light of day.

"I'm tired, Bronson. Let's try to get some sleep. We have to rebuild the house tomorrow," Catherine reminded him as she covered up and tried to forget what she'd been through.

"Are you sure you're okay, honey?"

"It's just a scratch. Now, let's get some sleep."

Bronson lay beside her as Catherine drifted off to sleep. He wondered about the mysterious visitor, and could not sleep for fear that the entity would return. He lay beside her with his eyes open, rehashing all that happened in his mind and searching for other logical reasons. Eventually, he also fell soundly asleep.

At sunup, a gunshot abruptly awakened Bronson. He opened his sleepy eyes to see Catherine pointing her rifle at the opening of the tent. The explosion painfully rang in his ears as he tried to understand what had happened. While covering his left ear with one hand, he grabbed the rifle from Catherine with his other.

"What the hell are you shooting at, Cathy? My ears are ringing!"

"I saw him! He tried to get into the tent. I killed him!"

"Him? Him who?"

"A man dressed up as a plant! I killed him!" She cowered under the blankets and pointed toward the tent's opening.

"You stay here. I'll go outside to see who or what you shot."

Bronson wiped his eyes and shook his head. Still holding his rifle, he rose to his feet and stepped outside.

Scared, Catherine quivered under the blankets, anxiously awaiting Bronson's return.

Bronson came back in and set down his rifle. "There's nothing out there, Cathy."

"Yes, there is! I shot him in the chest! He has to be dead!" she yelled, crying profusely.

"Look for yourself. There is nothing out there. I walked all around the area. There's no blood or bodies anywhere."

Catherine removed the blankets, wiped the tears out of her eyes, and cautiously walked outside in the blazing morning sun. At first, she sheepishly looked around, but saw nothing. She grew bolder in her search because she knew what she had seen and done.

Eventually, she grew angry that they had seen no signs that she had shot anyone or anything. She stomped around the tent twice and dropped to her knees, frantically searching the ground and underbrush for just a single drop of blood to validate her experience. Bronson saw how much she wanted to find anything and sat next to her.

She said through tears, "I couldn't have missed him. Perhaps I wounded him and he ran off?"

"That's possible, I guess, but there is no blood that I can see. Look, I have to start the boat's motor to keep it ready in case we see some form of rescue. Do you want to come?"

She stopped pushing back weeds, held her head in her hands, and cried, "There's nothing here. There's nothing here..."

Bronson saw that something more than her perceived experience was hurting her.

"What's really wrong, dear?" he asked.

"It's back! It must be back!"

"What's back, dear?"

"My disease is back. It must be!" Catherine cried even more, and grabbed Bronson and hugged him.

He forgot about everything else and hugged her harder. "We'll get through this, honey, I promise you."

Catherine's Alzheimer's disease had all but disappeared while they were on the island, but now she feared that it was coming back and making her see things that were not there. Bronson spent the next fifteen minutes hugging the pain out of her. He had never seen her cry that long.

He changed the subject because he could see that her biggest fear had reemerged in her mind. The fear of dying with no memories. Up until then, the island strangely reversed the onset of her dementia, but now, neither was sure her experience had really happened. He felt bad for her pain, stood her up, and gently kissed her head. Her pain transferred to him as he shed a few more tears. He hated seeing his wife in distress.

"You want to take a walk?"

Wiping her eyes and obviously still feeling the turmoil of assuming she was not getting better, decided to courageously go on. "Yes, I do, but let me water the garden first."

Early the next morning, Bronson was still worried about

his distressed wife. She had not had an Alzheimer's moment since they stepped foot on the island, but now he had notions that her issues lessened due to the serene tropical setting that the island presented. The soothing sounds of the surf and the sweet beach air calmed her as she sat on her favorite stump and read Bronson's journal; her book had long since disintegrated in the tough conditions.

Bronson righted the boat, poured a small amount of gasoline in the outboard motor, and started it.

Catherine looked over the top of the journal at him. "Why don't we take a trip around the island in the boat?"

He wiped his hands and turned off the motor. "We can't do that, honey, because we only have a little gas and we'll need it if we ever see a way to get off of here. I figure we have enough to make it to a boat if we see one, but not enough to escape the island. By the way, you're looking great today."

"I feel great. Look at my hands. It seems that these age spots are dissolving." She held out her hands.

"I know! Mine too."

"I think we should take the boat out once in a while to make sure it still floats. Besides, we don't want a surprise when we do see a ship."

Bronson scratched his head. "That's a great thought! I didn't think about that. Let me catch a few fish and we'll take it out for a bit. Besides, I do have oars, and my back feels great. Do you want to fish with me?"

"No, I still remember what I saw out there. I know we haven't seen the sand move for a while, but I still don't want to."

"Well, if we go for a ride on the boat, you'll have to walk on the sand to get to the boat."

"I'll run when it's in the water."

Catherine settled into her chair and watched for moving sand as Bronson strolled to the water's edge and readied his angler's gear. His body was tanned, and a slight breeze fluttered his tattered shirt as he flung his cast out into the deep, hoping to catch that night's dinner, all the while looking back at his wife disrobing on the edge of the beach, enticing him. He knew of her fear of the beach itself and that she would remain where she was. Their clothes, weathered over the years, were wearing out, so they often wore nothing when the weather cooperated. However, this time, the sudden removal of her clothes affected Bronson and reminded him of his youth. He would not be a man if he didn't notice the youthful change in her body. It did not seem to be important to wear clothes all the time, given they were the island's only inhabitants. They just wore clothes to protect them from the weather. There were clothes in the suitcase they found on the plane once their own clothes wore out, but there didn't seem to be a great enough need for them yet.

She sat at the beach's edge and wrote in Bronson's journal, waiting for him to gather dinner. However, on that day, he caught nothing due to his preoccupation with staring back at his naked wife and ignoring the task at hand. Ever cautious of the moving sand, he walked back to the boat and prepared it for his short adventure around the island with Catherine. She quickly helped him push the boat to the remnants of a once powerful wave that licked their feet.

The boat floated and they climbed aboard. They both wore shirts during their trip in case the sun got too bright. Bronson loved it when Catherine threw modesty out the window and walked around naked. The old feelings had strangely returned to them. Sex in their older years had never been a priority in their marriage, but since being on the island, the thoughts of such pleasures had resurrected themselves. They both thought about it often, though neither of them mentioned that their desires had changed.

Bronson rowed the boat a bit, then started the motor. He was wary of how much gas he expended, but he considered it a gift to his lovely wife. Boredom with island living got to her; they needed a respite from the tedium.

They looked at the island from afar for the first time since their landing.

They'd explored seventy-five percent of the island; the last part consisted mainly of the large mountain on the southern-most edge.

Age prevented them from scaling the sheer face of the huge peak, although they had tried a few times. A tall mountain, it jutted out of the island with sharp, rocky crags and loose stones that made an ascent nearly impossible, but they still they vowed to scale it eventually. They'd claimed the island as their own with all its strange attributes and eerie mysteries, and they wanted to tread upon every part of it, but the mountaintop proved to be an unreachable star or the last frontier.

With the wind in her hair, she leaned back and soaked it all in as Bronson steered the boat. They passed the mountain and started their return trip when Catherine perked up and saw something sitting, then moving on the precipice near the top. Intently staring at the bluff, she saw the object move with animalistic actions. She stood up in the boat, causing it to rock, and excitedly pointed to the mountaintop, but what she saw vanished before Bronson could see it. He turned off the motor and peered through binoculars, but saw nothing out of the ordinary. Catherine, excited in her belief that she had seen an animal, insisted that they stop to investigate, but a half hour later, Bronson still saw nothing.

"I know what I saw, Bronson! Something is up there!" she spouted, as Bronson shrugged off her discovery. It irritated Catherine that her husband discounted her claims and she demanded that he acknowledge her discovery. Humbled and angry, she sulked at the back of the boat with her arms crossed and an unwillingness to dismiss what she'd seen.

He noticed her demeanor and said, "If there is something up there, it knows how to scale a one-hundred-foot sheer cliff. Cathy, we need to get back," he muttered, as he started the motor. He thought that she was again seeing things that were not there. His patience wore thin and he did not feel the need to reason with her. Instead, he focused on getting them back to their camp.

Catherine, seeing that Bronson turned the boat around, stated angrily, "I know what I saw! I don't care about the gas! We need to find a way to get up there."

Raising his voice, he spouted, "Cathy, are you crazy? I'm seventy-two and you're seventy; how the hell are we going to climb that? There's nothing up there and I'm not going to risk our lives finding that out!" Bronson navigated the boat to their encampment. "Besides, we have to build our shelter."

Catherine, seeing that her suggestion irritated her normally jovial husband, relented. "Okay, Bronson! I know we have to build the hut and gather food. As for our ages, have you noticed that we don't appear to be aging?"

Bronson did not answer, but he knew what she meant;

however, he had no explanation about the phenomenon because he always believed that when something impossible happened, there usually lurked some dark consequences to counteract whatever fate planned for him. The strange, unexplainable aspects of the island caused him great tension. Every time he thought of a reason for the odd experiences, the island did something to change his mind. There were many thoughts of unseen supernatural entities playing with his mind and creating something that just wasn't there. Even his dreams concocted stories of aliens who attacked from the darkness, not allowing for rational thought.

The long trip back and Catherine's angry silence allowed him to think of all of it. It preoccupied his mind and marred his normally clear-thinking judgment. The strange occurrences mounted daily and he remembered and relived them constantly, struggling for a single hint of resolve.

He secured the boat on shore and thought that he had been too aggressive in his beliefs, but he knew that his assertions were closer to being real than Catherine's. Her thinking she shot someone, coupled with the fact that she'd had a vision of a mountaintop neighbor, Bronson felt convinced that Catherine's illness had returned. He concluded that her sighting of movement on the mountain had to be the result of another illusion brought on by the choppy water. He noticed a change in his wife that day because she stayed on the beach, not worrying about whatever stalked them beneath the sand.

They finished their shelter two weeks later, a rudimentary shack made up of broad leaves and bamboo stalks, but it served them well. He had used up the remainder of his rope, so bamboo strips, cut thin, held most of the shack together, similar to the way he had built the two chairs. He converted the remnants of the tent into a roof because the material repelled rainwater perfectly.

For the next five months, the couple settled into a daily routine of gathering food and water and fortifying the hut. They checked their garden daily, but nothing grew, not even a sprout. He tried loosening the soil, but nothing worked.

Growing vegetables in the sandy soil proved futile, but all around him plants thrived in the same soil, which disappointed them both, but did not prevent them from passing by the garden every day with hopes that something had sprouted.

Catherine, sad that the garden did not grow, cried all the time; however it wasn't the lack of a good salad that depressed her. It was everything else about the island that manifested within her. Her garden issue was just one more thing added to her pile of failures. Everything seemed to make her miserable.

One minute she felt fine, and then the next, an unexplainable torrent of emotion captured her. Bronson feared that a bout of island fever, mixed with her Alzheimer's disease, caused her world to topple daily, and she struggled to dwell in the world of the sane.

Chapter Five

Catherine's Perceived Dementia

Worried about Catherine's bouts with confusion, Bronson felt the need to be by her side constantly, to the point where he irritated her. One morning, Bronson arose as the sunshine crept through one of the many crevices in the makeshift dwelling. Looking around and wiping his eyes, he called out to Catherine, but she did not answer. He ran from the hut and gathered his rifle just in case she had ventured out on the beach and their only known enemy should attack once again.

Running toward the beach, he frantically called for her. He checked all their usual spots, but she'd just vanished. Hours went by, yet he still could not find her. He ran around the island and even to the mountain, but still, no luck. By late afternoon, he gave up the search and returned to the camp, thinking that she may have gone there and waited for him. Arriving, he leaned the rifle against a tree and entered the empty hut. He rested for a few hours because he could barely walk, much less carry on his search.

Three hours later, as the sun lowered in the horizon, he gathered up some water and food and set out on a more extensive search. He loaded up, but saw Catherine approach, singing to herself as she calmly passed Bronson, entered the hut, and sat on the mattress.

"Where have you been all day? I've searched nearly the entire island!"

"I saw my grandson and he took me around the island."

"Our grandson? Cathy, we've never met our grandson—or granddaughter. That world is hundreds of miles away in Florida. Besides, our grandchild is only two years old. I doubt if he or she can even walk yet. Don't ever go off like that again! I've been searching for you everywhere!"

"I'm never lost, Bronson. Not here on the island. He showed me where we shouldn't go. He's a beautiful little boy."

"Let me make myself clear to you. We are on a deserted and probably uncharted island. We are the only humans here. We spent nearly three years looking for inhabitants and we found no one. Why hasn't this boy made his presence known to me?"

"He's afraid of you because you always have your gun with you. He came to me last night, and we took a walk through the jungle and he told me how he got here. Then he disappeared in the jungle and I spent hours looking for him."

Bronson, still irritated with Catherine, stated, "There is no boy, Cathy! We are alone here. You are having issues with your sanity again."

Catherine angrily stated, "I was right about seeing the island, wasn't I? Why don't you believe me now?"

"Yes, you were, but I've lived with you and your illness for some time and I've seen you see things that aren't there many times. We are experiencing something strange here and even the island sighting was odd given its sudden appearance."

"Maybe it's you who are seeing things or not seeing things."

Bronson ignored her obvious insult, as he had many times during her illness-induced episodes, and asked, "Please just promise me that you will not walk away from camp without me again."

Confused and angered, Catherine wondered why Bronson scolded her. "Promise what? I'm not your slave. If I want to explore the island alone, I will!"

"I know you're not my slave, it's just that I worry when I don't know where you are. I don't want you to get lost or injured." Many things concerned Bronson. He admitted to being overly protective of her, but the fear of someone or something watching them heightened his senses and made him almost desperate.

"We've been together twenty-four hours a day for the last three years. I needed some alone time. I'm sorry that you worried and will tell you when I need space next time. I am sorry."

Bronson apologized as well, and decided to placate Catherine about her imaginary friend. He asked, "Now, about this boy you met out in the jungle?"

"I walked near the creek when he peered out from behind a tree and told me to beware of the tree I nearly leaned on. I don't know why he warned me about it, but then he ran away."

"What did he look like?"

"He's shirtless and has long blond hair past his shoulders. He has tattered oversized shorts on and shoes that appear three sizes too large. He said his name is Charles." She nibbled on a banana, knowing that Bronson did not believe a word she said.

"Well? Where is he? I wonder if he's the one who threw the coconut at you."

"No, he didn't do that. He is a very nice young man who seems well educated. I guess he's really not my grandson, but I think of him or her often. I pictured him that way. I don't know why I do that."

"Can you show me the tree he warned you about?"

"Sure, it's by the creek. I can take you now if you'd like."

Bronson, anxious to see what Catherine had discovered, grabbed his machete and his backpack. Catherine took off walking; Bronson gave her the machete to clear the underbrush, and followed close behind. She hacked a few vines along the way and Bronson noticed that the vines did not just fall; they reconnected with other vines and fused together before they hit the ground.

"Did you see that? The vines you cut fused with the others before my eyes. I've never seen plants do that before."

Catherine seemed unconcerned as she approached the tree. "Well, come on, the tree is right over here."

Bronson ignored the odd plant behavior and followed Catherine to the strangest of trees. A normal enough tree, but with an unusual blood-red trunk. He grabbed the machete and took a chunk out of it. The chunk fell to the ground and reconnected to the tree at its base. The tall, thick tree appeared to heal itself extraordinarily fast. The chunk that Bronson cut out completely filled in.

"What the hell kind of tree is this?" He looked up and saw

very few leaves on its branches. He looked at Catherine. "What did the boy say about the tree? Because I admit it's strange-looking, but what did he warn you about?"

"He just told me to stay clear of them, that's all."

Bronson, walking around the tree, placed his hand on the bark. It immediately sucked two fingers in.

Frantically, he tried to pull his fingers out, but the more he struggled, the more the tree sucked in his fingers. He felt intense pain, as the tree appeared to be eating his two fingers from the inside a little at a time. He screamed.

"What is happening, Bronson?" She tried to pull him away from the tree but she was not strong enough. He struggled to free himself as he winced in great pain, screaming and throwing obscenities at the strange tree. Sweat poured from his body as the unimaginable tense scene created a horror that he had never seen or felt. His eyes tightly closed, trying to do anything to ease the anguish he felt. Blood was seen oozing from where his fingers were inserted. His two fingers were in one knuckle deep as he pleaded with Catherine to do something that she could not do.

"Catherine! Cut my fingers off! Quickly! I can't pull them out and it's sucking my hand in further! The tree is eating them from the inside! Cut them off!" He let out another anguished scream.

Catherine frantically tried to help, thinking that there had to be a better way to extract him. "Cut off your fingers? There has to be a better way! I can't cut off your fingers!" She frantically tried to pull him away.

"Give the damned knife to me! Quickly!" he demanded.

Catherine, crying and frantic, hesitantly gave him the machete, knowing what he intended to do. She turned away because she couldn't watch his horrific resolve.

He intentionally calmed himself, took careful aim, and with a mighty swing, sliced the tips of his fingers off. He fell to the ground, holding his hand as blood gushed from his ring and middle fingers. He squeezed until the blood stopped, and his anguished screams echoed loudly throughout the jungle. Tears flowed down his face as he tried to calm himself to prevent shock and making the situation much worse. He tore off the remainder of his shirt and threw it at Catherine, imploring her to cut it into a bandage until he got back to camp and took care of his injury. She violently ripped the shirt to shreds and helped him wrap them around his hand.

Catherine stared intently as Bronson tightly wrapped his hand to stop the blood flow. Her emotions were all on display as she revisited what had happened.

They sped back to camp. For only the second time in three years, he opened the extensive first aid kit, grabbed the antiseptic, and poured it over his fingers. The pain subsided slightly, but he knew what he had to do next. He calmly told Catherine to stitch him up because he did not want infections to invade the exposed flesh. They had precious little medicine to combat an infection. With his other hand, he squeezed one finger, stopping the blood flow as she pierced the outer skin and brought it over the exposed area.

"I can't do this, Bronson!"

"Well I can't and you are the only one here. Honey, I know it's difficult for you, but I need you now."

"I know! I know..."

Catherine saw the pain he was experiencing on his face and knew that she would be supplying more pain by doing what he asked.

"Sweetheart, it's just like mending a sock. Please, I need you to do this."

His bloody nubs were right in front of her. Her heart beat so fast that it felt it would explode within her. She took a deep breath and began. Her hands shook as she made her first stitch. Bronson's eyes closed shut, trying not to show her what he felt so she could easily continue. After the second stitch, she felt confident, and from there, she performed the intricate procedure with precision. Bronson was both proud and relieved that she was able to continue without passing out.

She tied it tightly, re-sewing a few times to insure that it closed up completely.

Though the sight of blood made her squeamish, she sewed him up fast, trying not to think of what she did. The faster she sewed him up, the better. She stitched the last suture on the second finger and hoped that it held until it healed.

She threw down the needle and thread and walked away, vomiting and shaking her head. She felt anger that she had been made to do that, but she also knew that her thoughts were shallow and unfeeling. She was both ashamed of her thoughts and proud to have completed the task.

Bronson knew that it upset Catherine, but he had to finish. He soaked the cloth in antibiotics and wrapped it around the wounds. He went to Catherine as she wiped her mouth and eyes, because the vision of what she'd just accomplished still haunted her thoughts. She remembered every excruciating puncture of skin, every knot she tied, and every drop of blood that spilled upon her as she wove the seams. She shook at the remembrance.

"Oh, dear, Bronson, how do you feel?" she asked, holding his injured hand.

"It's throbbing, but it could have been worse. I'm proud of you, Cathy. I know you have an issue with blood, but you did a fantastic job in closing it up."

After the shock of his injury, he remembered the tree and that a mysterious boy walked around the island. At the realization that she'd told him the truth, he looked at her. "Dear, is there any way you can contact that boy again?"

"I don't know where he is. He contacted me! I think I have to lie down. I'm not feeling well."

"Sure, dear. I have to go fishing anyway. We are running out of dried fish and I should collect some more bananas and coconuts as well. You take a nap and I should be back soon."

"You have just suffered a traumatic injury! Give it a rest for a couple days. We have enough food for at least four days. I'm worried you will break the stitches. We haven't much thread left," she confirmed as she entered the hut. "Come on and lie next to me."

Bronson followed her, although the thoughts of the day still swam around in his head; he still had a hard time believing that a boy named Charlie roamed around the island offering wisdom.

Bronson noticed that Catherine's sex drive had returned because she flaunted herself in front of him daily trying to entice him into a reciprocal response. Bronson noticed changes in himself as well, although there were no mirrors on the island to determine how much. He did not care why the changes took place, because he effortlessly made love to his wife again and felt like a younger man.

The reappearance of passion in their lives made their existence on the isolated island tolerable, as the resurgence of another aspect of their love for each other replaced the tense and overwhelming desire to free themselves from the bondage of the isolated island.

Life as they knew it, prior to their island excursion, escaped their minds, but they had thoughts of each other's pasts for one night, and that mattered to them. They made love for hours and disturbed the loosely fitted leaves of their rudimentary hut by the energy released on the inside.

They woke up at dawn, but they stayed in bed well into the afternoon, incredulous as to what they'd accomplished the night before. They were equally proud of themselves as Bronson noticed a glow in his wife that he thought age had taken away from her decades earlier. He leaned over and gave his sleeping bride a kiss on the cheek. She stretched some seldom-used muscles, placed both arms around him, returned the kiss, and said, "I love you, Bronson Preminger. I can't move a muscle. You brought it all back to me last night. The way we used to be; the way you send me to that place where I feel safe and loved. What a night!"

"You were amazing last night. I used muscles that I thought had dwindled away years ago. It was a welcome return of something that I thought was lost forever. It took me back, Cathy. I feel young again and feel that anything is possible from this day forth."

"Oh, Bronson, I feel the same way. I also remembered those times in the throes of passion. Last night made me believe in magic."

Bronson gently kissed her again and, though he wanted to continue basking in her glow, there were tasks that needed to be performed, "We'll have to fix the hut. We're nearly out of food and water and I am hungry. I'll get the fishing done and you get the water. I'm taking the boat out. I want a huge tuna steak."

"I'm hungry as well. Let's get started."

They arose from the hut and realized that their muscles had not fully recovered from the previous night's calisthenics. Both were stretching and trying to recover, but after a few minutes, they returned to the hut and plopped onto the mattress, resolved to allow their muscles to recover slowly. In doing so, they fell asleep until dusk.

They did not dare fish or fetch water at night because the night teemed with movement and the island woke up and presented dangers that, up until then, had escaped them. They were still alive because they respected the island's mysteries and never ventured forth for answers to the ambiguities. They learned to fear the nighttime because the darkness brought unseen beings, but every time they felt threatened, Bronson bravely confronted their tormentors. However, all he noticed were eerie sounds emanating from windblown plants and an errant coconut falling from the swaying trees.

Still, an overwhelming sense that someone or something watched and stalked permeated his thoughts as he surveyed the area around the hut. He dared not venture far because of his experience with the red tree.

He still had not mapped all of them on the island, and walking around the jungle without knowing where they all were worried him because the darkness masked the bright red color of the trees' bark. They slept all day and were wide awake with nothing to do that night because they'd allowed their passion to overtake their desire to forage for food and water, and had to wait until sunup.

They talked all night about their future. Prior to their trip, they measured their future in days, but now that life seemed to be coming back to them, they craved civilization again and being in it.

Six months later, they had forgotten how long they had been on the island, and learned to adapt to the sparseness of their existence. Bronson sporadically entered the days in his journal and missed whole months, including their third anniversary on the island. Their days and months mixed with duty and fun, a daily routine made up of gathering food and water, and sex and passion at night. They had not seen the mounds of sand chasing them in a long time, so they ventured toward the once forbidden part of the island and played in the surf.

Bronson had just landed a huge fish. Catherine looked on, sitting in one of the lounge chairs while he filleted the fish. He sensed that Catherine was in distress and turned around. Standing up and frantically pointing, Catherine tried to scream to warn her unsuspecting husband. Bronson saw her erratic movements. He looked behind him and saw the lumbering mound of sand heading directly at him.

Catherine looked on in horror as the creature appeared to be aiming at her husband. Running away as fast as he could, his legs tangled with each other and he fell hard.

He froze as the sand dragon exploded through the sand with its mouth agape and aiming to thrust its massive head toward Bronson. The creature towered ten feet above him with the majority of its body still submerged in the sand. Its double set of fangs dripped in anticipation of the meal in front of him.

Bronson, still grasping his machete, narrowly missed its lunging bite as its head plunged in the sand. The turbulence of the sand dragon's dive threw Bronson's two-hundred-pound frame to the side, as if his weight had the consistency of a feather.

The dragon moved at lightning speed, not finished with the shaken Bronson. It wheeled around for another run. The dragon's quickness preempted Bronson's escape because he could not grab enough traction in the loose sand to scurry to a frantic Catherine, who implored him to run as fast as he could.

However, Bronson could not match the speed of the giant beast.

It cut him off, pushed its large head up through the sand once again, and stopped in front of him. It towered over Bronson, a beast that the world had never seen with five rows of very sharp teeth that glistened in the mid-day sun and moved independently within its gigantic mouth. It sized Bronson up for a defining and deadly strike.

Bronson waved his machete like a mad man, trying to intimidate the creature into making a mistake, but it did not fear his violent actions and lunged at him once again. Bronson fell on his back, still flailing his machete, hoping to hit something, anything, to slow his foe's advance.

Strike after strike, Bronson avoided the blows. The massive dragon appeared to tire and now moved much slower than its initial attack. Again, Bronson got to his feet and timed the next lunge of the monster, then dove under its advance, stood up beneath its neck, and with all the power he could muster, swung the machete and buried it deep in the dragon's neck, nearly decapitating it with his second swipe. It flailed on the sand. Gallons of a blue liquid drenched Bronson as he ran away from the thundering dragon. He'd killed the beast, but still danger lurked as another mound of sand sped to where Bronson's bold maneuver had taken place.

Catherine scampered to her husband as another dragon stormed its way toward him. She helped him to his feet and they ran toward the tree line and watched as a much larger dragon immerged from the sand and gobbled up the dead dragon. It instantly fled, leaving no trace, other than the blue-tinted sand, that an immense battle had taken place.

"Are you okay?" asked Catherine.

"I'm fine, but I can't see. Get this crap out of my eyes!"

Catherine handed him her shirt and he wiped his face clean.

"Did you see that monster? Wow! He nearly got me. I've never seen anything like that. He must have been twenty feet tall. Those teeth were moving in his mouth like a buzz saw! Is that the dragon you saw?" He still reeled and tried to catch his breath. All energy spent, he threw the machete aside and collapsed in Catherine's arms.

"I don't know if that's the same one, but now we know there's more than one. We can't go on the beach again. Bronson, we have to move our hut to the point where the water is closer to the tree line."

"Nonsense, I'm not going to let them beat me. I tired it out. It's slow when it's tired. I can beat them then."

"But I can't! We need to move so you can fish not fifty feet away from our home. I don't want to see those dragons again." She hugged her champion and returned to the hut to prepare to move their camp without any more discussion.

"Wait a minute, Cathy. I'm going to get that fish that I filleted. We need it and I'm starving," he said as he eyed the filleted fish drying on a tarp at the surf.

"Are you serious? Did you not see what's under the sand?

Let's go! Let him have the fish." Catherine grabbed his hand in hopes of leading him back.

However, Bronson let go of her hand, sped to the fish, snatched it, and ran as fast as he could back to Catherine. She saw turbulence further down the beach, but the creature did not approach Bronson, and allowed him his fish.

"That's crazy, Bronson!" Catherine admonished as a winded Bronson met her.

"Catherine, did you see what that animal just ate? I doubt that it's still hungry."

"That's a good point!" Catherine followed Bronson back to camp. The large fish fed them for three days. They used those days to pack up everything and begin their move to a safer place. They left the hut standing, because they thought that they might use it in the future, and now that he knew how to make rope, they did not need anything.

On the perilous hour-long trip to the new site, he noticed that there were many red bark trees he had not mapped because they seldom visited other parts of the island. Other mysterious plants he noticed along the path made him stop and look as they walked and Bronson hoped that this was the last hut he had to build. He waved his razor-sharp machete and cleared everything in his path. He came across an odd three-foot high stump with a single circular stalk sprouted from the center. The small stalk had five fern-type leaves branching out and Bronson wanted to investigate, but Catherine stopped him. "No, that's a helicopter plant. Watch."

She looked for a dead branch for a demonstration, but nothing existed on the jungle floor. All the plants that Bronson had chopped in making their path had already adhered to other plants, so she grabbed one of the tent poles that Bronson carried. She cautiously approached the plant. Bronson intently looked on. She touched the plant with the tent pole and Bronson saw why going near the plant had serious implications. The ferns began to rotate like a helicopter blade during startup and then moved faster and faster until the broad, rotating fern leaves sliced the aluminum pole cleanly in half. The plant amazed Bronson; however, it irritated him that she'd sacrificed a valuable tent pole for the lesson.

"Okay, how did you find out about that plant? I could have walked right into it and been sawed in half!"

"You won't believe me if I tell you."

"Try me! Sit on that rock over there and explain it to me." He dropped what he carried.

"I'm not sitting on that rock! No, not that one. I'll sit on the ground. Come sit next to me and I'll tell you." She sat and patted the ground.

"No, sit on the rock and I'll sit on the one next to it," Bronson demanded.

She sprang to her feet and tackled him. They both landed on the sandy ground about a foot from the moss-laden rocks.

"What the hell has gotten into you, Catherine? Why did you tackle me?"

"Because that's not a rock!" She grabbed the remnant of the tent pole and dropped it on the rock. Bronson stared in amazement. The rock instantly turned into a gel. The tent pole sank into it, and it hardened back into rock again, capturing the tent pole for eternity.

"How the hell do you know these things?" Bronson asked as he and Catherine arose from the ground.

"Charles told me yesterday when you were at the surf. He talked to me while you were fishing. As I walked around, he showed me the plant and the rock and then followed me to the tree line where you were fishing. He doesn't trust you."

"Again with the Charles nonsense? Show me the boy! Take me to him!"

"I can't. I don't know where he is. He comes to me at odd times. Bronson, he exists! How else did I know about the plant and the rock?"

"I don't know." He scratched his head, wondering if he could have possibly been wrong about the strange boy. "Did he say how he got here?"

"He said that he came here in a plane about thirty years ago. He thinks that he, like us, has lost all track of time, but he did mention that the island is trying to kill us and has been trying ever since we landed."

"A plane? It must have been Corker's plane! But I don't understand how that could be because Corker's plane crashed decades ago and you said he's about fifteen years old."

"More like twelve, I think. He appears to me to be

younger every time I see him. It's getting late. We have to get all this stuff to our new location and you have to get the boat to the inlet before it gets dark. I don't want to be walking around these woods at night because he told me that there are other dangers that he hasn't spoken about. Now, let's get going!" She gathered up her bundles and began walking toward their new home. Bronson could not resist one more tug on the tent pole stuck in the center of the rock, but it did not budge. It made him think of the sword in the stone during King Arthur's reign.

Catherine and Bronson went back for several more trips. Catherine did not answer any questions while they delivered everything to the new site, but that did not prevent him from asking. Taking the usual path, Bronson watched every step he took. However, the vines and brush grew back instantly, so he had to continue hacking away every time.

After five trips, all the supplies were there, with the exception of the boat and the nearly empty trunk. Catherine loaded up on water, glanced at her ill-fated attempt at gardening, and sighed at the thoughts of fresh vegetables eluding her taste buds, but she sauntered on. They ran to the boat fast to evade the sand dragons, pushed it to the waterline, and hopped on board. Bronson lifted the five-gallon gas can and placed it in the boat. Catherine carefully arranged a place for them to sit. Bronson started the motor and they sailed to their new destination, a mere fifteen minutes away.

"At least we don't have to go through that torture path again," Bronson stated. "I want to have a talk with you after dinner about Charles and some other things that have been happening to us."

They slowly fought the small waves, but took the fastest course to a little inlet. It seemed like a long voyage. Bronson noticed a few small leaks in the boat. He plugged them as much as possible.

The suspicious-looking holes had not been there the last time he'd used the boat. Looking closer at them, he noticed that they were bullet holes.

"Catherine, where's your rifle?" he asked as he filled in the holes with torn strips from his shirt.

"It's right here." She held it up.

"Is it missing three bullets?" he asked, thinking that she

may have put the three holes there during one of their many disagreements.

"I don't know, Bronson! What are you really trying to say?" she asked with disdain in her voice.

"I'll talk to you about it when we get there. Here, help me plug up these holes. I can't steer and do this at the same time!"

Catherine got on her knees and plugged the holes as Bronson steered into the little cove. They emptied the boat and dragged it up on a sliver of beach, capsized the boat to get rid of the water, and then Bronson tied it as best he could. He spied three separate holes, perfectly aligned. He decided to let it go until they settled into their new home.

He and Catherine had found the perfect location. Ten trees equally spaced apart formed the walls; they covered the walls and the roof with broad leaves plucked from a tree. They built their hut, and just in time, because they saw another nasty storm forming on the horizon. Bronson worried about the old lifeboat, which floated in the shallows. Bronson wanted to pull it closer inland, toward their camp. As he struggled to get the boat moved, he noticed its deterioration because of time and neglect. Their survival depended on the boat's viability because it offered the only hope of rescue if they saw a ship on the horizon.

Catherine still held the view that they were already where they were supposed to be because she had grown accustomed to her new younger look and that the island's regressive attribute made her age backwards, eliminating her illness and saving her life.

Chapter Six

Charles Reveals Himself

Bronson, seeing that the storm may pass them by, reinforced the hut and prepared to patch up the three holes that apparently his wife had put in the boat. He made a fire with what he had available. No underbrush to speak of existed on the island, so he piled up coconut shells, felled a tree, and cut it into pieces. Cutting trees on the island proved to be a much bigger task than it should have been as the trees sealed up cuts as he sawed, so he had to chop the smaller trees. When they'd arrived on the island it had been easy to gather things for a fire, but now that they were there for as long as they were, the island appeared to refuse to allow them easy access to its resources.

Soon, he had a large stack. He used a small amount of gasoline to get it started.

He noticed a slight chill in the nighttime air, which he considered strange given that the weather had always been seventy-five to eighty degrees. The large fire counteracted the chill and after a day's hard work, they settled into each other's arms and talked about their future and their past. Catherine cooked the fish over the large fire and a new vegetable that she discovered on the island that looked and tasted like potatoes. The salt supply ran low, but they decided to use a little. Any new things to eat warranted a celebration.

"These are great, Catherine! Where did you find them?" He stuffed himself with the new food.

"They are everywhere on the island. They are good, aren't they?" She slid the fish filets onto Bronson's plate. "I can't believe how much you can eat, dear. You've certainly got your appetite back."

"I don't know why, but I feel as if I got it back years ago. However, I'm not gaining weight. In fact, I've lost a lot of it and so have you."

"I know, I love my body again."

"It's more than that, Catherine. I've been meaning to have a talk with you about the way we look and feel. Since we've been on this island, I feel as if we're getting younger. I mean, I'm at least seventy-three, maybe seventy-four, but can do all these things without getting winded. You're just two years younger than I am, yet you look like you're in your late fifties."

Bronson had noticed many strange things over the years, but their age regression still confounded him the most. Catherine appeared younger. Her once solid silver hair had even more streaks of dark auburn, the hair color of her youth, and the lines, which marked her years, had inexplicably faded away. Her quick smile reappeared on occasion between her bouts with dementia, and her energy level soared off the charts.

Bronson lay next to her. They snuggled like newlyweds.

"I don't know why, but I think that we've possibly found the fountain of youth. Do you remember the old explorer, Ponce de León? He searched for it in Florida for years. Do you think that this island could be that fountain?"

"I know you have changed. We don't have mirrors, so I can't tell how much I've changed, but think about it, Bronson; suppose we are in the fountain of youth? I attribute much of our weight loss to the sparse food supply and the fact that we are working hard to survive. How long do you think we've been here?"

"I don't know. I filled my journal up a long time ago. I think it's been about three or four years. We may never know for sure, but I'm not complaining. I need to know, how did you know about these potatoes? These are delicious!"

She struggled with her words for fear that he would think it was her dementia rearing its ugly reality again. She felt embarrassed to tell him what was on her mind, knowing that he would doubt what she had to say.

Regardless, she stated, "I really have a problem telling you this because when I do, you look at me as if I'm crazy.

Charles told me about them. He came to me while you were tying up the boat. He brought a whole pile of them. He's worried about his life." She waited for Bronson's normal response.

"Again with the Charles reference. I told you he is a figment of your imagination. How could a boy be on that plane and still be a boy?"

Although he knew that some mystical happening caused their appearance to change for the younger while being on the island, he did not think that the same magical occurrence applied to Charles. To him, Charles was simply a harmless manifestation conjured by Catherine to help her cope with not being with her children. Bronson generally did not fight with her about his existence because it appeared to give her a happier outlook in their bleak but comfortable surroundings. Most of time, he allowed her believe all she wanted, but sometimes the constant narrative irritated him. He did what he could to ease her out of such sightings by using logic rather than constantly dismissing her notions. They had conversations about Charles, and the more she talked about him, the more he wanted to justify how Charles could have been there. Being on the plane appeared to be the only logical answer if Charles really did exist.

"Maybe he wasn't a boy on the plane. Maybe he was a grown man and regressed in age like we're doing. Regardless of how he got here, he seems to need us and he is helping us survive. He's just a boy. Every time I ask him to come live with us, he runs away. I don't know where he lives, but I feel like he's all alone."

Bronson rubbed his unbelieving brow. A mounting body of evidence suggested that this Charles did exist, though he stubbornly refused to believe until Charles presented himself. "Then why doesn't he show himself? If he's seen us together, he should know that I'm not a threat." He stood up and yelled into the darkness, "Charles, come to the camp! I will not harm you. Let us help you!"

Bronson mocked Catherine and did not expect an answer; he still thought that Catherine's disease continued to play tricks on her mind, although she amazed him with what she knew about the dangerous plants, rocks and, now, edible roots.

"Bronson! He's real! Why can't you just believe me? I'm

not hallucinating. I wish he'd come here, just so you won't think I'm crazy." She teared up.

Bronson, seeing that his rant hurt her feelings, mustered a sincere apology. "I'm sorry, sweetheart. Please forgive me. Listen, I know that someone told you about all this. They had to. Perhaps I should listen to you more. I love you, sweetheart. I've always loved you, so I apologize for not believing you. Tomorrow we will explore the outer reaches of the island and try to find him and bring him back. I want to believe he exists because we can possibly find out more about the island."

On a whim, he thought that he would give Charles a chance to show himself and somehow reassure him that he would not harm him. Bronson yelled again out into the void of darkness, never expecting a reply. "Come in, Charles! It's safe here. I will not harm you!"

Catherine reiterated Bronson's announcement and implored him to join them.

Bronson looked at Catherine, shrugging his shoulders, he turned back to the darkness, but there, standing before him, a little boy approximately twelve years old, emerged clad in makeshift shorts and oversized tennis shoes with holes everywhere. He had long blond hair past his shoulders and a weathered look about him.

"Charles? Are you Charles?" Bronson asked as he stumbled forward, trying to find soothing words that would entice the boy to stay. He stood there, stunned that, once again, Catherine was proven to be right, and made him look like an unbelieving fool.

Catherine ran to Charles and hugged him, looked at a stunned Bronson, and said, "Yes, Bronson, meet Charles. Charles, don't be afraid, he will not harm you."

The young boy walked toward Bronson and held out his hand. "Hello, sir."

Bronson, still amazed that Charles existed, shook his hand. "Son, what took you so long to come to us? I assure you that I'm no threat to you. How long have you been here?"

"I don't know. Maybe fifty years? When did you get here?" He eyed the boiled potatoes still simmering in the pot.

"We were marooned here in 2013. When were you?" Bronson asked.

"Then I'd been here for thirty-six years when you landed and you've been here for three, so, I'm twelve."

"That doesn't make sense. How could you be twelve?" Bronson asked.

"It's complicated. I will explain later, but I'm terribly hungry."

"Oh, I'm sorry! Catherine, fix him a plate," said Bronson, both excited and confused. He never took his eyes off the boy.

Charles went to the simmering potatoes and sat beside Catherine.

They both stared at him as he devoured the meal. He ate as if he had not eaten in days, ignoring Bronson's stares. Ten minutes later, he started to answer questions.

"When did you come here? I mean, how long have you been here?" Bronson asked.

"I've been here for thirty-nine years, I think, but I'm not really sure. My airplane crashed in the jungle, but you know that because I saw you and Catherine go inside. My pilots died instantly."

Bronson looked at Catherine in disbelief. "That's impossible, son. You said you're only twelve years old. How can you have been wrecked thirty-nine years ago? It doesn't make any sense. What is your last name?"

Charles smiled. "What? You guys haven't figured it out what this island does yet? I spent ten years avoiding this cursed island's attempts to kill my wife, my brother, and me. Since they died, the island is still trying to kill me, but I now know what it's trying to do and I'm real good at avoiding its dangers. My name? I believe you may know me as C.K. Corker. My first name is Charles."

"C.K. Corker? The philanthropist? Impossible!"" Bronson prodded.

Charles lowered his head, seeing that Bronson had a hard time believing him. "You see a boy, but I'm really a man. I am ninety years old, but fifty-one when my plane crashed. My wife Karen died three years ago. I am fifteen years her senior, or at least I used to be."

"The island killed her?" Catherine asked.

"No, she died of young age. So did my younger brother, Frank. He died just last year."

Catherine saw grief reflected in the young man's eyes and reached over and hugged him.

Bronson suddenly stood up in disbelief. "This is impossible! Are you saying that people age backward here?"

"Not just people. The plants also age backward. Did you notice that a lot of the vegetation is disappearing?" Charles asked. Bronson's sudden move obviously frightened Charles.

Bronson held up his hands. "I'm sorry, Charles. Please don't run away. I will not hurt you. We want to help you."

Charles sat down and listened to Bronson's questions. He felt at ease knowing that he was there and talking to both of them, but he was struck that Bronson still did not appear to believe him and his assertions.

"Where are your wife and brother's graves?" Bronson asked.

"Graves? Don't you get it? My wife and brother died because they ran out of time. Just like I'm going to die, and so are you and your wife. You both are aging backward and both of you will continue to get a year younger for every year you're on this island! My wife turned thirty-six a few weeks after the crash. I turned fifty-one just before. I protected her from that point through infancy and one day she turned into a mass of cells. A few months later, all remnants of her disappeared. The same thing happened to my younger brother. I have lived in a cave for the last twenty-five years and the only reason I'm here with you now is because I'm too young and weak to make the climb anymore. My brother and I fought the sand dragons as you did. They are the hands of this island. They clean up beached fish and prevent anything living from penetrating the beaches. I don't know why they allowed you onto the island."

"The hands? Are you saying this island is alive?" Bronson asked in astonishment.

"Yes, it is. It is a living entity. It breathes carbon dioxide like a plant, near as I can figure out. This island has been here for thousands of years. I wrote about my findings in a journal."

Bronson rummaged through his backpack and held up the journal that he'd kept when they discovered the wrecked airplane. "I have it here."

"That's the first one I wrote before we crashed; the others are in the cave up in the mountain. That's where we all lived for a long time."

"You protected us. You told Catherine about the dangerous plants in the jungle and you told her where to find the potatoes. Why are you helping us?"

"Because, as you noticed, I'm a boy now. I have to get off this island. I figure I have twelve years before I die. I'm getting weaker and more uncoordinated with every passing year. I saw you two land on this island in the boat. We need to use that boat to get out of here, or at least I do. Otherwise, I'll die. I hoped that if I helped you, you'd give me your boat so I can be rescued before I dwindle to nothing. I assume the aging reverses back to normal as soon as I set foot off the island. It's the island that is doing this. I saw my brother and my wife dwindle down to nothing. It's fully documented in my journals."

"How do you know it reverses when you get off the island?"

"I don't. All I know is that I was aging normally before I got here and I started regressing in age when I crashed. My only hope is that I'll start aging again once I'm off this island."

"You want us to give up our boat?" Bronson asked.

"Yes, I hoped we all could use it, because, as you can see, I'm too young to row that boat alone. I need both of you. Please understand that I could have stolen it a long time ago, but I didn't. I'm not afraid of death. As a middle-aged man, I saw what my wife and brother went through, and that's not the way I want to die. I feel as if I should at least try."

"That old boat won't make it past the breakers; besides, it has three holes in it," Bronson announced.

"I know. I saw Mrs. Preminger shoot it. I stopped her from completely destroying it."

Bronson looked at Catherine for an explanation. She stood up and walked a few steps away. She muttered something that neither could hear.

"Catherine, you told me that you didn't shoot the boat!"

She knew that Bronson had caught her in a lie and she struggled to find the words to rectify her deception.

"I did shoot the boat," she confessed.

Bronson stood up as well and asked in astonishment, "Oh, dear God, Catherine, why would you do such a thing?

That boat was our only hope of getting off this island!"

"I know. That's why I shot it. Bronson, my vanity drove me to do it. Being on this island took my pain away. It made us younger and alive once more. I do not want to leave yet."

"Why didn't you tell me that rather than blasting holes in it?"

"I just couldn't say anything knowing how badly you wanted to leave. I felt that it would happen soon. Without the boat, I knew that we would have to stay."

Bronson thought hard at what Catherine said as Charles sat and watched the interaction, "We've been here three long years. We've suffered through strange and deadly things. We saw things that people are not allowed to see, and yet you want to stay?"

"I just wanted us to live again. I wanted another lifetime with you. Oh, I guess I'm stupid. Bronson, the last eight years my life have been hell with my illness and living here. Now we have a chance to capture our lives all over again. I want to be young and full of life again to make up for the years I lost due to my illness. Through all this, I know that you are right in being angry with me. I hope that you understand and I apologize for lying to you."

Bronson took her in his arms and said, "Okay, dear. I think I know what to do now." He left Catherine's embrace, walked over to Charles, and said, "Son, you've looked after us for years. The boat is yours, but we won't be going with you. It's better that just you go, because you can stock it up with food and water. If we go, it's two more mouths to feed. Besides, we have a lot of time left before we suffer the same plight as your wife and brother." Catherine looked at her husband, wide-eyed and stunned. When Bronson's act of undying love sunk in, she suddenly cried as hard as ever. She ran into his arms and kissed him, not caring who watched.

"Bronson, are you sure?" she asked.

Bronson smiled and stated, "As sure as the day I married you."

Charles interrupted their romantic moment and said, "I don't have to leave. I just have to stay on the boat and off the island. I'm asking to anchor it offshore. I want to live on it."

"That boat won't last that long on the surf, even if I can fix the holes. It is very old and it won't last a month before those waves destroy it. But we will accommodate you as much as we can."

"Thank you, Bronson. Maybe one day when I get a little older and you get a little younger, we can figure out how to get out of here before it's too late for all of us."

Bronson placed another log on the fire. "What else do you know about this island?"

"I know it's dying because we are on it. Have you noticed that there are no small animals or insects scampering around?"

"Yes, we noticed that," Catherine acknowledged.

"The island ensures that no animal survives because anything alien to the island, reverses the aging of the plants. It needs the plants to survive. The fewer plants, the less oxygen the island gets. It needs the plants to grow, not regress. That's why it's trying to kill us."

"There's plenty of oxygen all around us."

"The oxygen gets to the island through the plants roots. No plants equal no oxygen, and no oxygen means that the island will die. It's trying to save itself."

Bronson's logical mind was again transfixed and confused, and he had to hear it again, "You're saying that this island is actually an animal of some sort?"

"Yes, that's exactly what I'm saying. I don't know where it came from or if it originated here. You have a lot more time than I do, and that's why I need to be off this island. If I don't get off soon, there will be an infant that you'll have to care for and that infant will be me."

"Okay, I think I speak for Catherine as well. We'll have to fortify the boat if you're going to live on it. We'll swim food out to you when you need it. I think we can do this as long as you're within waving distance. I certainly hope that old boat has a few more years in it."

"I'm hoping it has ten more years in it so I can grow strong enough to help all of us escape. Right now, I just have knowledge, because the island took my strength."

"Well, son...I mean, Charles, tomorrow morning we'll get that boat seaworthy, or at least surf-ready."

They all stayed in the hut that night, but Bronson could

not sleep. He stayed up staring at the sleeping boy in utter amazement of what he'd dealt with all those years. Regardless of the circumstances, he believed Charles, and had to make sure that he, Catherine, or Charles survived to tell the story.

He muttered to himself, "We are growing younger. I get to live my life all over again with Cathy and, if we are rescued, another full lifetime together. How did I get that lucky?"

Unable to sleep, he walked to the water's edge and watched the moonlight glistening off the calm surf. He remembered his twenties when he'd met and married Catherine and found himself wanting to relive it. Pondering those things in such a beautiful setting made the remembrances much more special.

A few minutes later, Catherine joined him and gently held his hand. "It is beautiful, isn't it, Bronson? To think that we've been together for all these years and get to relive it all makes me happy. How old do you think we are right now?"

Bronson smiled. "I think, really, that we are in our seventies, but the island will allow us to revisit our fifties, and who knows after that."

Catherine added, "If Charles is correct, then I'm sixty-five and you're sixty-seven. I wonder if we'll see Brooke and her family again."

Bronson said, "I suspect not, but perhaps when we're younger, fate will allow us an avenue off this island to see her and Murray again, and perhaps meet our grandchild."

"I hope so, but as for now, I'm intrigued about our future."

"It's funny that we've been together for over fifty years and we still have an entire lifetime to look forward to."

"I felt that way before we landed on this island, dear." Catherine tried to reconcile her desire to remain on the island within her mind. She contrasted her desire with what she would have to sacrifice. That sacrifice being never seeing Brooke or her family again. "Look at Charles. Doesn't he remind you of Bradley?"

"What made you think of Bradley?" asked Bronson.

"Oh, honey, I haven't stopped thinking about him or Brooke. I guess I'm just an old woman longing for my past. We had a nice life, didn't we?"

"Had? We are experiencing something that no one has.

We are reviving our youth. It's a gift and I feel the need to stay here for another forty years. I'd love to spend it all over with you again. I remember all the time I missed, being in the Navy while you were bringing up the children. Ah, honey, I missed it all. Never a day went by that I didn't think of you and the kids. The Navy took all that away from us, but now I feel I can at least get my time away from you back. I know that I also spent time away from Bradley and Brooke, but there's not much I can do about that right now. My attention and concern lies with you now. We raised Brooke well and she has a life and family of her own now. As long as we still have our memories of them, they are not that far away."

"I just think that it is strange that we wanted to die together and now, we could have two more lifetimes ahead of us. I haven't seen a boat or a plane. I'm afraid we may die here."

Bronson proudly stated, "Maybe, but we will also live here. I married you wanting to spend the rest of my life with you and now I get to spend three of them with you. How could a man be so blessed?"

"Hey, I'm pretty lucky myself. Now, we really should be getting some sleep. We have a lot of work to do tomorrow if we're going to get that boat ready. I sense that he really wants to get it done as fast as possible."

They walked back to the hut hand-in-hand as slowly as they could, because they knew they had all the time in the world and then some.

The next morning came with the bright sunlight shining in Bronson's eyes as the sound of chopping breached the leafy walls.

Catherine and Charles were already up felling trees and gathering supplies.

A young boy, Charles possessed strength beyond his years. Obviously, he did not possess the strength of the man he used to be, but as a twelve year-old, he more than pulled his weight. He and Catherine had already cut down ten trees and freed the branches from them. Each tree equaled the length of the boat.

Bronson had a plan for what he wanted to do with the boat. He wanted four trees on either side to allow Charles to have a front and back porch.

He got to work, placing four trees on either side of the boat and connecting them in a V-shaped configuration that the boat slipped into. Then he tied the boat to the eight trees, making a floating home with an area where he could place a chair or two. The reinforced boat had a carriage underneath.

Three days later, they loaded it up with supplies and watched as Charles rowed out fifty feet from the shore. Catherine cried as he left, because it brought back memories of her son going off to war. She cried into Bronson's chest; he consoled her and pointed at him a mere fifty feet away.

Charles waved at them when he reached the spot where the waves did not smash against the side of the boat and anchored it. They ate lunch and watched the little boy sort things on the boat, then lie down, out of view of a sad Catherine and her stoic husband.

"Did we get him everything he needs?" Catherine asked.

"Yes, we did. Come on, Catherine! He's only been out there ten minutes. He's going to have it tougher than we do. He has to live in that confined space for the next ten years and we have the entire island. I don't envy his future."

"Perhaps he can visit us on occasion," Catherine interjected.

"I'm afraid he can never set foot on this island again. He told me last night that he thinks he will die if he ever comes back. He didn't want to worry you. I'm sorry, sweetheart."

"That's not right, because we did it a couple of times and we didn't die," Catherine asserted.

"I know, but we weren't twelve years old, which is what he thinks he is. He told me once that he thinks the aging process speeds up slightly if we leave and come back. Although, he told me that was just guessing."

"Yes, but we are older and will visit because we have the time. He cannot come here again because he doesn't have much time left before he regresses to nothing."

Bronson took her hand and walked her back to the hut. "We still have to fend for ourselves because we gave him everything he needs to survive if we're not around. I told him that if we die, to take up the anchor and leave as soon as possible. It's the only chance he has."

They still took daily walks. Bronson took the opportunity to mark all the hazards around the island.

One day, they approached the mountain. Bronson put down his backpack and began to climb, but fell back onto the soft sand. He wanted to find the cave where Charles had lived, thinking that something up there could help them, but Catherine talked him out of it, saying that in perhaps twenty years he could try again because, at the time, they were still too old to make the ascent.

Two weeks later, they got a shock as they looked to where Charles had anchored the boat.

They were missing!

He had ventured back onto the island and left a crudely written letter telling the Premingers that he could not wait any longer and took off, allowing the tide to take him to a certain death or a better place to see a passing ship.

"Oh dear God, Bronson! He's just a boy!"

"I know, dear, I only hope he knows what he's doing. I guess he just didn't want to live that kind of life."

"Do you think we'll ever see him again?"

Bronson looked at Catherine with a sullen expression and said, "No, I don't suppose so, dear. Come on, we need food. I'll get my fishing gear."

They went their separate ways to perform their duties of the day. Both of them gave a last stare to where Charles had anchored, and hoped that he survived.

The mountain remained unexplored for the next year. They had long forgotten to worry about Charles and assumed that he'd died, if not from the storms, then from starvation or suicide. They were thankful that because of him, all the dangers within the jungle were marked.

Bronson slept late due to strenuous work the previous day. A shrill scream woke him up and he found Catherine missing again. He exploded out of the hut screaming, "Cathy! Cathy, where are you?"

She did not answer. He grabbed his machete because the gun did no good on an island where their foes were plants.

He ran around the camp frantically, calling her name, but again, no answer.

He ran into the jungle and onto the makeshift path, frantically looking for Catherine. Then he realized that Catherine had possibly visited the mountain and tried to climb it without him.

Minutes later, he looked up at the mountain and yelled her name, but she did not respond.

Scared and worried, Bronson ran everywhere. Judging by her scream, she seemed to be in great pain. He remembered the garden that she'd planted and ran along the vine-covered path to their former camp.

Bronson ran through the dense jungle where dangers were just an errant step away. He frantically yelled for her, but not a peep echoed back to him. He spied a filled water jug and thought that she'd gone to refresh their water supply. He called to her for the next hour and could barely speak because of the strain placed on his voice. Exasperated, he sat on a rock, crying. He walked to the brook to get a drink of water. He easily saw the bottom of the creek, but accidentally kicked a rock into it and it disappeared. He threw in a larger rock and it also disappeared. Reaching with his hand, he could feel no bottom to the small creek even though he could see it. Then, something clamped onto his hand and tried to pull him in. He struggled until whatever held his arm released it.

"I hope she didn't fall in that," he muttered to himself.

He leaned his machete against the water container, sat on a rock, placed his head in his hands, and cried openly. He did not hide his sorrow.

"Catherine, just give me one more scream to give me a direction to search."

He wearily stood up and noticed movement in front of him. The vines on the ground moved slightly, as if they blocked something. He ran to the movement, ripped the vines apart, and saw Catherine's hand. The vines were actually eating her!

She tried to scream, but the vines had wrapped around her mouth so tightly that they nearly split her jaw. Bronson grabbed his machete and hacked the vines as fast as he could. He sliced the ones across her mouth. She immediately screamed in pain because the vines were trying to penetrate her abdomen.

The vines were regenerating as fast as he cut them. His muscles tired from swinging the machete, so he put it down and relied on pure adrenaline to rip them up by their roots. He made progress. He ripped the vines apart and threw them aside; they reassembled as fast as he pulled them apart. Sweat dripped from his brow as he struggled to pull the vines off.

Catherine panicked. She pulled away enough of the vines to help herself. Together, she and Bronson grabbed and ripped them from the sand.

They were able to get Catherine free, but her head was bleeding and a vine had penetrated her leg and her arm. It grew through her leg and exited the other side of her calf. Bronson pulled the vine from both her leg and arm and, seeing it being removed caused her to collapse. He grabbed her in his arms, but could not move because the vines wrapped around his ankles. He fell backward, placing her on top of him. He grabbed the machete, cleared the vines from his ankles, and tried to stand up, but the vines had permeated her hair, trying to pull her back to the ground. He chopped off her long hair and ran with her to a safe area devoid of vegetation.

"Are you okay, sweetheart?" he asked, with no response. Laying her down gently, he ran to the water pail, sprinkled some on her wound, and gently wiped the blood from her face. Catherine had a large gash just above her hairline, so he applied pressure with his last shirt. She woke up crying in because her leg and arm still hurt badly and were bleeding.

"We've got to get you back to camp. Your head is going to need stitches. What happened to you?" he asked as he wiped the blood out of her eyes.

"I got hit with a coconut, I think. I remember it bouncing on the ground before I blacked out. Then I woke up and the vines were all around me. I couldn't pull them off. Bronson, I need to get away from here," she begged, sniffling.

Bronson kept pressure on her head and said, "Okay, let's get you back to camp and get you sewed up."

"No, I mean off this island! I used to love it here, but now I feel as if the island is trying to kill us. We need to find a way. I don't care how much of my youth I'm recapturing."

"Honey, according to Charles, the island has been trying to kill us from day one. We'll be fine if we fight. Let's get back."

Bronson placed the top on the filled water can, lifted Catherine to her feet, and they staggered back to the camp. Catherine kept pressure on her head and carried the machete, but her leg bled badly, which made it important to get back as fast as possible. Bronson did not tell her that treating her wounds would nearly deplete the first aid kit. He knew that they had little antiseptic lotion, antibiotics, and sutures left. Something that was odd to Bronson was the fact that, as she got younger, her wounds did not appear to heal as fast. Just the opposite of getting older.

They walked for ten minutes. Catherine collapsed from blood loss as they entered the camp. He dropped the water can, carried her into the hut, and gently placed her on the mattress. Her head wound had stopped bleeding so he concentrated on the other two wounds. He hastily stitched her leg and arm up without stopping, to take advantage of her unconscious state.

With all her wounds sewed up and antibiotics injected, Bronson waited for to wake up. He had used everything in the first aid kit, outside of some aspirin and a few gauze bandages.

After he covered Catherine up, he walked outside the hut and broke down. Bronson did not cry often, but the potential loss of his precious wife scared him beyond his masculine limits.

He still worried about all the blood that she lost and prayed he had stopped it in time. He dried his eyes, walked back into the hut, and sat by her side, wiping her brow when needed.

He tended to her for three days. He did not get water, he did not fish, and he did not eat. The more she slept, the more he worried because he had a lot of time, but he had only one Catherine.

On the fourth day, she awoke and called his name. Seeing him asleep, she gently pulled their lone blanket over the both of them and drifted off again with her husband by her side.

The next morning, Bronson was weak from lack of food. He left the hut to get a cool cloth to wipe the beads of sweat from her face, but when he walked back in the hut, Catherine sat, waiting for him to return.

"Oh dear God, you're awake!"

He ran to her and questioned her about her condition, but she just held up her hand and said, "Calm down, Bronson. I'm fine, but I'm starving. What do we have to eat?"

"We have nothing in camp but a few bananas. I'll be right back with them."

One minute later, he brought the remnants of a banana stalk with just three bananas on it. He plucked them off and gave her all three.

"Bronson, have you eaten?"

"No, I didn't. I forgot. I'm fine."

"No, you're not fine! Let me fix you some of the potato root. I know where they grow. You lie down and I'll get it."

"You can't do that. Tell me where they are and I'll go get them."

Catherine smiled. "I tell you what, they are near us. Let's both go. We need the exercise. My old bones have been still too long."

Bronson knew that he needed help. He could barely stand, but he kept it together for her and they walked the few feet to a familiar plant. She pulled it up and freed the root. She found many more and placed them in a pot of water. Bronson lit the fire, and they sat and waited for it to boil. Later, they ate and went over what had happened.

They ate their fill and, afterward, Catherine asked, "Bronson, how old do you think we are?"

"I don't know. Wait a minute! I have two photos of us. One taken in 1993. I'd just turned fifty and you were forty-eight." The other one was taken just after our wedding. Remember? At that fair? We were in our early twenties."

She asked, "You still have them?"

"Of course I do. I had them laminated, so they wouldn't get wrinkled. They stayed dry all the way though our shipwreck and though all those storms. It's sort of ironic that they survived just like we did. Yes, here. I've had them in my wallet the whole time. Do I look like that now?"

Bronson handed her the photos and she looked at the 1993 photo and then up at him. "That's it! You look exactly the same as you do in the photo. We must be back in our fifties." She looked at their wedding photo and longed to feel the way she'd felt that day again.

"I have to tell you, you look better than in the photo. We have been here for only four or five years. At the most, I'm in my mid-sixties. I'm so proud of you over the last four years. You have weathered so much, and you are still just as beautiful. We both have been able to stay alive and that's all I care about. Now, let's go fishing."

"That sounds fun."

Chapter Seven

Conquering the Mountain

They happily talked while Bronson fished, but something bothered him. He wanted to find the right time to tell her. She marveled at how he looked as he snapped a hundred-foot cast far out into the surf.

Catherine seemed happy and Bronson knew that she had not had much to be happy about since Charles left, so he wanted to prolong it for as long as he could.

Hours later, Bronson reeled in his catch. Normally, he stayed to catch more, but the ones he caught had plenty of meat to fill their stomachs.

Catherine gathered a pot full of seawater to boil down in order to coat the bottom of the pot with salt. They had long run out of salt and all other spices, so they improvised. Once the pot cooled, she filled it with the roots that she had collected earlier, then poured fresh water in it and brought it to a boil again. Bronson gutted and filleted the fish, placed them in a pan, and seasoned them with the salt he had earlier scraped off the pot. It smelled so good that she wanted to eat the fish partially cooked, but Bronson, ever worried about their lack of medical supplies, stopped her for fear of the both of them getting sick.

An hour later, they had finished all of the roots and the fish. He wanted to relax, but he had to attend to Catherine's wounds.

"Let me take a look at how well you're healing, dear. My, you heal fast. I wonder if being on the island makes injuries heal so much faster?" Bronson said, as he started to take the bandage off her head.

"How does it look?" she asked, seemingly in no pain.

"It looks great! Another week or so and I'll remove the stitches. This is our last gauze bandage. I'm afraid it's the last of a lot of things."

"What things?"

"Pretty much everything in that survival trunk. The pots, pans, and dishes are still okay, I guess, but the first aid kit and everything else is done. I have one lighter left, some of my tools are broken, the machete has dulled, our last razor is getting too dull to use. Soon, we'll have to think of other ways to survive. I think we've had it easy up until this point. I can't believe the trunk lasted for over four years. I still have the cigarettes, stale as they may be, the guns, and two boxes of ammunition."

"We'll get by, Bronson."

"I've noticed that the banana trees are dwindling, and how long before those root plants dry up? Cathy, we are getting younger. I know it's unexplainable, but it's happening and, soon, we'll need more food. Do you remember how much I ate forty years ago?"

Catherine did not seem worried, but said, "I forgot to tell you, the pot has holes in it. They're small, but it's hard to boil water in a leaky pot. Can we fix it?"

"Yes, I guess so. You see this fish bone? I'll just push it through the hole and I'm sure it will plug the holes. The frying pan is fine, but the cigarettes have already been tapped."

"You're smoking again?" she asked with an angry stare.

"Yes, it takes the edge off hunger and I couldn't stand it. I have three cartons, so I know that they won't last long."

"Okay, well give me one. I stopped fifty years ago and I can stop again." Catherine adjusted the bandage on her leg and felt stubble. "Bronson, I need the razor again."

"Okay, you can have it. I won't be shaving anymore."

"I wonder what you'll look like with a beard."

"You'll find out in a month."

"This is just a thought, but what about the mountain?"

"What about it?"

"Well, Charles lived there for twenty-five years. Do you think he has anything up there that could help us?"

"Well, Charles said that his journals could help us. We've tried to climb that mountain but still do not have the strength.

We're still too old to climb, but maybe in a few years, I should be able to."

Bronson's idea to fix the leaky pot worked to the elation of Catherine.

"I tell you what...after I sharpen the machete, let's take a walk over to the mountain and get a good look at it. Maybe there's an easier way to get up there."

Catherine said, "That's a good idea. I'll get the honing stone from the tool box."

Later, they strolled their normal well-traveled path toward the mountain. Dangers existed all around them, but the path had proved to be safe many times over.

She mentioned that she'd seen many new plants during her search for the root, and a few odd-looking flowers. Bronson, wary of anything new in the jungle, made Catherine promise to leave the flowers alone, regardless of their beauty or scent, and she agreed.

Approaching the base of the summit, he pulled a few rocks away and noted that there were many loose ones to contend with should they make the attempt.

"I'm afraid we're many years away from tackling this. I hope desperation doesn't make us try sooner, but we'll see. Did you notice that each time we tried, we got farther and farther? Neither of us have ever attempted to climb anything, so we have to be careful and make further attempts when we are ready."

"Yes, but I almost fell a dozen times. I don't think I'll ever be strong enough," Catherine said as she climbed to one of the lower-level areas.

"Oh well, it'll be dark soon. Let's get back to camp. I don't want to walk back at night." He held out his hand to help Catherine off the ledge.

They walked back, but Bronson worried about starting a fire without his lone lighter. The gasoline that he had saved for the boat motor had gone with Charles, so he had no way to start a fire to cook their food. Not to mention, a mere scrape could cause an infection and he no longer had the medicine to combat it. For the first time, he felt scared and vulnerable.

He saw the anxiety on Catherine's face when she had to struggle to find any more of the root that, along with the fish, had sustained them for years. Many of the edible plants dried up, and the dangerous ones replaced them. To Bronson, it seemed that the island dried up along with them. They were in good physical shape for their age, but not yet able to seek the survival treasures that may lay at the top of the mountain. However, he knew that it could not last forever. Bronson did not want to worry her, so he kept her in the dark about the dwindling food supply. As long as he could catch fish and feed them, he did not quit. There were many times when he thought of suicide rather than to fight a fight that he could not win, but her exuberant attitude toward their fate stayed his hand. They had two guns and many shells left for that last act, but for now, he just wanted to hold his wife's hand and walk back to their camp.

It took approximately an hour to get back; they took their time. For years, they had lived on the southern part of the island, and seldom explored to the northern part, but now, to relieve the boredom, they made plans to explore it more thoroughly. The jungle had gotten increasingly more dangerous as time went on and he did not want to tempt fate until necessary.

That day neared.

Six more years went by and nothing new happened. The boredom got to them; their required day-to-day activities created a rut that needed to end. Catherine got angrier faster and Bronson sometimes fought back. They'd lived a lifetime together, but ten years on a small island complicated their relationship. In the day-to day hardships of trying to stay fed and alive, they never explored the northern part of the island, nor did they climb the mountain due to their advanced age. They just yelled at each other and tried to survive. A year earlier, they'd still cared deeply about each other, but now they lived more apart than together.

The coolness of their relationship lasted another year, but deep down, both of them yearned for the way they had been. Bronson assisted in building another hut for Catherine, because staying in the same one caused the problem to explode to levels never before seen or contemplated. They decided to separate for the first time since they'd said, "I do."

They'd spent eleven years on the island, but the last year had tested them. Regardless of their animosity, Bronson still supplied food and Catherine still cooked it, but eating together created too many opportunities to communicate, and that usually led to one of them storming off to the quiet of their own hut.

After a particular tasty meal, Catherine started an argument about the size of the fish he'd caught and Bronson complained that she tried to find things to be angry with him about. They went back to their respective huts, waiting for the other to end the torturous turmoil between them. Living apart for another year created a period of them not even talking to each other.

Bronson, at times, did not come back to the camp and slept under the stars at their very first camp. Many things there reminded him of how their relationship used to be. During those times, Catherine worried about him so near the sand, and being alone scared her.

Bronson went over to where Catherine planted her garden with hopes of a bounty of fresh vegetables. The small mounds of soil still existed. He dug them up and found the seeds had done nothing. They lay dormant in the sandy soil after all the years that had passed. He gathered them up and placed them in a small piece of cloth cut from one of his old shirts. The cloth still held bloodstains from Catherine's previous brush with death. It brought back the remembrance of how he felt when he'd seen his lovely wife in such pain and how helpless he'd felt trying to ease it.

In the quiet of the original camp, he resolved to end the stalemate and win back the woman he loved. He stood up, determined to get back to her and make things right. He looked at the seeds tied within the cloth and realized that a seed without fertile soil would never reach its potential, and two people, angry about their plight, could never resolve their differences without the fertile ground of compassion. Living apart exacerbated the problem. He started back to the camp, but stopped. Catherine stood in front of him.

"What are you doing here?" asked Bronson.

"I worried that the sand dragon got you."

"Are you nuts, walking through the jungle at night? You

could have been killed!"

Catherine was tired of the yelling and accusations that had dragged on longer than any argument they had ever had. She seldom ever fought back against Bronson, but in a moment of clarity in their strained existence, she resisted the urge to fight further and wanted the harsh tones to ease and get back to where they had been.

"Bronson, I don't want to argue. I want you back. I'd walk through fire to be with you. The jungle seems tame in comparison."

Bronson walked over to her and hugged her, kissed her, and vowed never to catch a small fish again.

Catherine laughed and said, "Pretty harsh, wasn't I?"

"Yes, but I was just as bad. I can't remember if we have ever been separated in the past."

"We haven't been, and I cried every time I thought about it and wondered what brought all of it on. We have lived and loved together for nearly fifty years without a worry or care. Now that we have to be together, we have problems. We are all we have right now. If we can do it for all those years, we should be able to live and love each other on this damn island. Those fifty first years were the best of my life. This hardship does not seem as bad as long as I have your hand, your shoulder, and your heart."

"All of that you have, but I need you much more than that because, without you, I would have died years ago. Without you, I'm nothing, a shell of a man with no soul. With you, I'm Superman"

"Yes, you are, as long as I'm your Lois Lane."

Bronson laughed as well and took her hand and they sat in the two chairs he'd built, which had begun to fall apart; they stared at the stars, as they had on so many happy nights. They stayed at their original campsite that night, made love passionately, and lay in each other's arms until dawn. Instantly, all the anger and worry left them and they enjoyed being together once more.

Bronson said, "It's funny when you think about it."

"Think about what?"

"Well, most couples look toward a future together, but we are gifted in that we have our past to look forward to. Honey, we haven't made love like that in decades."

"It will only get better the younger we get," Catherine added.

"I know it will, but how far back are we going to go? I hope that we don't wait too long to get rescued."

Catherine reasoned, "Let's not think about it. We have more time than not right now and I see a glorious past and future."

Bronson looked up and saw that clouds had darkened the sky. "Look, a storm's coming in. Let's get back to camp. I don't want to go through it here."

They scurried back to camp that morning and made a vow to never separate again.

The bad storm rolled in that night and it came with ferocity not seen since the first storm that had devastated their boat. The high wind howled throughout the day and into the night. Bronson misread the severity of the storm and knew that they were in the midst of a hurricane, with winds so strong that much of their supplies were propelled high in the blackened sky. The pots and pans flew all around the camp.

Their hut weathered the onslaught because all the leaves that they used to construct it had fused with the live trees and now were actually a living part of their new home.

They strapped the door shut, but the noises outside told them that much of the camp and its components either blew away or had been destroyed. The rain came down hard. Being close to the water, the rising tide permeated the hut's walls and eventually, the mattress, which represented their last vestige of comfort.

"Bronson, the water is coming in. We have to get to higher ground." Catherine stood as their hut flooded.

"I know, but I don't want to go through the jungle in this storm. Honey, we can't see where we're going. If we run up against one of those red trees or the vines catch us, we will not be able to escape!"

"Everything we have is out there and probably being destroyed."

"We have to stay here and deal with it. It's just water. We will be all right if we wait it out. The wind alone may get us. In here, the wind is blocked for now. The tide will subside eventually. We will get through this. Trust me!" He screamed so his voice could override the loud gusts of wind.

They resolved to sit on the submerged mattress and hold each other until the storm passed. Several hours later, the wind subsided. Walking out, they saw the devastation. Everything they had splashed out to sea. They had no pots or pans, their food store was destroyed, and their camp turned into a muddy mess. Just as desperation set in, fate stepped up and delivered them a floundering tuna, thrashing near the water line. Bronson ran toward the water and tackled it just before it made its escape back to the depths. However, the cooking utensils were gone and all the wood in the area lay wet and unburnable.

"Bronson, everything is gone! We have nothing left!"

"I know, but we have this," he said as he presented her with the large fish.

"How are we going to cook it? Do you still have the lighter?"

"Oh damn, the lighter! It's in my pocket!"

Bronson dropped the now-dead fish, put his hand in his soaked pants, and pulled out the lighter as the clouds parted to reveal the warm morning sunshine. He held his breath as he tried to ignite the lighter. It failed to light.

"Okay, dammit! Light!" he yelled as he tried over and over again. "It doesn't work! We will have to allow it to dry out and pray that it works later." Setting it on a stump, he focused on the fish. He pulled out his knife, cut it up into sections, and placed it on the same rock as the lighter. The island had no insects or crabs, so he placed the meat in a shaded area to protect it from the blazing sun until he found dry wood to start a fire, depending on whether or not the lighter worked.

He needed to find wood or anything that burned before the strips of fish went bad. He busted off the metal top of his toolbox for a makeshift pan to cook in.

"Catherine, I have to go into the jungle to find wood. I should be back in an hour or so," he said as he gathered his saw from the water-filled toolbox and hung his machete on his belt.

"Oh, please be careful, Bronson, and hurry back. I'll do what I can to clear an area for the fire. If you're not back in an hour, I'm coming to look for you."

"Maybe you should go with me in case you see any of

those edible roots and you can help me carry them back. Besides, we're better together in these situations. The fish will be fine. Do you want to go?"

"Yes! I want to go! Let me get my shoes," she said as she entered the hut. She walked out wearing her soaked shoes, but she did not care; she didn't know what she would do if Bronson didn't come back. "Suppose we can't get any wood?"

"Then we'll eat the fish raw!" Bronson yelled, frustrated and scared, an angry scowl on his normally pleasant face.

Instantly, Bronson knew that he had gone too far in his frustration; he grabbed her, hugged her hard, and whispered, "I'm sorry, sweetheart. I didn't mean to yell at you. It's just that everything is going sour at the moment.

"I know you pretty well, Bronson. Outside of our year-long fight, I can count on one hand the number of times you've yelled at me in over fifty years with you, and I know four of those times were my fault. I think I can give you a pass on the last one. We are here together. If one of us died, the other wouldn't last a week." She hugged him back.

"You and me. That's the way it's been and that's the way we'll end," Bronson said as he walked beside her into the jungle. He hacked away at the brush to make a path as they made their first advance.

Later, they got to the part of the island where the flood waters did not reach, but they were shocked to see no wind damage to any of the plants or trees.

He spied a few trees and began sawing on one of them, but Catherine felt uneasy where they were. "Hurry up, Bronson, I don't like it here. I get this feeling that something bad is going to happen. Can I help you?"

"This one may be enough because I feel the same way."

He felt that the island moved in for its final attack now that they were destitute. He handed Catherine a log, and he grabbed one as well; they turned away from the fallen tree and began their trek back to their camp. Bronson looked back after a few steps and noticed something that shocked and scared them. The tree that he had just cut down stood erect, as if he had not taken the logs from it.

"Catherine, look! The tree is still there!"

"If the tree is there, then where did these logs come from?" She looked at what she carried, and the log vanished.

She screamed and held out her hands.

"What's wrong? Are you...? The logs! They're gone! I felt the weight of the log and then it vanished!"

"I know. Mine did too. Bronson, what's happening to us?"

"It's not us! It's this damn island. First it tries to harm us physically and now it's trying to take our minds."

"We are not going to let that happen, Bronson. Tonight we eat sushi!"

They walked back to camp empty-handed, but they were not depressed. They realized that they had each other and that they were each other's reason to take what life handed them.

That night, they ate well. Catherine seasoned the meat with sea salt and other spices that ten years on the island presented to her. They coped with the day's conundrums with laughter.

They turned the mattress over to dry the other side. Bronson spied the lighter, tried it, and it lit.

"It worked the first time! Everything is going to be all right, dear."

Bronson flicked it one more time and placed the lighter in his now dried-out shorts.

The boredom of everyday life on the island had clouded what they loved best—to sit on the sand and watch the sun set. They had nothing, but for one night, they were back on their boat and watching the reds and yellows of a glorious sunset. The mattress had dried in the hot sun and Bronson gathered it up as they went back into the hut. To cap the evening off, they made love again and reinvigorated their desire to beat all the odds and fight back.

The next morning, they veered from their normal routine. Bronson did not go fishing and Catherine did not forage for roots or any other edible plants. They simply stayed in bed and held each other. No longer were they going to live being afraid of what the island had in store for them.

They spent the rest of the day cleaning up the camp. They were hungry, and decided to take a break. They walked to the mountain again and tried to scale it. Each time they tried, they got farther up, but cancelled the ascent when one of them nearly fell. Bronson still felt that they were not young enough.

Another ten years went by before age, energy, and muscular development presented a viable attempt at scaling the large peak.

They vowed that both would scale together or not at all. They made plans to visit the northern part of the island because they wanted to discover new things. It had been nearly two decades since they had visited Corker's crashed airplane and the surrounding area. Regardless of their long stay on the island, parts of it were left unexplored, and now that they were invigorated and stronger, they decided to take some chances and see what else they could discover. They were anxious to find new things and possibly a new banana tree or two, or a better fishing location. The banana trees growing closer to camp were depleted and no new ones grew in their place. They took other unused paths during their walks, not worrying or caring about the dangers, and they discovered something new every time in their sterile environment.

The walks and the new attitude were great, but they still needed to eat, and lately, Bronson failed to bring in the big catches he used to. They cut their walks short and concentrated their efforts on resupplying their food stockpile. Regardless of their day-to-day hardship, they still regressed in age. No longer did gray hair grace their heads, and their age-related wrinkles faded away into the smooth skin they remembered from their youth. They were thin from the lack of food, but, otherwise, they were as healthy as they had ever been.

The next morning, they decided not to take their usual walk. Catherine foraged nearby for anything edible, and Bronson grabbed his fishing gear, and, ever cautious, ran to the surf.

He cast his line for an hour, and then it happened. He snagged a large fish, but struggled to reel it in due to its size. It taxed his ability to hold on to their most precious tool. The fishing rod bowed badly as Bronson fought the massive fish. Try as he may, he could not reel it in or release it; he screamed for Catherine to get him his knife so he could cut the line.

He had other lures and bait, but only one fishing rod.

Catherine scurried inside the hut, found the knife, and ran with great haste to Bronson, but he'd vanished. She frantically called for him, but he did not respond. Tremendous fear came over her as she ran to the surf calling for him, unconcerned as to what lay beneath the sand.

A few minutes later, Bronson called back as the waves crashed into his back. The great fish had taken his fishing rod, and now they had nothing to catch the only sustenance they had left. Fate dealt them a serious blow. Catherine ran to Bronson as he slogged out of the surf, bloodied hands dotting the foam.

"I tried to save it, but the damn fish took it. A tiger shark, I think. Now what are we going to do?" he asked, as he hugged his wife on the pristine sand.

"Well, I guess we'll have to adapt without it."

"Adapt? Catherine, we needed that. I can't catch fish anymore. The roots and bananas are drying up. I'm scared!"

"Nope, I'm not scared! We'll get by! We always do," Catherine said, trying to comfort Bronson.

Bronson, angry that he'd lost his fishing rod, took his frustration out on Catherine. He sulked as he walked into the hut and stayed there the entire afternoon. He prided himself on the fact that he had always provided for his wife, but now, his abilities suffered and he did not know how to deal with it.

She saw how hurt he felt, but she did not say a word. She sat beside him, held his arm, and listened to him rant about his fight with the big fish. The rest of the night, nothing got done. They did not eat, but Catherine knew the importance of him getting his confidence back.

A few hours later, he realized that he acted immaturely and focused on the positives. He had a healthy wife and a mind made for invention, so he adapted to another hardship and thought of ways to overcome it.

"Please, Bronson, don't let this be our end. It's not! We'll get by. We always do."

"You know, that's why I love you so much. We are faced with hardships every day, and you always make me see another way out. You're right, we'll adapt! I love you so much, sweetheart."

"I love you too, Bronson. I think we have to find out how Charles survived all those years. We have to climb to the cave. He mentioned that it saved his life. Maybe the cave will save ours as well," she said as she grabbed his arm to let him know that she still had confidence in him.

"You're right as usual. Tomorrow we will make it to the cave. We have to!"

The next day, they forgot about all their troubles and endeavored to accomplish a goal that had eluded them for many years. They readied their haggard minds to offer the greatest effort to scale the rugged mountain and visit the cave that Charles had described. In it, according to Charles, existed all they needed to know about the island, but getting there had proved impossible, until now. The push to explore outweighed their need for safety, and their need for food outweighed everything else. They hoped that, in his journals, they could find descriptions of all the edible plants on the island to replace their normal fish fare.

The sanctuary of the mountain appeared to be the last vestige of a desperate couple longing to be together for many years to come.

Still determined but weary, they set forth to the mountain cave. Their survival depended on it.

Bronson carried his rope on his back; he attempted to make the climb himself first to secure the rope for Catherine because she did not possess the strength to climb the peak on her own.

Time passed before they made it to the base, twenty-five feet up from their starting point. Bronson quickly climbed to the first level as Catherine watched from below.

Standing on the level landing, he yelled back to Catherine, "There's a lot of loose rock here. Don't stand there or they will come down on you. Step back a bit just in case."

"Okay, please be careful!" She moved back a few steps.

His weight loss made the climb much easier. His hands were strong enough now to pull his lesser weight. He found small divots, placed his feet in them, then slowly placed his full weight on the divots to see if they held, and they did. He mapped out the stronger rocks and marked them with drops of fish blood. He climbed farther than he had ever traveled in prior attempts. Each grasp resulted in small rockslides that eluded his waiting wife, but when the loose rocks gave way, the ones that held firm emerged.

He had brought a hammer to loosen rocks as he ascended. He made great progress and stepped onto the second landing where he could rest his burning legs and arms.

Seventy-five feet up the mountain, he yelled to get Catherine's attention, but she could not hear everything he said. She quivered with every rock hurtling downward, thinking that Bronson came with them.

He had one more rocky level to tackle before he could rest. The hardest and most taxing to strength and mind of his climb came next. A sheer face made of smooth rock with no apparent footholds, seemingly impossible to scale, stared him in the face. Bronson slammed five or six mighty blows with his hammer, causing some rock to give way, creating a foothold.

Each step seemed to take an eternity to Catherine as she looked up, fearful for her husband's daredevil tactics. He hugged the face of the mountain and slowly and carefully climbed one perilous step at a time.

Then, a seemingly solid rock gave way and left him hanging by his hands with no crevice to get his foot in. Dangling by his arms and struggling to find even a tiny split, his hands and arms tired and burned for a respite. His body wanted him to give up because his muscles ached, losing strength by the second. He had one chance to survive the climb and he hoped that his sturdy hammer held up.

Catherine could not watch and she screamed when saw her husband in distress and struggling mightily. She turned away because she could not bear to see the love of her life plummet to his death.

However, he wedged his hammer into a small crevice as he dangled with one hand. With his hammer firmly wedged, he placed a foot on it, and it held his weight. The hammer's makeshift step allowed him to stop and rest for a few minutes. He leaned his body against the rocky face, released his grip on the rock above his head, and rested his arms, one by one, dropping them limp and numb by his sides. A mere twenty feet from the cave, he reached for a jutting rock he could hold onto. He did not want to spend too much time with his hammer bearing all his weight. He grabbed the jagged rock, pulled himself to other footholds, and cleared the sheer part of the mountain. He climbed the rest of the way up with ease.

He swept aside loose rock; he did not want Catherine to use those as footholds when she made her climb. He cleared as much as he could to make her path easier than his.

Catherine lost sight of Bronson as he ascended closer to the top, but she knew that he did not fall. She speculated that he had reached the top or had gotten stuck somewhere just below it. Sometime later, she did not notice any more loose rocks coming from the top and he never returned her pleas for information. She did not know what to do as she ran around the bottom to get a better view of the cave, but she did not see Bronson at all. Her pleas garnered no responses because her voice did not travel to such heights.

She made a decision to attempt to climb by herself. She had no problems in reaching the first level, as she had done so on many prior visits, but the rest of the way looked too daunting without help.

Not thinking clearly, she blindly tried to scale the mountain because she thought that Bronson needed her. As soon as she made a critical first step, a knotted rope that he had made from tree bark dangled, nearly striking her in the head.

Bronson had made it all the way up to the cave, but would not explore it until he assisted his wife's climb. He tied the other end of the rope firmly to a huge boulder at the entrance of the cave.

He noticed that his wife had lost a lot of weight, and it reminded him of the one hundred pound woman he'd married in her twenties. She was strong, fit, and lean, and climbed in earnest.

Bronson was also much stronger and gathered enough strength to lift his wife past the sheer part of her climb. He hoped that her arms were strong enough to hold on.

The knots, placed about a foot apart, eased her ascent to the second level rock. She rested her arms and hands then tied the rope around her waist.

Bronson wrapped the slack around the boulder as she scaled the mountain.

She made it to the third level and, for the first time, they could talk to each other. Prior to that, he knew that Catherine had made her attempt because the rope tensed up. Bronson rested enough for her to continue climbing.

"How are you doing, Catherine?"

"My arms are tired. Oh, Bronson, I don't think I can do this!"

Bronson yelled, "Oh yes you can, Catherine Preminger! Just don't look down! I've got the other end of this rope! I will not let you fall!"

"Okay, I'm ready."

"The stones are marked. Look for them."

She made it to the sheer face, and a rested Bronson started to pull. Catherine helped him as she placed her weight on some of the footholds. She saw the hammer wedged in the mountain and stepped on it, allowing Bronson to rest his arms.

"Wait, Catherine!" he bellowed, needing a break.

After a few minutes, he pulled again and hoisted her up the rest of the difficult climb. When she got above the sheer face, she sat amid the sharp rocks and rested her tired muscles, having a mere ten feet to go.

Bronson had no more energy; he asked her to stay there for a while as his muscles recuperated. He waited for a bit, then pulled until the rope broke loose. He fell backward, hitting the solid rock floor. Horrified, he stood up, thinking that his wife had plummeted to her death.

Catherine climbed up the rest of the way under her own power. When he saw her emerge over the edge, he helped her up the last step. They fell into each other's arms and lay at the entrance of the cave, not wanting to move until their muscles stopped throbbing.

"I'm glad I didn't have to climb any higher. That tired me out." Invigorated, she sat up, looking at the cave.

They stood and looked around at the island. From their vantage point, they could see almost the entire thing; tall trees blocked their view of the northern-most part. They saw the sand dragons moving on all the beaches, clearing beached whales and dolphins. They also noticed the island's sparse vegetation in areas, creating open sandy patches for the dragons to roam throughout the outer rim.

They turned their attention to the cave. They were anxious to explore it. Initially, they saw nothing to indicate that anyone had lived there. It appeared to be naturally formed and not man-made, as they originally thought. They pushed aside rocks that blocked much of the opening, but easily squeezed through the narrow areas.

The small opening gave way to a large room. Charles had lived there for many years; a few faded photos of himself, his wife, and brother on the island and in the plane were strewn all over the cave. Later, they found the broken Polaroid camera that he had used to take the photos.

A bed made of dead leaves and cut wood nestled in the corner of the cave. They found many useful items, including a dusty pair of binoculars with a cracked lens, carved utensils, plates, and various pots and pans made from metal parts of Corker's airplane. Bronson speculated that Charles had used the binoculars to spy on them.

He'd lost his own binoculars years earlier, so finding another set, despite the cracked lens, made him happy.

They found only one journal and opened it up. He turned to Catherine and said, "Well, we have an easy way of climbing down. Apparently, he and his brother created a stairway on the back of the mountain, but it ends at the water's edge. They had to swim to get to the stairs, but he also mentioned an easier way, and that is through the basement."

"The basement? There's a basement here? Does the journal say anything about food and edible plants? I'm starving," Catherine asked as she sifted through the clutter of artifacts from the nineteen-seventies.

"According to the journal, the basement is through that opening in the rocks." Bronson pointed the way.

They started their trek.

"It's dark in here. I can't see that much," Catherine said.

"Here, wrap what's left of this cloth around this stick. Maybe we can make a torch to light the way."

Catherine did as he suggested. She wrapped it very tightly to make it last longer. They left the binoculars and journal behind because he intended to return for them after their exploration of the basement. He lit the torch; it gave off plenty of light to allow them to venture deeper into the cave's crevices.

Eerily quiet, the cave had provided an excellent view of the island, many items associated with eating, and reading material, but thus far, no food. The grumbling of their hungry stomachs broke the silence. They inched their way through the small spaces and climbed over rocks, but, as they proceeded, the torch expended its fuel and extinguished. However, they were surprised to see light fifty feet ahead.

They easily made their way toward the light and after they traversed a small stone bridge, they saw an amazing sight—a pasture the size of a football field right below them. They looked up and saw bright sunshine caressing the lush green grass, gently swaying in a slight swirling breeze.

"This is not just a mountain! This is a volcano, although it appears to be a dormant one. Just look at the grass, Catherine! I feel like we landed in Oz."

"It's not just grass! Look! A garden with vegetables! Am I hallucinating?" Catherine asked. "How can we get down there?"

"I can't believe it! He stole some of our seeds and didn't tell us."

"So what if he didn't tell us? We couldn't have climbed the mountain back then. He may have not told us to prevent us from trying and, thus, killing ourselves. The vegetables are growing here. It's beautiful!"

Bronson surveyed the surrounding walls and noted a man-made stairway created by piled rocks leading to the pasture.

"Look, there are stairs! Let's go and check it out," Bronson said, pointing. "This must have taken years to construct."

"He had his brother and his wife to help, I guess."

They walked down the stairs and ran to the garden. They saw corn, tomatoes, cucumbers, carrots, and an apple tree sprouting right out of the grassy field.

"Bronson, there's something odd here. These plants are actually growing. Could it be that, in here, the island has no control over what grows and what does not?"

"I don't want to think right now. I want to eat!" Bronson plucked a green apple off the tree and took a huge bite. They gathered the ripe vegetables and sat in the foot-high soft grass as they filled their stomachs.

"They won't grow on the island, but they grow here. This is how he lived as long as he did. He ate the way we did for years, saw us plant the seeds, and came in and stole some of them."

Catherine ate as much as she could, and then walked in

the cool grass until she came across two graves. Makeshift crosses adorned them. The epitaph, written on cloth, read, *Here lies Karen Corker and Frank Corker. They assisted me on my journey but fell into infancy.*

Catherine knew what that meant. "By the looks of the damaged crosses, made of decaying vines, they died a long time ago."

It made her think about how long they had been on the island. Catherine repaired the fallen crosses as best she could, and said a quick prayer. She walked over to her resting husband in the tall grass. He smiled because, coupled with a full stomach, the grass had a soothing effect on him. She lay next to him and fell asleep instantly.

It was the most restful sleep they had in years. They slept there the entire day, and by the time they woke up, darkness covered the grassy area. The stars supplied light, but still not bright enough to attempt going back toward the cave.

"Dammit! We slept too long. I can't see ten feet in front of me. I guess we'll have to stay here until tomorrow morning before we look for an exit," Bronson explained.

"Well, what difference did the height of the climb make to him if an easier way to get here existed?" Catherine asked.

"I don't know. I suspect we'll find out tomorrow. I wish I'd brought the journal with me. We have to go back to the cave to get what we need."

They made plans to make the cave their new camp; it provided food, shelter, and safety from the island's dangers, but they had to get their guns and everything else they'd left behind. They spent the night in the high, cool grass with stars twinkling above through the opening of the volcano. The next morning, they filled their pockets with apples and made their way back to the cave to find the basement door.

Bronson stumbled in the darkened narrow passageways; Catherine held his hand firmly, until, once again, they saw light from the cave entrance. Bronson went straight for the journal and read that a secret passageway that led to the base of the mountain existed somewhere in the volcano.

"Here it is, Catherine. The passage leads to an underground pool. We have to swim underwater for just a few yards to get to shore. It's a glorious day. Look at the shore. The waves are small today."

Catherine took the binoculars and scanned the beach to find their camp. She looked out over the horizon and saw smoke emanating from the water, "What's that? It looks like smoke," she asked as she pointed out to the ocean.

She gave the binoculars to Bronson. "That's a boat and it's on fire! We have to get back to camp because I'm sure that we'll have visitors soon who may have cell phones!" He placed the journal in his pants and the binoculars around his neck.

He and Catherine gathered what they could carry, walked through the narrow tunnel to the massive opening, descended the stairs, and searched for the secret tunnel.

They found an old bucket and decided to bring the new visitors a gift of corn, cucumbers, tomatoes, and carrots, thinking that they may be hungry. A cave-in appeared to block the basement exit, but Charles had written about it. Bronson speculated that when the cave-in occurred, Charles did not have the strength to move the tons of rocks to clear the passageway, and neither did they.

"Well, that's why Charles had to climb up and down the mountain. It will take years to clear all this," suggested Catherine.

With the passageway blocked, they chose the other way out—the steps that Charles and his brother had built prior to the discovery of the basement exit.

They had to go back to the cave entrance and took another passageway to the edge of the mountain. The steps were wide apart and not easy to navigate, but it seemed safe. They started down the trail.

"Wait, we can't jump in the water with the journal. It will get soaked."

"You're right, Cathy. Let's leave it here."

"What about the bucket of food?"

Bronson looked around the cave, found the lid of the five-gallon bucket, and securely placed it on the bucket. "There, it will float."

The trail ended at the ocean. They jumped in and swam around the mountain to the shore with the bucket in tow. They swam to shore and walked up the beach, soaking wet. They ran to the camp and hid the guns until they discovered what kind of people came ashore. Excited, they saw two boats approach their former camp on the eastern shore.

Chapter Eight

The Visitors

They were excited to welcome humans again in their lives. Anxiously, they awaited the first boat's arrival and met it at the surf line.

The new castaways were weary and shaken. Three men and two women staggered to the shore. One man carried an injured woman. Bronson had no medical supplies, but still could help. She had long blonde hair and a shapely body, dressed in only a bikini. Obviously, she had no time to change into something else prior to the disaster. Another man held up her broken arm. The other man and woman seemed to be a couple, and the last man, who appeared to be part of the crew, directed them up the beach and toward the tree line.

"Hello, welcome to Preminger Island. We saw that your boat caught fire. Is everyone okay? We have food if you're hungry." Bronson presented the vegetables to them.

"Thank you, not just now. I'm Mike Stanton. I don't know about the others, but I see another boat coming toward us. This is Angela Burgon. I believe her arm is broken. Is there a doctor on the island?"

A large man, Mike appeared to be a weight lifter who was close friends with the captain and owner of the ill-fated yacht. Later, Bronson found out that Angela and Mike were dating.

"I'm sorry, but we are the only inhabitants here. I'm Bronson Preminger and this is my wife, Catherine. We landed here after our ship sank many years ago. What year is it?"

"Why, it's 2035. We were out on the ocean for a friend's

New Year's celebration. How long have you been here?"

"2035? I'm ninety-two years old," muttered Bronson to himself, astonished that they had been on the island that long. "We've been here twenty-two years."

Bronson held out his hand to the couple and shook their hands.

"I'm Dan Stagis and this is my wife, Pepper. Our friend's boat exploded. I don't know where the others are. I think we need to get Angela someplace where she can sit."

The last man heard Bronson state his age. "Pardon me, I'm Jeff Smith and I thought I heard you say that you were ninety-two years old. Did I hear you right?"

Bronson thought for a second and replied, "Yes, that's right, ninety-two."

At first, the island's newest residents appeared fearful to see a very bearded Bronson and his scantily-clad wife, probably thinking that they were cannibals or members of a tribe who didn't appreciate visitors to their tropical isle, but soon after speaking to Bronson, their fears diminished.

Bronson guided them to their hut and Angela sat on the mattress, with the women trying to assess the damage to her arm.

Catherine asked Pepper if they'd brought any medical supplies, but she said that they had not. Catherine found out that Pepper had studied to be a nurse.

"We are the only people on this island?" Pepper asked.

Catherine, tending to Angela's arm, confirmed, "Yes, I'm afraid so. Is there anyone else coming in?"

"Yes, the captain and his wife have their own lifeboat. My husband and I were their guests. I can't believe that you and your husband survived for twenty-two years here," said Pepper.

Catherine did not tell her of the island's strange attributes, thinking the story too unbelievable, so she kept it to herself while she tended to Angela's broken arm. With Pepper's help, they were able to set her arm and splint it with the few tent poles they had left.

Meanwhile, the men talked as they waited for the captain's lifeboat to arrive. They and Bronson asked a million questions back and forth. None of new visitors believed Bronson's age, and Jeff said, "Sir, I still can't believe that you're that old."

"It's true. I had just turned seventy when our yacht went down. We've been here ever since. We have to get off this beach. Let's talk at the camp. It's just beyond those trees," Bronson explained.

"Why, you don't even look sixty. How can you explain that, and why do we have to get off the beach?" Jeff asked as he looked at Mike in astonished disbelief.

He did not tell them about the dangers. They already did not believe most of what he told them, so he kept it to himself. They did not need to know the aspects of the island yet. He changed the subject many times, but Jeff did not let it go, to the point of being arrogant.

Bronson did not want to test the young man's resolve and decided to check on Angela and Catherine.

After Bronson had gone, Jeff and Mike had a conversation about their hosts.

Jeff, helping Mike tow the lifeboat to the shore, said, "I don't trust him, Mike. There's something very strange about him and his wife. I certainly know that they haven't had a bath in a long time."

"Isn't that the truth? I could smell him before we landed, whew!" said Mike.

"Why lie about something as simple as his age? Also, why is he so worried about us spending time on the beach?"

"I don't know. Maybe later on we can ask him to elaborate. I have to see if we have cell service way out here. I don't want to stay here very long. There are Mitch and Jocelyn. I wonder if they saved anything before their boat sank."

"I don't know, but knowing Mitch, I'm sure he saved the booze," explained Mike.

Dan said, "That's great! I hope he did, because I could use a good stiff drink right now. There they are, and they were able to save Trent as well! After last night's bender, I'm sure he's still passed out. I'm going to get Pepper and tell the rest that Mitch is here, and also check on Angela."

Dan entered the hut to see Angela smiling as the pain in her arm subsided. "Pepper, Mitch just pulled up with his wife, Jocelyn, and Trent. Bronson, you and Catherine want to meet the captain of the boat we were on?"

Mitch hailed his friends as their larger lifeboat floated to the beach. Bronson and the previous arrivals met the captain and his wife as they stepped ashore, but the captain did not seem interested in Bronson or his story. Most of Mitch's crew had perished in the explosion, but he did not appear to care about them as much as he cared for his friends.

Bronson and Catherine walked to the surf and saw Mitch Rodgers, who was dressed in a white jacket with a glass of cognac in his hand. His clothes were dry and he didn't seem to understand his situation. Bronson knew well the type of man Mitch was as they talked among themselves about the boat blowing up.

Mitch was an arrogant twenty-six-year-old who'd sold his website for millions and retired early. Bronson saw that Mitch needed to be in charge and started spouting orders without even acknowledging Bronson and Catherine's presence. Catherine had equal opinions about Mitch's self-centered and high maintenance wife, Jocelyn. She immediately noticed her need to have attention thrown at her from all angles. She appeared to Catherine to be a twenty-one or twenty-two-year-old beautiful yet shallow socialite dressed in a fine designer gown. Just like Mitch, she was dry and ready to party on the island. Catherine saw how she treated her friends and caught a part of the conversation where she disparaged people who had less money than she did. She did not know if she was speaking of herself and Bronson, but noticed that her female friends disliked her for multiple reasons. Catherine sensed that they never let on about how they felt for fear of being kicked out of the millionaire club.

An emboldened Mitch immediately declared that the uninhabited, uncharted, and undiscovered island was in his control, discounting Bronson and Catherine's many years of being marooned on it.

They all were young, tanned, and obviously trained in the art of drinking. They were part of the beautiful set who cared little of lesser people, though the hierarchy was obvious to Catherine and Bronson. They all were dressed to party without a care because they all had cell phones and knew rescue was a phone call away. Later, they found out that none of them worked, but they were certain the phones would operate eventually.

The new visitors congregated outside the hut, but Bronson and Catherine could easily hear all the ugly comments about their appearance, the laughter when they talked about their ages and what they'd told them about the island's strange attributes.

Bronson had enough and stormed out of the hut.

"Do you idiots know how bleak your situation is? We welcomed you here! We brought you food and you sit there drunk and disparage my wife and me?"

They drank and talked loudly; Bronson's pleadings did not seem to result in any kind of concern. They simply ignored him.

Bronson stormed back into the hut and prepared to take Catherine away.

He demanded, "Come on, we're getting out of here!"

Catherine sat up and wiped her eyes. "Why? What's going on?" she asked.

"These idiots haven't got a clue of the danger they are in. I don't trust them."

"Bronson, calm down. They are the first human contact we've had in I don't know how long. They will come to understand their plight."

"Okay, I'll give them a few days, but if they don't change their attitude toward us, we're leaving."

"Where would we be leaving to?"

"Back to the mountain. For now, I'll cut them some slack, but they are walking a thin line with me."

The last member of the group, who Bronson had not met, represented the worst of them. Bronson noticed that Trent was the problematic alcoholic, and never a meaner man existed when he got a belly full of Mitch's finest whiskey and vodka.

The first few days, the new arrivals were cordial to Bronson and Catherine when they were face-to-face with them. The Premingers supplied them with plenty of food and water.

However, once the Premingers were beyond earshot, they continued to mock Bronson and Catherine. The longer they were there, the more arrogant and mean they got. They took advantage of their hosts' hospitality and eventually ordered them to fetch more food. Try as they may, Bronson and Catherine could not keep from hearing their rude comments. Bronson finally reached his boiling point.

They'd endured their snide comments and their bravado as long as they could. They needed to get back to the mountain, but they surely did not want to leave their guns behind. Guns in the hands of drunk, obnoxious people was not a good combination on a deserted island where there were no laws to protect them. Even Angela, who Catherine assisted in helping, called her some very hurtful names when the topic of odor came up.

Bronson finally could take no more of the abuse. He ran out of the hut and confronted them. "Do you idiots know how serious your situation is?"

Trent staggered toward Bronson. "Listen, prick, you don't own this fucking island, we do. So, why don't you scuttle your old ass back to your stinking wife so you can smell each other?"

Incensed, Bronson swung his mighty fist, landing squarely on Trent's jaw, and instantly knocked him unconscious. The other men ran to Trent's defense, not knowing why Bronson had slugged him. Mike, the body builder, lifted Trent to his feet and placed him in one of the newly repaired chairs that Bronson had made, then strolled back over to Bronson and did not say a word as he swung a his fist at Bronson. Bronson sideswiped the punch and Mike went tumbling into the sand.

Angry that he missed, Mike staggered to his feet, lumbered menacingly toward Bronson, and again tried to connect with a right cross. Bronson slipped the punch and landed a haymaker to his head. Mike staggered backward, surprised that Bronson could hit him as hard as he had. Bronson stunned him, but Mike did not go down. He bullrushed Bronson, driving him deep into the sand. A hulk of a man, Mike weighed too much for Bronson to handle on his back. Mike swung a punch sitting on top of Bronson, but, again, he just caught sand. Bronson hit him in his crotch.

He screamed at Bronson's low blow and lay on his side yelling and holding his crotch.

Unharmed, Bronson moved toward the group again.

After Mike's pain subsided, he ran up behind him and tackled him once again.

Bronson eluded him, got to his feet, and squared his fists, ready for a prolonged fight. Bronson fired off five consecutive punches. Mike fell, bloodied and exhausted. Bronson moved forward, but Mike held up his hands, indicating that he'd had enough.

Bronson turned his back to him and, once again, Mike took the coward's way out and sucker-punched him in the back of his head. Bronson fell hard, to the cheers of the drunken group.

Mike breathed heavy, and could not stand up straight due to the beating that Bronson handed him. Catherine ran to Bronson, who was lying face-down in the sand, and turned him on his back. She felt pride in him for standing up to Mike. She ran to get some water from the rain bucket and swabbed his face until he woke up. Groggy, he asked what had happened and Catherine told him.

Bronson had fire in his eyes as he stood up, and he wanted to end the fight with Mike, but Catherine convinced him to go with her to the hut. The new people scared her, and she did not know what they were capable of.

"We go to the mountain tomorrow morning. To hell with these people. They are throwing the vegetables around as if they are toys. They have no clue what they're up against. We have to smuggle these guns out of here," Bronson stated.

Meanwhile, the others in the camp were talking by a fire one of them had started. They'd broken the wooden crate that held the booze and ignited it. They'd also thrown the chairs Bronson had made into the fire.

Trent, having awakened from the knockout punch delivered by Bronson, said, "I will kill that son-of-a-bitch."

Mike said, "He's a tough old bird, but I got him. Angela, how's your arm doing?"

Angela, still in her bikini and drunk, stated, "I don't feel a thing other than being horny; I'm fine."

Mike perked up and said, "Oh, I can take care of that, baby. Let's go explore the jungle a bit."

Mike and Angela walked out into the dark jungle. Jeff and Trent commiserated that they had no woman.

Mitch said, "Well, if you just want sex, there's a woman in the hut."

Trent, still drunk, said, "I don't think I can take him on,

being drunk off my ass, but if I can get him out of there, I can do her in any condition."

Jocelyn, through drunken slurred words, said, "Yuck, why anyone would want to have sex with her is beyond me. She's old and she stinks."

Jeff said, "Still, she's a pretty good-looking woman if we can look past all the other problems."

Dan asked, "Are you saying that you want to rape her?"

Jeff slurred, "No, I just want sex, that's all. How I get it doesn't matter. Call it what you want to call it. No one knows they're here. We can get away with it. Mitch, remember that idiot who tried to date your wife? What did you do with him once you found out?"

Mitch smiled and said, "We don't know anything about that, do we, Trent?"

They clinked their glasses together and winked. "Come on, let's get Jeff and Trent laid. I think all of us can get that asshole out of there."

They waited to attack. Accompanied by the women and still wildly drunk, they quietly allowed Bronson to fall sleep. An hour later, they entered the hut and saw Bronson sleeping with Catherine behind him. Trent hit Bronson over the head with a vodka bottle. The bottle did not break, but it disabled Bronson long enough for them to drag him out of the tent. A small trickle of blood streamed down his face.

Catherine awoke immediately and fought the men as they removed Bronson from the hut. Trent smacked her across the face and she fell back onto the mattress.

Catherine fought hard, though, and was strong enough to throw the young girls aside as they attempted to hold her on the mattress.

Jeff and Trent left Bronson out on the beach, then returned to the hut.

"I'm going first, Jeff, and there's not a damn thing you can do about it!" Trent said as he removed his shirt. He told Jocelyn and Pepper to leave as he drunkenly walked toward a trembling and vulnerable Catherine.

Meanwhile, Mike and Angela returned to the camp and wondered why everyone was hanging around the hut.

Mike asked, "What's going on, Dan?"

"Nothing much. Trent's getting himself some."

Angela asked, "He's getting what?"

"He found out that Catherine had a crush on him, and he's sealing the deal," explained Mitch.

Jeff piped in, "I'm next because I heard the same thing, except she really likes me."

"You assholes aren't doing anything!" Angela ran toward the door of the hut.

Mike caught her. "This is none of our affair. Let Trent have his way."

Angela looked to the beach and saw Bronson on his hands and knees, trying to focus on what had happened to him.

Inside the tent, Trent moved closer as he took off his shorts. He grabbed Catherine and ripped off her tattered shirt. Her screams alerted a still-dazed Bronson. Trent mounted her, trying to kiss her neck, but she resisted mightily and kicked him in the groin—hard. He winced in pain and fell off her, holding his crotch. Incensed, he hit her, full fist to the jaw, knocking her back so hard that she partially went through the rear wall.

Stunned, she got up to run away, but he caught her mid-stride and hit her in the face again. She went flying against another wall.

On the beach, Bronson rose to his feet and ran toward the hut, but stumbled badly.

Suddenly, a gunshot rang out, shocking everyone. Catherine came out of the tent topless with blood coming from her eye and mouth; the others ran when they saw her pistol still smoking from the barrel. She walked over to Bronson and gathered him up as she saw the others scampering about and hiding behind anything they could find. Bronson leaned heavy on her, but she still held the gun up, pointing it at whoever showed themselves as they escaped into the jungle.

Catherine could not think clearly due to the trauma she'd suffered at the hands of Trent, and led a still-stunned Bronson in the wrong direction. She just wanted to get far away from the group as fast as she could, no matter the area.

Bronson, too injured to confront their drunken guests, captured his equilibrium and ran with her into the darkness. After some time had passed and Catherine and Bronson were beyond eyesight, the others walked into the hut to see that Trent had a bullet hole right between his opened eyes. The women screamed at the sight of their friend in that state, left the hut, and gathered nearby to console each other. Mike and Mitch were enraged. Mitch spied the rifle leaning up against the wall and checked it to see if it was loaded.

"We'll get them!" Mitch stated.

Mike asked, "Is it loaded?"

"Yes, but it only has a few bullets. Check and see if there's more."

They searched until Mitch found a box full of bullets. "I got them," he bellowed.

"Let's go get them!"

"Tomorrow morning, Mike. They have a home field advantage at night, but we'll hunt them down tomorrow."

Because of Catherine's earlier confusion and hasty retreat, they had to double back through the camp to get to the mountain.

"Go to the plane, Catherine. I can't see straight," Bronson said, staggering to stay upright while they ran.

"I think they got the rifle! I killed one of them! He tried to rape me!" Catherine trembled badly as she assisted Bronson.

"It's okay, sweetheart! I'd have killed him if they hadn't knocked me out. We'll be safe when we get to the plane because they don't have the stomach to go through this jungle to get to us and we both know the jungle won't allow them to pass through it cleanly." Bronson stopped to rest.

Catherine had so much adrenaline going that she practically carried him further. They stopped about a half-mile away and Bronson attempted to sit on a rock, but Catherine stopped him and said, "Not on that rock, remember?"

"Oh, damn, I forgot. We only have a half-mile to go. I don't think they will chase us tonight, but when they get hungry, they will. They will want to know where we got the food that we gave them. How many bullets do you have left?"

Catherine opened the revolver and counted.

"Five. I'm sorry, I forgot to take the box of shells."

"We'll be fine, sweetheart. The island will get most of them anyway. Let's get to that plane. It's completely covered with vines; they will never find us there. We need rest. We'll plan tomorrow."

They arrived at the plane later and climbed in. Bronson decided not to ask Catherine how she felt about what had nearly happened to her, but after some time, she looked at him and said, "He tore my shirt off, but that's as far as he got. I put a bullet in his head. He painfully begged me not to pull the trigger, but the gun relieved him of that pain."

"That's my girl," he said proudly.

"They knocked you out while you were sleeping. I grabbed my gun just in time."

"Well, let's get situated in here and plan what we're going to do."

Just as Bronson finished his sentence, Catherine left the plane and lay in a meadow nearby. He followed her out and asked what she was thinking.

"Bronson, I can't stay in the plane because of the pilot and co-pilot. It's not the smell. It's not right that they weren't buried properly."

"Catherine, those people mean to kill us, especially now that their friend is dead. We have to get some sleep to deal with them. We don't have the time to bury these two."

"Please help me lay them to rest?" she asked.

"Well, I guess they won't start looking for us until daylight, and this plane is so well hidden with the vines. Okay, we will bury them."

"We have nothing to dig with, though," Catherine muttered.

He said as he looked around, "The sand is loose and there are plenty of metallic parts of the plane that we can use as a shovel. You're right, it is the right thing to do, I guess, what with all that's going on..."

Catherine stood up before Bronson finished his thought and walked toward the plane. "Come on, Bronson; besides, it will take my mind off the fact that I killed a man. I've never done that before and I hope to never do it again."

The moon shone bright that night and showed them a small clearing where they could bury them.

Walking into the dark fuselage, they removed the pilot first. "His name is Smoky Richards, according to the name on the tag on his shirt," noted Bronson.

A mere skeleton, Bronson picked him up and he came

apart. Bronson made a few trips to gather all his bones and placed them on the ground as Catherine dug with a piece of the plane wrenched loose on impact. He could not be certain that he got all of Smoky Richards' bones, but vowed to return the next morning to make sure. Bronson arranged the bones as best he could. He assisted Catherine in digging and, later, they laid Smoky to rest. Once they covered him up, they used whatever the plane provided to make a simple cross. They placed his nametag on it, not having anything to write an epitaph with.

Catherine used to be a religious woman. Though the experiences on the island had shattered many of her beliefs, Bronson could tell that she wanted them back.

He brought out the co-pilot the same way and they dug another grave beside Richards and placed him in it. "His name is Patrick Johnson. I checked their wallets, but there is no indication who their next of kin are."

Catherine said a few words over the dead men and grabbed Bronson's hand and they entered the fuselage just as a few sprinkles started to fall.

"Bronson, I'm scared!"

Bronson assured Catherine that the new people on the island did not follow them. "Relax, Catherine, they aren't going to attempt revenge in this downpour."

Catherine felt secure and they slept.

Back at the camp, the men in the group prepared to track Bronson and Catherine down and kill them; however, they had a dead body that needed burying. They placed Trent on the blood-spattered mattress, dragged him to the beach, and laid him on the sand. Just like Bronson and Catherine, they had no tools, so they took turns digging in the sand with their hands next to the body. The women wanted nothing to do with burying Trent, although they did shed a few tears for their fallen friend.

Night fell with the hole not nearly deep enough to bury Trent, so they quit for the night and started drinking again. The rain got so intense they took refuge in the hut.

Eight people crammed into it. The next day, they planned

to hunt Bronson and Catherine down for killing their friend, but first they needed to finish burying Trent. Going to the mattress on the beach with the blood-soaked blanket covering his body, the men saw that the rain had filled in the hole they'd dug, much to the dismay of Mike who had done most of the digging. They also noticed something odd. The blanket covering the body only had a small bulge.

Dan removed the blanket and they all jumped back in horror to see that just Trent's head remained. The rest of his body had vanished.

"What the hell happened to the rest of him?" asked Mitch as he covered up Trent's head.

They looked around in confusion, then Jeff saw movement farther down the beach.

"Look! There's something moving in the sand," he said.

"I see it, but I don't see anything else. Come on, let's go check it out! Wait, first I'd better get the rifle," said Mitch as he ran back to the hut to retrieve it.

Dan met him on his way back and said, "It's gone now. I'm hungry! Any of those vegetables lying around?"

"Nope, none that I can see. I'm a little hungry myself. When we go hunting for the Premingers, we'll find out where their garden is and, if we find them, I have ways to make them talk. Maybe this island has game on it."

Mike scratched his shaven head and asked, "But how did Trent get in that condition? Do you think those two could have done that to his body?"

"I don't know! Unless there are other inhabitants of this island. Cannibals?" asked Dan.

"Cannibals? Shit, that's all we need. We had better stay together, just in case. Or maybe we should just wait here until a rescue boat comes by. You did radio in a mayday before you left the boat, didn't you?" asked Jeff.

"I couldn't do that because the explosion took out the entire cabin. Relax! We have cell phones. I'm sure one of us can get through. After all, we aren't that far from Florida," explained Mitch.

Mike threw his hands in the air and stated, "Dammit, Mitch! None of our phones work out here! We're stuck here!"

"Well, let's get Trent's head buried before the women find out," said Jeff, and they walked toward the mattress. "Where the fuck is it? I just saw it here a few minutes ago!" He scratched his head. "Mitch, there's some serious shit going on here! Who takes a fucking severed head?"

"Headhunters? I don't know. Listen, the answers are in that jungle. I don't know what is fucking going on! All I know is there are two people who know where food is. We have to get their asses to talk!" Mitch demanded, kicking at the sand.

At the plane, Bronson also made plans. He and Catherine awoke from a restful night's sleep. Hungry, they knew they had to pass the island's newest inhabitants to get to the mountain.

Bronson checked the pistol to make sure he really had five bullets.

"What are we going to do?" Catherine asked as she stretched her muscles.

"We are going to take back what took us twenty-two years to get. We don't have to confront them at all. All we have to do is slip past them and get to the mountain. They will die of starvation or they will kill themselves, I don't care which. The sand dragons will take care of the rest."

Catherine agreed. "They are vile people. I don't care what happens to them. I felt the safest I've ever felt in the green grass at the mountain. Can we go now?"

"I feel like we should wait a day to start. You know, to make sure they are good and hungry. They are weaker when they are hungry and that Mike guy packs quite a punch. If I do encounter him, I want him to be weak," Bronson said.

"We haven't eaten either," Catherine reminded him.

"Yes, that's true, but we're used to being hungry. We've gone days without food; they haven't. I imagine they are scraping the sand for those vegetables they were tossing around. Probably even fighting over them."

"Yes, they probably are."

"Besides, they want to find us, and the sooner they leave the camp, the easier it will be for us to slip behind them. I'm not worried, are you?"

"Yes, I am a little, but I know you're right. We can't let them know about the mountain or we'll have no place to go."

She and Bronson searched the plane for anything they could use in the coming days.

Mitch and the others searched the jungle. The women were asked to stay behind, but they were just as hungry as the men, and they demanded that they come along. Mitch agreed. He had the rifle; Jocelyn followed close behind.

Angela, still with her makeshift cast on her arm, stayed behind because she had no shoes to trample through the jungle and no proper clothes for the search. Mike, protective of her, demanded that she stay in the hut. She did not have the same killer instinct as the rest of the group and felt differently than the others toward Catherine because she'd cared for her. She did not express her opinion for fear of reprisals. Also, she had not known Trent as the others had. She waited for Mike and others to return, with the hope that they hadn't found Catherine and her husband.

None of them had any tracking abilities, but after reaching the eastern side of the island, they knew two things—the island appeared to be a large one, and possibly uncharted.

Mitch said, "Hey, all of you. If you come across them, at least leave one alive so they can lead us to the food."

Jeff, not convinced that they should go into the jungle, said, "This is not a big island. A garden that has corn in it can be found if we search for it."

"Hey, they killed Trent. I don't want to be worried about them taking potshots at us while we search. I want to eliminate them first. Let's kill them and be done with it. Then we can search for the garden on our own," said Mike.

Mitch smirked and said, "Okay, suppose we kill them and can't find the garden? Then what?"

"Okay, I see what you mean," said Mike.

"I hope we find them soon because I'm starving."

Jeff added, "So am I!"

Thus far, they had not noticed anything different about the island other than it appeared not to have animals of any kind.

They wanted to find a wild hog or something they could hunt and eat, but they found nothing, so they continued their hunt for Bronson and Catherine. They found a freshwater stream, and made camp for the night next to it. They drank the much-needed water, but hunger still tortured them. Mitch passed around a bottle of whiskey and emptied it. However, without food, the men got drunk fast and started acting stupid right away. Dan staggered to the creek and urinated in it, not realizing that he had urinated in their water supply. Regardless of the slow-moving water, the thought of drinking from the stream after he urinated in it sickened them. Drunk, Pepper and Jocelyn danced around the men, trying to entice them sexually. Mike missed Angela and he decided to return to the camp to be with her. He didn't have anything to hold water, so he couldn't bring any back for her.

"Tell her that we'll be back with food," stated Mitch.

"I hope so. Angela and I will search around the camp. There has to be something to eat on this damn island," said Mike.

Mike left and the rest of them bedded down for the night to continue their quest the next morning.

The whiskey helped, but it did not fill their need for solid food. It only made them stop thinking about it. Little did the rest of them know that Mitch and his wife had a stash of cookies, chips, and various other snacks hidden in Mitch's backpack, and they chowed down on the snacks while their friends slept with empty stomachs.

Bronson and Catherine opened their eyes, stretched, and planned their return to the mountain. The small space inside the plane caused their muscles to ache, but the pain ceased when they exited the plane into the still-dark morning. They packed what they needed and started on their way. Bronson did not see the group as they approached the camp quietly at mid-morning, but Mike watched them from behind a bush. He noticed the pistol on Bronson's hip and decided to take him out with an oar salvaged from the boat. Quietly, he eased up behind Bronson, and swung the oar with such force it chipped the wooden edge. He hit him hard on the back of the head, then grabbed the gun as Catherine screamed and fell to her knees to tend to her husband.

He stood up, pointed the gun at Catherine's head, and

said, "Look, you bitch! Here's how it's going to go. You are going to take me to wherever you got the food right now. You hear?"

"Why should I help you? You've hurt my husband and I'm going to help him," Catherine uttered defiantly.

Mike, in no mood for compromise, bellowed, "Listen, bitch, I will put a bullet in his head right now, then you won't have to worry so much about helping him. Now get up!"

"Okay. I'll show you where it is if you allow me to at least stop the bleeding before we leave. You go over there, sit on that rock for five minutes, and I'll show you potatoes, carrots, and anything else you can eat. I promise you!" She sat Bronson up and leaned him against a stump.

Mike agreed to give her five minutes, but he kept the gun trained on Bronson. He sat on the rock, but it instantly changed to a gel-like substance and he fell into it. The gel covered his abdomen and re-solidified with only his arms, head, and lower legs coming from the solid rock.

"What the fuck is this? Help me! Get me out of here!" He screamed as he moved violently, trying to free himself.

"Sorry, you son-of-a-bitch, I can't help you. You aren't worth my time."

She grabbed the gun, spit on him, then walked back to Bronson.

Bronson regained consciousness and, groggy, he stood up and staggered over to the rock, which held a frantic Mike.

"What happened?" Bronson asked.

"He came up behind us and hit you with an oar," Catherine explained.

"Where's my gun?" he asked.

"Right here!"

"We have to get out of here! The others probably heard that commotion. Let's go back to the mountain a while. We don't know who else is in camp. Hurry, Catherine, go back to where we were, run! I'll be right behind you!"

Catherine took off running. Bronson quickly moved behind Mike and said, "Sucker-punched me again, did you? You damn coward! Enjoy the rest of your life stuck in that rock. I don't expect it to last that long."

Bronson ran after Catherine.

Mike had difficulty breathing heavy as the rock began

constricting his chest. He mustered one very loud scream before screaming was no longer possible.

Mitch and the others heard him and backtracked to where they thought the screams came from.

Angela arrived first and saw Mike deeply emerged within the rock. "How the fuck did this happen?"

"I just sat on the rock and I sank into it. Get me out! I can hardly breathe! Hurry!"

"How the hell am I supposed to get you out of that? It's solid rock!" She hit the rock with the oar. The third time, the oar broke in half and she could do nothing other than wait for the others to get there. When they did arrive, they were shocked at what they saw. They tried in vain to release Mike, but they could not. Mitch pointed the rifle at the rock and fired a shot.

It took a tiny piece out of it, but the rock kept Mike firmly trapped. He began to turn blue. Just as Mitch aimed to take another shot, Mike screamed in pain.

"What is it, Mike?" yelled Dan.

"There's something moving around my ass and stomach!" He let out a blood-curdling scream as whatever moved around his mid-section increased in intensity. "It's eating me! It's eating me!" he bellowed as pain contorted his face. "Fuck! Make it stop!"

Blood oozed from around the holes where his legs and his chest were protruding.

Frantic, Angela pulled his leg in a vain effort to extricate him from the rock, and she suddenly fell back, holding his severed leg. She screamed. Pepper fainted and Jocelyn screamed in anguish at seeing her friend's hopeless demise. Once the leg fell away, the hole filled in with the gel and solidified back into solid rock. Mike had a look of death on his face, but was still alive. Slowly, an arm fell off, and then the other, and Mike twitched. His eyes were eerily wide open, but he couldn't speak. He did, however, see his body being picked apart.

They stood there and watched him die with a horrifying expression on his face as blood rushed from his ears, nose, and mouth and soaked into the rock. His expression changed drastically from horrific to relaxed as he took his last breath. The remnants of Mike, which protruded from the rock, fell into the bushes, including his head, which bounced a few times, spraying the last of the blood and settling in front of them. His friends stepped back as hundreds of vines appeared and engulfed the last remains of Mike.

The rock closed up and appeared to be a harmless boulder once again.

"We have to get out of here!" shouted Jeff. "What happened to Mike is not possible, but we all saw it and I feel like I'm being watched."

They heard a branch snap.

Mitch spotted Catherine and Bronson watching a short distance away and started shooting. He barely missed Bronson. Catherine ran in another direction. Bronson felt his pistol drop, but he had no time to retrieve the valuable weapon from amidst the tangled vines.

All of a sudden, coconuts rained down on them. Unfortunately, one of them grazed Catherine and she fell.

Mitch shot from a covered position and thought he hit Bronson, but when he investigated, he saw a topless Catherine trying to get to her feet and he knocked her out with the butt of the gun. Dan woke up Pepper from her fainting spell, carried Catherine back to the camp, and threw her into the hut with a still frantic Angela. Catherine had a small cut on her head and Angela applied pressure to stop it. She also retrieved one of Mike's shirts and covered her up.

Mitch fired a few shots in the air to get Bronson's attention and called into the jungle, "Preminger, we got your wife! She's unconscious but alive. Bring us food and you can have her back! I know you're out there and I know you can hear me!"

"What assurances do I have that you will not harm Cathy?" shouted Bronson from a hidden position.

"You're in a lousy negotiating position, Preminger! We have the upper hand!" Mitch spouted. "Jeff still thinks your wife is attractive! Perhaps I'll let him have his way with her while she's sleeping!"

"Okay! I'll get your food, but if you harm her in any way, I'll use every bullet I have on you. I've got you in my sights!"

Mitch took refuge behind a tree with the rifle trained to where he thought Bronson's voice came from. "Okay, she will not be harmed!"

"I'll leave your food on the beach tomorrow morning and you allow my wife to walk into the jungle. Agreed?" Bronson had no choice, but he did not allow them to follow him. He watched Mitch give Jeff instructions before he went into the jungle. He needed to pass by the camp, and needed a distraction to get past Mitch. He spied Jeff peeing behind a tree and quietly snuck behind him. He knocked him to the ground, stunning him.

Jeff scrambled back up.

Bronson said, "Let me pass, Jeff!"

When Jeff blocked his way, Bronson punched him in the face and Jeff went flying. Dazed, he wandered close to the marked red tree. Bronson tried to push him against the bark, but could not get him close enough.

Jeff got up, tackled Bronson, and landed a few heavy blows of his own. They fought far away from the camp; Mitch and the others could not hear the melee.

Bronson, worn out from all the injuries he'd suffered, swung at air as Jeff avoided the haymaker. Bronson fell to the ground, exhausted. Jeff picked him up, dazed and defenseless, Bronson watched as he reared his fist back for a final punch. Bronson closed his eyes, waiting for the finishing blow because he had no energy to block it. However, shockingly, the blow did not come.

Jeff released him.

Bronson opened his eyes to see Jeff's fist against the bark of the red tree. The tree had sucked his hand into the bark.

"What the fuck is this?" Jeff tried to pull his hand away from the tree.

"That is one of the red trees, asshole. It's a man-eater. You're done! Once it has you locked into it, it will never let you go until it eats every fucking bit of you." Bronson smiled and ran toward the beach just outside the camp.

He waited for Jeff's scream so he had an opportunity to enter the camp unobserved to rescue Catherine and continue toward the mountain. Sadly, despite Jeff's screams, Mitch held his ground. He did not relinquish his position and sent Dan off to find out what had happened. Bronson saw the rifle trained on the hut and did not take the chance of Mitch indiscriminately shooting into it.

He continued to the mountain to gather the food, but with Jeff in the perilous clutches of the red tree and Mike dead, he did not have to bring back as much. The red tree provided the diversion Bronson wanted as it slowly sucked Jeff in. The tree needed a few hours to finish him off, and he speculated that it continued to eat him as he returned with the food.

Bronson ran past the camp when Mitch left his position, and continued to the mountain. He rested a few times due to the tiring fight with Jeff, but arrived sometime after his altercation. He dived in the water, swam to the back of the mountain, quickly scaled the heights by pure adrenaline, entered the cave, and dropped from exhaustion.

However, he had no time to waste relaxing because he wanted his wife back as soon as possible. He grabbed a five-gallon bucket amid Charles' cluttered belongings. He gathered himself together, ran to the clearing, ripped up as much food as the bucket could carry, and placed the lid on it.

Climbing down the mountain, he skipped the last four steps and jumped in, holding his arm over the bucket. He swam one-handed the short distance, lumbered onto the beach, and walked as fast as he could.

Chapter Nine

Mitch Changes the Rules

Bronson positioned himself so he could talk to Mitch upon nearing the camp. He placed the bucket filled with food into Mitch's lifeboat, which was moored near the camp. He noticed a compartment in the boat and opened it. In it, he found a stash of food and snacks.

He saw Mitch and Pepper talking; he could not hear what they said, and dared to creep closer to find out.

Mitch asked Pepper, "What's going to happen after we finish the food and we don't have a hostage anymore?"

Pepper said, "That's a good point..."

Just as they realized their mistake, they heard Jeff's deathly scream. Dan went to investigate.

"Mitch, Pepper, come quick! It's Jeff! I need your help!" Dan shouted from somewhere in the jungle.

Mitch, ever vigilant over Catherine, shouted back, "I can't come out, but Pepper is on her way!"

Pepper ran toward the screams. After some time of searching, she saw what Dan yelled about. The tree that Jeff touched had swallowed him shoulder deep, vying to suck in the rest of him. It had devoured his left arm, shoulder, and part of his left leg. The tree slowly drew an agonized Jeff in farther. Dan and Pepper could do nothing but watch the slow, painful demise of their friend. No blood leaked from the tree, but Jeff's anguished expression indicated the level of pain he endured. They tried to pull him away from the tree, but that just made the tree pull him in faster. Up until then, it had not affected any of his vital organs, but it quickly approached his lungs.

Pepper screamed when the mysterious tree unmercifully pulled Jeff's head into itself, and he fainted before death slowly and finally came to him. They felt helpless as his eyes fluttered while the tree ate his head and brain, post-death. Pepper fainted, and awoke soon after. Dan helped her to her feet, but by the time she woke up, the tree had eaten most of Jeff save half his leg, which was left dangling but still moving into the bark. They sat, watched, and cried as the last of their friend disappeared within the tree. Then, the tree changed to a brighter shade of red with no sign that it just devoured a full-grown man.

Dan and Pepper ran back to camp to inform Mitch about what had happened. Out of breath, they hurried back so fast that Mitch thought Bronson chased them. They stopped and tried to talk, but they were terrified as they tried to communicate what they'd seen.

"A tree ate Jeff! We saw it with our own eyes. The fucking tree ate Mitch, we have to get off this island," Dan explained.

Mitch did not believe them at first, but soon realized by their terrified expressions that they had seen something unspeakable.

"A tree ate Jeff?" he questioned. "How does a tree eat a person?"

"Listen, I saw it and so did Pepper. I say we get in those lifeboats and get the hell off this island! There's an evil here that I can't explain and I have a feeling that Bronson and Catherine are somehow making all this happen," Dan reasoned.

"We can't go now! Look at the sky. There's a storm moving in. We need a few days," said Mitch.

"We'll die of starvation if we stay here," Pepper said.

"We'll die of starvation on the open seas too. I say we wait out the storm and get fed when Bronson comes back. I really hate that old guy!" Mitch confessed.

Just as he said that, Bronson yelled to the group that the food had been delivered and for them to allow Catherine to go free.

"How do we know that you did what you said you'd do?"

Mitch yelled out into the jungle.

A minute later, Bronson heaved an apple as far as he could throw and hit Mitch in the back. He tried to get it close enough for them to see it, but he did not complain when the tossed fruit hit Mitch in the back of his head and stunned him. Dan and Pepper saw the bright red apple rolling around on the ground and both dove for it, ripping it into pieces.

"We have a change of plans, Bronson! We will need a week's worth of food! Don't worry, we'll feed your wife!" Mitch yelled in the general direction of where the apple came from.

"We had a deal, Mitch! You son of a bitch! I did as you asked, now let her go!" Bronson bellowed.

"Today is day one, Bronson. Five days from now, you can have her back. Today is just the first installment. There's a storm coming in and we can't leave. In five days, we will get in our boats, get away from this hellhole, and leave it to you and Catherine. We want no part of this island. It's killed Mike and Jeff and your wife killed Trent, but something or someone decapitated him," Mitch explained.

"Okay, I agree, but I will be watching you. I will make sure that you're feeding my wife or I'll come in there and cut your throat while you're sleeping. Bring her out in the open so I can see her eating. The food is in your boat. Send Dan to get it," Bronson agreed.

Mitch conferred with Dan and stated, "He doesn't have that pistol anymore. Did you hear him? He said that he'd cut my throat. We may get food for the rest of our stay here as long as we keep Catherine. Here, hold the gun and I'll go get the food."

Mitch did not dare allow Dan to see inside his boat for fear that he might notice his and Jocelyn's stash. He handed Dan the gun and ran toward his boat.

Mitch picked up the bucket and noticed that the compartment that held his secret had been opened. He knew that Bronson now had information that could splinter his group of allies.

He carried the food back to the hungry bunch. They could not wait until he put the bucket down before they grabbed what they could. Mitch ordered Catherine out of the tent and into the open as Angela gave her a few apples. Angela quickly ate a few apples as well.

A bond had formed between the two women and they talked about how they'd gotten there.

"I don't really know these people. This is my first date with Mike and that idiot, Trent, tried to rape me the night before the explosion, but Mike stopped him. I'm glad you put a bullet in him. Does your head still hurt?" she asked as she placed a cloth over Catherine's head.

Catherine asked, "Why are you being so nice to me?"

"Because you were nice to me when setting my arm."

"Bronson and I greeted and were nice to all of you. We were so excited to see you and it turned ugly fast. We've been here twenty-some years waiting to be rescued. We've encountered and dealt with horrific things, but none as bad as Mitch and the others."

"I don't know these people. Mike asked me out on his friend's boat. I didn't know how horrible they were until I saw them treat you the way that they did."

"Thank you, Angela. You're not like them. I'll tell you a secret about this island."

"What's that, Catherine?"

"As long as you're on it, you won't age."

"How is that possible? You mean I'll remain twenty-five years old?" she asked.

"Not exactly. You will age, but backwards. You will get younger here, not older. I am ninety years old, Angela."

Amazed at the fantastic story, Angela asked, "Ninety? Why, you don't even look forty."

"I know my husband well and I know he's worried sick about me being here as your captive. I must tell you that I will try to escape if the opportunity presents itself."

"You're not my captive, Catherine. I know you will. Take me with you! We'll both escape!" she whispered.

Sensing that she could trust Angela, Catherine drew closer to her and whispered, "We will take care of you, Angela. We have plenty of food and I'll tell you all about this island. It's a dangerous place here and you must know where to go and when. We have another camp about a mile from here, near the water. We left this camp because of the dangerous beach. Whatever you do, do not venture on the beach because there's something there that you do not want to see.

Trust me, I've seen the creature that lurks beneath the sand. It will eat you whole."

Angela did not know what to say, but she could tell that Catherine had serious concerns for her safety. She did not believe the tale of a monster beneath the sand, though, and thought that she referred to the sun's rays and its harmful effects on her skin. She wanted to leave with Catherine and Bronson, and vowed to help her escape that night. However, they had to leave while the others all slept in the same hut as they did.

Mitch brought out the liquor as a nightcap; that turned into a drunken orgy. The party lasted well into the night as Mitch fired the rifle in the jungle, threatening to kill Bronson and allow Catherine, or make her, join the food-fueled sex party.

Catherine and Angela could hear the debauchery going on outside. Dan and Pepper tried to get Angela to join, but she refused. Mitch angrily stepped toward the hut and pulled her out by her hair, demanding that she dance for them. Angela no longer had Mike to protect her, and she was frightened. The other women wanted her as much as the men did. They did not care that she said no and they did not have a problem with Dan and Mitch coercing her to strip down to nothing. She only had a bikini and they were hell-bent on getting it off.

The rest were naked and dancing around without a care in the world. Stripping Angela's bikini off embarrassed her. Nude, she tried to run away when Catherine turned up with an oar in her hand, swung it wildly at Mitch, and caught him on the side of the head. However, Catherine did not have enough strength to put that much power behind the swing.

Mitch backhanded her across the face and she went flailing against a tree. Angela ran to her and helped her up.

Just as the still-naked Mitch reared back to slap her again, Bronson burst out of the jungle with his machete and swung it wildly, striking Mitch in his crotch with one wild swing and causing a serious injury to his manhood. A drunken Dan could not help Mitch. Mitch held his groin, but still kept the rifle close. Bronson had to get Catherine out of there before Mitch got the rifle cocked.

"Come on, Cathy, we have to get out of here, now!" he bellowed, grabbing her hand.

"Wait, we have to take Angela with us. They will kill her." She reached for Angela's hand.

"She's one of them! Now come on, Catherine."

"No, she's one of us! Please, Bronson, let her come with us!"

Bronson relented, "Okay! Okay! Let's get out of here."

The three ran into the jungle, on their way to their other camp. They did not dare try to climb the mountain at night, nor did they enjoy walking through the jungle at night because there were many perilous things in the dark and they did not know where they were. Angela stumbled a few times because she lacked shoes, and she no longer had any clothes.

As they scurried away, Mitch, in serious pain due to Bronson's partial castration, begged Jocelyn to help him, but she declined saying, "That's not in the trophy wives' handbook."

"Dan, can you help me here?" Mitch asked as he tried to stop the blood loss.

"Dude, what do you want me to do? Your balls are hanging out of their sac. I don't know what to do other than push them back in and I don't do that!" Dan said, disgusted.

Pepper was a student nurse and she took over and did the deed, but she did not have anything to sew up the wound with. Dan went back to Mitch's boat and searched around for anything that they could close up the wound with. In the process, he found their stash of food and a roll of duct tape.

He brought both back to the camp, threw the roll of duct tape at his feet, and held up a large bag of potato chips.

"Pepper, wrap the tape around his sac to close the wound because I want him to live long enough to explain this," Dan said in a disgusted tone.

Pepper grabbed the tape and wrapped it around Mitch's testicles, all the time eyeing the bag of potato chips.

Mitch said, "I wanted to surprise you all when we got desperate. That's all we've got and it has to last until we get rescued. Bronson and Catherine will not help us now and I don't want to chase them through that labyrinth of a death jungle. We have to ration it all."

Dan accepted Mitch's excuse, but he still did not trust him. The duct tape stopped the bleeding and sealed the wound, but the unsanitary bandage would not stop an infection.

Just the four of them remained. The rifle seemed useless, but Mitch kept it close anyway. Now he had something else to guard. Dan and Pepper were always hanging around the boat hoping to get something to eat. Jocelyn handed out daily rations, but secretly, she and Mitch ate as much as they wanted.

Dan worried about the gun. He confided in Pepper and she asked, "Why does he always have to carry that thing around, dear? The Premingers are long gone and don't appear to be a threat now."

"That gun is not for the Premingers anymore. They don't need anything from us. That gun is to protect Mitch and Jocelyn from us. I predict that soon, they will not be giving us any more food. Sadly, I think they are plotting our demise to make their food supply last longer."

Mitch and his group did not chase the others further after Jeff's death. Bronson mastered the technique of catching fish with his bare hands after he lost his rod and reel and Catherine marveled in her husband's ability to provide for her.

Bronson waded out into the shallows, waited for a medium-sized fish to come near, and pounced on it. He emerged from the inlet with a thirty-pound fish. The only kinds of fish he could immediately identify were tuna and sharks. He didn't know which kind this one was. He brought up the wriggling monster, killed it instantly with his machete, and filleted it with the precision of a master sushi chef. Bronson's angling technique amazed Angela, but the speed at which he readied it for the fire shocked her. Catherine seasoned it and they talked as the fish cooked. They ate until they could not eat anymore and the rest he left out to dry to eat later.

"This is so good," said Angela as she licked her fingers.

The sun had set; Bronson did not start a fire in the blazing sunshine of day because of the fear that Mitch would see the smoke and give him a clear path to where they were. He also made sure that the wind did not blow the aroma of their meal toward the troubled group.

"How have you two survived all these years?" Angela asked.

"Bronson planned all this out when he packed his survival trunk in our lifeboat. Without that, we'd have been dead many years ago," explained Catherine.

Bronson, shirtless and bearded, said, "Well, it's a lifeboat, and I hoped that we'd never have to use it. Cathy and I have been sailing since we got married and have been through many storms, but I guess fate finally caught up to us. Mostly, I guess we've just been lucky."

"Have you thought about leaving here or trying to get rescued?" Angela asked.

"Once we found out the secret of the island, I wanted it to cure my wife and it appears to have happened. We've been aging in reverse ever since, and personally, I like the idea of living our entire lives together once again, if we ever get rescued, that is. Mitch's boat is the first one we've seen since we've been here." Bronson placed another log on the fire as the embers crackled.

Angela started to cry, fearing that she did not have as much time as the Premingers. "Are you saying that I will be getting younger here too?"

Catherine confirmed, "Not if we get off this island."

"Good, because I don't want to relive those years. Do you have a plan to leave?" she asked.

Bronson looked at Catherine and saw her nod her head. "Yes, we plan on taking over their boats once they die and making an attempt. The boats are big enough to store as much as we can. It will be a long, hard voyage with no guarantees of success, but we have angels looking after us. I really believe that. Our story will go on and on." Angela shivered in the cool night air and Bronson asked, "Cathy, do you have anything left to give to that poor girl in the way of clothes?"

"I think I have some cloth somewhere. You have one extra pair of shorts and so do I; we can fashion something and, once we get to the cave, there's a lot we can work with. Angela, I know being naked in front of us is embarrassing, but we're in a difficult situation and if it makes you feel any better, we'll get naked too. It's okay, I trust my husband and we have a daughter about your age, or at least, we had one your age. She's fifty-six by now and our grandchild is twenty-two. You see, we last saw her and her husband just before we left Florida. That's when she informed us of her pregnancy. Oh my

God, Bronson! Brooke is ten years older than I am! Am I a bad mother for not thinking about her very much all these many years?"

"Cathy, look where we are! Do you recall what we had to do to survive all these years? I'm sure she thinks that we are missing at sea. I'll bet she still thinks about us still," Bronson asserted. "Hey, she's older than me as well. Strange the way things turn out."

"I hope she does. Angela, what's happening in the world now?" asked Catherine.

"Well, all the wars ended and we nearly had another civil war, but it turned out to be just a political one. Social Security ceased for a year or so, but because of an upheaval, Congress restored it. One of the political parties came into power and soon got voted out. Once the people realized the harmful effect, they rioted everywhere. Even the people who voted them into power came to Washington D.C. with guns drawn and blasted the Capitol Building. Everyone has a gun now, and they shoot first and ask questions later. It's a scary world, but I've been shielded from much of it. My father is a senator from Florida and he saved Social Security. They had good intentions, but didn't care enough how it impacted the people. I didn't know the ins and outs of it, nor did I care. The trains now run on air in tubes and cars on hydrogen even though fuel is plentiful and cheap. I wish I had reception on my phone and I could show you what has happened since you have been here."

"Stop! I don't want to hear anymore. It sounds like the country has gone to the dogs," Catherine stated.

Angela continued, "It's not that bad, really, but poverty is everywhere. Greed will always be a part of our society. Regardless of the troubles, it's still the greatest country on the planet and I want to get back to it. Bronson, do you really think we'll be rescued soon?"

"You have a cell phone? Where is it? Well, we'll try our best. I think Cathy and I are ready to go. For now, I just want to survive while we figure out how to get off this island, and to do that, we have to get to the cave. It's late and I think we should get some sleep because we have a good walk and climb tomorrow morning. Catherine, we have to get something on her feet," Bronson stated as he poured water on the fire.

"My cell is on the boat I came here in," she said as she and Catherine entered the smaller shelter.

"We'll have to go get that. You two sleep. I think I'll go to their camp and try to retrieve it. They should be asleep by now, so getting it should be easy."

Catherine, wary about Bronson going back around the visitors, protested, but allowed him to go without too much complaining; besides, she trusted that he knew more about getting around the island than anyone else.

The moon supplied enough light to allow them to find their way around the camp, and for Bronson to find his way back to the boats while Catherine and Angela went to sleep.

Mitch and the others turned in for the night after they had drunk the last of the whiskey. They made plans to take off the next morning. Jocelyn packed most of her belongings on the boat.

An hour later, Bronson quietly walked to the boat by following the tree line north along the beach.

The waves supplied sound cover. Bronson saw Mitch, with the rifle at his side, watching the boats. However, the liquor had taken full effect and he'd passed out.

Bronson did not risk waking him up by trying to retrieve the rifle and just stuck to his goal of finding Angela's cell phone. He collected the phone and started back, but stopped to see if Mitch's boat held anything else they could use. He rummaged around and found a pair of Jocelyn's sneakers and some of her clothes. Just for good measure, he confiscated all the food he could carry. He tied the pant legs together and filled them with food. He closed all the compartments and made his escape back to his own camp.

Running full force and getting there in record time, he settled in beside Catherine, who awoke at his presence. He showed her what he'd brought back with him.

The next morning, Mitch and the others readied to take off, but they needed to load up on water first. They all made their final trip to the creek; however, the trip took longer because they still had vivid memories of what had happened to Mike and Jeff.

They filled up everything that could hold water, but Pepper got too close to the creek. She stepped in the water and immediately disappeared.

Dan saw his wife vanish. "Where the hell did she go? The creek is only a few inches deep! I can see the damn bottom of it."

He frantically dipped his arm in the water, and it kept going well past the creek bed.

"I feel her hair. I got you, babe! Just hold your breath a little while longer," he said to himself while Mitch and Jocelyn looked on, not lifting a finger to help him.

Dan pulled and, finally, she came up. One last tug and he thought he'd saved her. However, he pulled up her severed head. Horrified, he fell back and threw the head in the water. It slowly sank and disappeared. Dan cried and held his head in his hands, completely overcome with grief.

"Mitch, I don't know what to say! I lost my wife! How the hell could that happen in just inches of water?"

Mitch and Jocelyn did not want to hear him anymore.

Jocelyn kissed Mitch and said, "Get it over with and let's get out of here. I'll be back at the boat."

"Get what over with? What's she talking about, Mitch?" Dan asked, still whimpering and not believing what he'd just seen.

"It's just this, my old friend. We don't have enough food for the three of us and it will be a long sail to find a boat to rescue us, so we must say our goodbyes now," Mitch explained as he raised the rifle up to Dan's head and fired a single shot. Dan fell across the creek. Shocked, Mitch saw something underneath the water pull Dan in.

Mitch ran back to camp and met Jocelyn at the hut. She'd heard the shot and knew that Mitch had done the deed. She was anxious to set sail.

"Come on! Let's go, Mitch!" she screamed as she stepped into the boat.

"Well, we still have to get all the water on board. Are you just going to sit there and make me do all the work? Get your ass up here and help me!" Mitch stated angrily.

Jocelyn climbed out of the boat and went to grab the last bucket of drinking water. Mitch placed his bucket on the boat and watched as Jocelyn stopped mid-way on the beach and stared at something coming toward her.

"What are you doing? Come on! Pick up the bucket and

let's go!" Mitch demanded. However, she froze and stared at the shuffling mound of sand coming at her. Mitch angrily stormed in her direction because he felt that she ignored him, but she just pointed toward the rolling mound.

Mitch took a few more steps. A huge dragon crashed out of the sand and devoured a stunned Jocelyn in one bite. Mitch fell on his back in shock, but another dragon skimmed the sand with him in its sight. Mitch got to his feet and ran toward the boat screaming, but the dragon beat him and bit everything off above the waist while another came and finished off the remains.

Bronson heard the screams a mile away. He stopped his pursuit of the mountain and shepherded Catherine and Angela to where they'd started.

"Why are we going back, dear?" asked Catherine.

"I think Mitch met the sand dragons. We should go and get what they left behind. They still had a lot of food in that boat. Let's go take a walk to see if anyone's left. If they are dead, we'll sail the boats around to the mountain and moor them here."

Catherine and Angela agreed and started their trek back to Mitch's camp.

Upon arriving, they were cautious to make sure Mitch and Jocelyn were gone. They saw one lifeboat tethered to an anchor dug into the sand, bobbing in the surf, and no signs of anyone scurrying about. Bronson ran over to the boat. He did not care about the buckets of drinking water. Their mountain home provided a lifetime of clean drinkable water, but they needed the food. He ran back to the tree line, ever watchful for mounds of moving sand, and pushed the other lifeboat into the surf beside Mitch's boat, then tied the two together.

Catherine explained, "When Bronson gives us the word, we have to run as fast as we can toward the boats."

"Why do we have to run, Catherine? No one's here."

"It's not people I'm worried about. It's what's under the sand that scares me. It's best that you don't see it. Trust me, run!" Catherine demanded.

Angela saw how serious Catherine appeared, so she did what she was told and ran to the ankle-deep surf as fast as she could. Catherine followed her closely. They climbed into one of the boats as Bronson grabbed the anchor, placed it in the boat, and pushed off the shallow sand bar. He stayed in the water, pushing the boats farther away from the island, until he cleared the waves and climbed in. Angela and Catherine assisted Bronson in rowing the boat with the other in tow.

They never visited their former camp again.

They arrived at the mountain some time later. Each climbed off the boat onto the lowest step on the side. Catherine went first to show Angela where to walk. Now that Angela had shoes, she climbed it easily. Catherine gathered the rope and sent it down to Bronson. He loaded what he could, and Catherine and Angela pulled it up to the cave entrance. With the boats emptied of all useable items, Bronson took them to the shore on the island side of the mountain and beached them. He swam around to the stone ladder and climbed up. As he arrived, he saw the women trying to make the cave a home.

Angela asked, "Where are the vegetable plants and the water?"

Bronson smiled. "Why are you two cleaning up the cave? Our home is the valley below."

"Valley below?" questioned Angela.

Catherine said, "We'll get to that. I imagine both places will be our home. Angela, follow us. We'll show you a heavenly place."

They walked the narrow hallway that opened up to the most beautiful place that Angela had ever seen.

However, they observed a troubling phenomenon. Because they had left the island and then returned, Bronson and Catherine regressed in age instantly. Angela did not notice that her body had changed slightly, but the older couple saw the changes immediately. The Premingers did not change outwardly that much; however, they remembered what Charles had told them about speeding up the regression process if they left the island and returned. They had not the heart to tell Angela what had happened to her.

Catherine pulled Bronson aside and whispered, "We have to get her off this island, dear, as fast as we can. She is such a sweet young girl. I can't bear to see her dwindle to nothing. We've left the island a few times and returned, and I didn't notice a change before, but I noticed this one. Look at my skin!"

"I think Charles said that age regresses a few years, but this time, you look five years younger. Maybe the age regression varies. I mean, the times we left the island before could have only regressed our age a month or just a few days. If we lost about five years this time, Angela doesn't have that much time left. We are going to have to limit our time away from the island. We have two boats; perhaps we should try what Mitch wanted to do," he said, as he saw Angela run though the tall grass with all the excitement and energy of a much younger woman.

Angela once had her whole life in front of her and Catherine thought that God Himself took it back year by year. "Well, we certainly cannot allow her to leave the island again. We have a few more years to give."

"Agreed! We'll get settled, and tomorrow I'll reinforce the boats for a long voyage. It looks as though we made it to our thirties. I remember you like this. You were stunning then and you're stunning now," Bronson stated proudly.

Catherine gave him a faux punch on the arm and said, "You look pretty good yourself, for an old man."

Chapter Ten

Angela's Stolen Future

That night, they feasted on Mitch's stash of snacks because they hadn't had such food for decades. They slept
among the tall green grass, but were rudely awakened when
a lightning strike narrowly missed them. It streaked through
the opening of the dormant volcano and struck the inside
wall. Small stones rained down on them as they scurried to
the protection of the cave's thick stone walls. Uninjured by
the falling rock, Bronson mentioned the incoming storm and
reminded Catherine that the storm could change their plans
of strapping the boats together and finally leaving the island.
The previous night, they'd decided to risk open water to save
Angela from getting any younger.

"This is a massive storm. Can you imagine where we'd be
right now if we'd left yesterday?" Bronson asked as he looked
out through the cave entrance at the torrential downfall and
the angry seas crashing against the mountain.

"Yes, we'd be at the bottom of the ocean."

Something else entered Bronson's mind as he trained his
binoculars on where he'd moored the boats. He saw that, for
the first time, water had overflowed the island, causing the
mountain and the island to be parted by a wide swath of
shallow seawater.

"Dammit! The boats are crashing against the rocks. One
of them is destroyed. I think I need to go down there to save
the other one."

Catherine very rarely questioned her brave husband's de-
cisions; however, this time, she put her foot down and demanded that he not go. Her justification seemed sound, as

the two women needed Bronson, and scaling the mountain in a perceived hurricane appeared to be a suicide mission.

She and Angela pleaded with him not to go, but he said, "I have to save the boat! It's more important than I am." He dismissed the concerns of the women and started his way down the backside of the mountain.

Catherine, looking through the binoculars, informed him that the other boat had just exploded on the rocks as well. It had crashed one too many times, shattered into a hundred pieces, and scattered over the violent surf. Bronson climbed back up and looked through the binoculars to see that Catherine did not exaggerate. Both boats were gone, as well as the thought of escape.

They looked at Angela and their hearts sank, because now she realized that she had aged the wrong way and that the only hope she had of stopping the aging process lay in a million pieces on the beach.

"Please! Can you stop this? I want to live my life," she pleaded with tears in her eyes.

Bronson walked over, hugged her, and said, "By my estimation, we have twenty-one or twenty-two years to get you out of here. I will use all my knowledge to try to make that happen, dear. Catherine and I will find a way. Wait! Your cell phone! I forgot all about it. Maybe we can get through now that we are here on top of a mountain."

She spied it on a stone bench in the cave and tried to make a phone call, but still received no signal, even as high as they were. It had plenty of battery life, but was useless without reception.

Bronson made another death-defying suggestion. "Maybe we aren't high enough. There's another fifty feet above this cave that I can try to climb to possibly get a connection."

Catherine's and Angela's eyes widened at the possibility of getting a response, but Catherine did not allow him to do it in the deadly storm. Bronson acknowledged that the storm raged too much to start scaling the rest of the mountain, but he left the idea open for when the weather cleared. He made promises to Angela and he intended to fulfill those promises, but he had no idea how.

A day later, the skies cleared and bright sunshine replaced the blackness of the storm. He looked for the boats, but saw no signs of their pieces, just the ropes still tied to rocks that held them. The tides lowered.

"Okay, it's time I find out if we can get reception from the top of this mountain. I think I can reach the southern-most rim of the volcano. It looks to be the tallest."

Catherine looked up to where Bronson wanted to go. "I guess that doesn't look too bad of a climb. Please be careful, Bronson!"

He gathered all the rope he had to start his ascent to the top. The fifty feet he had to climb were simple and he reached the halfway point in mere minutes. He continued his climb. One step at a time, he reached the top and took the phone from his pocket. He turned it on, but sadly, did not receive a signal.

He yelled to Catherine, "Sorry, there's no reception up here either. I'll stay a few more minutes, but I don't think it's going to work."

"What did he say, Cathy?" asked a concerned Angela.

"I'm sorry, dear, but there's no reception. He's going to stay up there a little while longer just in case."

Bronson yelled, "It's no use. It's not working. I'm coming down."

Catherine looked at Angela and said, "He's coming down. It didn't work, but don't you worry, dear, my Bronson will figure out something."

"I hope so."

Bronson jumped off the last step and handed the phone to Angela. In a fit of disgust, she threw it off the cliff and into the ocean below.

"I guess you deserve to be angry, Angela," Bronson said, and he reaffirmed his promise to get her off the island.

Catherine looked out over the jungle and asked, "Do you think you can build a boat out of all of that?"

"I think I can, if the rope holds up and the island doesn't kill us first," Bronson stated.

For the next year, they concentrated on surviving as they diligently replanted the vegetables and cared for their food supply.

Bronson noted that Catherine got more irritable; she lashed out at him for very small things, not telling him why. He hoped that her old illness was not making a comeback. One day, she gathered water, and Bronson noted that the pail leaked. She threw the pail at him and angrily shouted, "Well, do it yourself then!" She stormed away.

He gathered the water, held his finger over the hole, and poured it in a larger vat that he had made of stone. He walked over to Catherine and put his arms around her. She recoiled in anger and stormed off again, not explaining her actions. After a few days, he cornered her and demanded that she tell him what bothered her.

She started crying uncontrollably. "It's back!"

"What's back?"

"My period! It's back!"

Bronson remembered when she'd had bouts of angst when she menstruated, and it had completely slipped his mind that the younger she got, it inevitably had to return. He just did not think that it would affect her so strongly.

"I know I've been a bitch lately, Bronson, but I can't help it. I remember when I lost my period and how sad I felt, and now that it's returned, I'm confused as to how to react. I apologize for taking out my confusion on you."

Catherine dealt with her menstruation issues; however, five years later, Angela lost hers. She told Catherine that she'd bloomed late at fourteen when she'd gotten her first one, and by getting younger every day, she felt like much of her life left along with her period.

Depressed, she stayed away from the Premingers even though she came to think of them as her parents. Too young to climb down the mountain, she suffered from loneliness. She did not have a pet or even a stuffed animal to keep her company. Bronson and Catherine tried to comfort her, but she knew what came next.

Bronson tried in vain to construct a raft or something to get off the island so they could stop her age issues, but the island fought him all the way. Many times, he shimmied down the mountain to continue what he had accomplished the day before, only to see his efforts destroyed overnight. Upon his visits to the main part of the island, he noticed that the sand dragons were very active and new dangers were cropping up everywhere. He saw bright yellow flowers that gave off a sweet aroma and thought about plucking a few of them to present to Catherine and Angela, but stopped and tested his fears by grabbing a stick and poking at them. The delicate petals clenched onto the stick and spouted a stream of pungent acid onto whatever reached in to get a better whiff.

The trees appeared to be talking to each other and trying to get him to cut certain ones, but he did not bite. Fighting the island proved futile because there were too many unknown dangers and he dwelled in the only place where the rest of the island apparently had no say.

He pondered his promise to Angela; it preyed on his mind constantly. He even fashioned a leaf-centered platform just to get her off the island, but upon testing, it fell apart with the gentlest of waves. Dejected, he had to go back to the mountain with the bad news of his failure once again.

Another five years passed. Angela forgot about the urgency of getting off the island and wanted to just play among the tall grass. Catherine and Bronson watched her prance around chasing imaginary butterflies and talking to the apple trees as if they were listening. Angela's quick smile came back to her when she forgot about her plight; she couldn't understand why Catherine cried so much, but always hugged her in an attempt to dry her eyes, which, at times, made her cry more.

Angela turned into a beautiful ten-year-old girl, but still possessed some of the memories of a young woman, though the remembrances waned as she grew younger. Angela's innocent spirit made the Premingers' lives worthwhile because it brought back many fond memories of their own children at Angela's age.

A remembrance of a Christmas morning and their children's excited little faces filled their hearts with joy and happiness. She brought cheerfulness to their bleak outlook. Her antics and playful nature entertained them, but at the same time, made them sad that she supplied them with laughter and a loving spirit and they could do nothing to give her a life that she deserved. They cursed the island's will to allow it to happen to such a deserving young girl.

"Look at her, Bronson, isn't she the most precious little girl? I remember Brooke at that age. You know she called me Mommy last night when I put her to bed?" Catherine stated as she sat in front of Bronson with his arms firmly around her shoulders.

"She's confused as to who she used to be. I see her acting more like a little girl than a young woman. I guess she considers you to be her mother now because you have been her mother all these years. I remember the promise I made her a long time ago. I tried to apologize for not being able to help her, but she didn't remember it." A lone tear streamed down his face.

"How old do you think she is?"

"I'd say nine or ten."

"That means we'll have to go through what we went through with Bradley when he died," she said as she grabbed his arms, bringing her closer to him.

"Yes, but Brad didn't die as a child and I didn't see him die like I'm going to see her die. Hey, let's not dwell on that because here she comes. I don't want those eyes getting sad because we are thinking back to our past. We still have one, and hers is muddled in confusion. Let's make her last years happy ones, okay?"

"Look what I found," she said as she presented Catherine with a doll she'd made from sticks fallen off the apple tree.

"She's beautiful, dear! Did you name her?" Catherine asked.

"Yes, she's an angel and I named her Brooke," she said sweetly.

"Brooke? What made you name her that, sweetheart?" Catherine asked as she looked back at Bronson.

"Because you call me that all the time," she innocently stated.

Catherine immediately got up and walked back to the cave, crying profusely.

"What's wrong with Mommy?" she asked.

"She's just loves you too much, that's all," he said.

"I love her, too. She's funny sometimes. What is down the mountain?" she asked.

"Nothing, dear. We are here because there's food here,"

he stated.

"I like the apples here and it's fun to run through the grass."

"I'm happy that you are happy," he replied.

"Are you my daddy?" she asked, not looking in his eyes, but at her new doll.

"Do you want me to be your daddy?" he asked.

"Oh yes, I do. You're funny too. I wish we can go somewhere else someday."

Bronson wished that Catherine had not left because he teared up as well, remembering his unfulfilled promise to the little girl, but he did not walk off and leave her alone. He just hugged her as Catherine showed up and apologized to her for leaving.

"I missed you. Do you want to play with me in the grass?" she asked.

Bronson stood up and said, "Both of us will play with you. Come on, Catherine. Let's go play with her in the tall grass."

The three of them relished the opportunity to laugh. Whenever they played hide-and-seek with Angela, it brought out the child in them, and they laughed hard and long.

Angela tired eventually, but she saw that the adults were having more fun than she was. She wanted to go to sleep and asked if she could bring her doll with her to bed.

"Sure you can," said Catherine, and she took her to the soft bed that Bronson had carefully and expertly made for her.

Catherine returned to Bronson lying in the grass and looking up through the opening in the mountain. "What's on your mind?"

"I'm just thinking that we will face this sooner or later. Honey, I don't think we'll ever see another boat. I think that we will die here." He plucked a few grass blades and threw them aside.

"I know, but we've lived two lifetimes. No one else can say that. I know the second one sucks, but we are still here and we are still together, and if we ever do get away, we will live another. You realize that one day Angela will not be able to eat solid food. It's a few years away, but it's something to plan for. I saw that she lost a few teeth over the last year."

"That's a shame because she loves those apples. I guess

we'll have to adapt to her. Cathy, right now, I feel that she should be our main focus. She's earned it."

"Still feeling guilty, huh?"

"Yes, a little."

"Bronson, you did all you could to get us off this island. Stop beating yourself up. We will make her time with us the best it can be. We can't fight what is to be. I'm not happy about it and, when the time comes, I know that I'll fall apart. I'm depending on you to get me through it."

"I'll be here," he assured.

Another five years passed. In bed one night, Catherine and Bronson felt restless as they went over the day's events and spoke about Angela getting younger and younger. Angela expressed a desire to Catherine to play in the water many times, but Catherine feared it accelerated her age regression. At five years old, they denied her requests.

Catherine dreamt about Angela all the time, but for some reason, her dream that night of Angela's deadly plight made her awake in fear. Her maternal instinct took hold and she had to see Angela to make sure she was okay.

"Bronson, get up! Where's Angela?"

"I don't know where she is. Look over by the apple tree. She's probably over there."

"No, Bronson, she's not there. I can't see her anywhere! Help me find her!"

Bronson got up and called for Angela, but she did not answer. They searched every square foot of their home and suspected that she had gone to the cave. They did not see her there until Catherine heard her crying by the cave entrance. She ran to it, looked out over the edge, and saw Angela dangling over the rocks.

"Bronson, oh dear God, she's over here."

Bronson ran over. "Where?"

"She's down there!"

Bronson yelled to her, "Hold on, Angela! I'll come and get you. Don't let go!" He scaled down and grabbed her arm just as she let go. He pulled her to his chest and told her to hold on. Crying, she held onto him tightly as Bronson climbed back up. She climbed over the last rock and though she safely stood on solid ground, she did not let go of Bronson; she cried and hugged him harder.

Catherine cried to see Angela in such distress and they tried to comfort her. Bronson hugged her back and, remembering his promise to her years earlier, he relented.

"I tell you what, sweetheart. Tomorrow, we'll take you to the beach and we'll stay there as long as you want."

Catherine, stunned at Bronson's promise, said, "Bronson, we can't do that! Remember why we can't do that?"

"I know, Cathy, but I also know what the odds are. I say allow her to have some fun."

They all went back to the grassy field and played with her the rest of the day. They planned to take Angela to a safe stretch of beach the next, an area between the island and the mountain where they never saw dragons rolling under the sand, as a present to her. They hoped that leaving the island and returning did not take too much time away from her.

The next morning, Angela woke up before them, looking forward to playing in the water. Bronson made a special harness for her when he climbed down the side of the mountain. She did not weigh much, and Bronson got stronger as he got younger, which made the climb easy. Catherine followed. Bronson splashed into the sea and swam with Angela on his back the few feet to the beach. Catherine joined them soon after. Angela ran into the surf, played, and built sand castles, to the delight of Catherine whose wistful thoughts always went back to her own daughter, who, by their recollection, should be extremely old or dead by then. Catherine knew that Brooke had at least one child and speculated that she probably had more. That excited her because it gave her hope that the possibility existed they could eventually meet their grandchildren should a boat come to their rescue soon.

They saw to it that Angela had the time of her young life. They enjoyed the pristine white sand beach, and she pranced around as if she had never seen such a playground.

Bronson thought about trying to catch a fish, but playing with Angela gave him a greater joy. He threw her up in the air and she splashed down into the shallow water, to her absolute delight. Hours later, Angela missed the green grass at the mountain and asked, "Can we go home now?"

Catherine responded, "Sure, sweetheart."

Bronson still had to climb the mountain with her on his back, but vowed to return with her to the beach someday, though he knew that it would probably be the last time they would play in the surf.

Three painful years went by. Angela had lost her ability to talk. Catherine could understand her baby talk, but she also had difficulty walking and eating.

They knew that she had just a few years left.

She crawled more than she walked, which alerted Catherine to pay more attention to the toddler. Her curiosity about everything she encountered amazed Catherine. She asked questions about everything. Whether Catherine held an apple, a blade of grass, or the doll that she made for her years earlier, Angela asked about it, and Catherine dutifully answered her questions.

Bronson saw Catherine interact with Angela as she had with Brooke.

Bronson figured correctly that they were in their mid-twenties and, as Angela's time drew near, he intently thought of ways to get off the island, but could come up with nothing.

Approximately two years later, they lost Angela amid the bright sunshine in the tall grass. The remnants of her vanished before they had a chance to bury her at a place where she loved to play. They were heartbroken; they had become Angela's family, and they suffered a loss as devastating as their son's passing. It hit them hard, but Bronson bore most of the hurt at seeing her little body dwindle until she was comprised of a conglomeration of pink, indistinguishable cells. They dug a hole, placed what was left of her, her hand made clothes made by Catherine from pieces of cloth tied together, and her doll in it, and erected a small monument to her existence.

The grief they felt stayed with them for the rest of their time on the island, because they were starting to feel as Angela did when she got younger.

Bronson, still two years older than Catherine, vowed once again to kill himself when she died. They thought that they were in their mid-twenties and destined for the same fate. Bronson's abilities had not waned and Catherine saw a strong man who possessed an exorbitant amount of energy. She remembered him at that age, after several years of marriage.

"God, you look good, Bronson," she admitted.

"Me? Look at you! I remember you when you were this age. We had been married for about four years or so," he said as he pulled out the wrinkled picture taken on their wedding day. He handed it to her.

Catherine retrieved the other photo of them from her pocket, taken decades after their wedding day, and said, "I liked this version of you as well." She showed Bronson the photo and he traded with her. They treasured the old photos depicting them as young adults and as older citizens.

They lived their lives to the fullest for the next ten years, leaving nothing undone or untried. They threw caution to the wind, and visited the island many times, daring it to kill them. They talked, walked on the beach, and made love under the stars. They prepared themselves for the inevitable, but they did not squander the time they had.

They spent a lot of time visiting the beach, tempting the island with their presence. They did not care about living if it meant dying like Angela, but they did not voluntarily submit to the island's terrors either.

They lost the ability to climb up and down the mountain soon after Bronson turned thirteen. The mountain proved to be their final home and their final act.

The next remaining years went by quickly as they barely held on to life. They instinctively fed each other, but the food supply had dwindled to nothing.

Bronson, a toddler at two, and Catherine an infant, could not get back to the cave, and spent their last days in the grassy field. They had forgotten about their lives together, but he still looked after her as best as a two-year-old could. He still remembered her name, but could barely talk, and was thoroughly confused about their situation. Catherine did not cry much, but still possessed a sparkle in her eye that Bronson enjoyed. Bronson fed, cleaned her, and managed to play with her when she needed company, but she could not talk and, what she did utter, Bronson could not understand. Instinctively, he knew to be by her side at all times and, when she went to sleep, he slept beside her. There were times that storms and rain scared him, and Catherine crawled to him and nestled close.

They did not wear clothes anymore as nothing fit them. Months later, he forgot everything. Catherine could no longer crawl and Bronson did not do much better.

He forgot her name in the waning year she was alive, and they did not know words. Desperation replaced the child-like innocence and the need to play.

They only had each other in the final days, but they stayed together until both went to sleep, never to see the dreaded island again.

PART 2

Chapter One

Worlds Away

As Bronson and Catherine dwindled away on the island, Murray and Brooke raised their daughter, Chelsea Parsons. As her daughter grew older, Brooke wrote *The Premingers: A Family at Sea*, which became an international best seller. Chelsea and her husband, Bret Worthington, made sure their son Frank knew his family's proud heritage and would safeguard the literary inheritance.

In his grandfather's honor, Frank convinced his wife Penny to name their son Bronson, and he passed on the countless stories of Catherine and Bronson's many voyages and their ultimate loss at sea over seventy years ago.

Frank fell asleep many a night to tales of Grandma Brooke's adventurer-parents' lives on the high seas, and the many ports of call that they visited in a lifetime of traveling to the vast corners of the aquatic world.

"When my mother died, she left me all the rights to her book, and when I die, I'm leaving it to you, Frank," Chelsea said to him at a young age.

After Chelsea and Bret's untimely deaths, the valuable rights to Brooke's bestseller belonged to Frank.

Hollywood came calling, and in 2083, Frank sold the movie rights of the book to build a college trust for his young son.

Bronson, from the very start, showed signs that he was gifted. He started walking at six months and talking at two. Penny, his mother, could hardly keep up with his antics; he always ventured far beyond his mother's set limits. Frank held him on his lap and told him stories about Bronson's great-great-grandfather, and Bronson listened intently. He sat still because the stories mesmerized him. Penny thought that Frank's soothing voice made young Bronson calm down.

Four years later, in grade school, his teachers saw potential beyond the normal intellect of a typical young boy.

Bronson met Richard Marlowe in 2098, his junior year of high school. Unknown to Bronson at the time, Richard was two years older than him. He was an underclassman by one year. The polite, quiet kid looked up to the star quarterback and all-around well-liked student. Despite his popularity, Bronson had few friends, and Richard and he has similar likes. They both loved sports, but Bronson excelled as an athlete. Richard liked everyone, but a secret haunted him, so he did not socialize much. Bronson's parents liked having young Richard to their house. The boys were inseparable at school and they played baseball and football afterward, though Richard lacked the skills and coordination to compete on Bronson's level. Richard liked Bronson's family and he always stayed for lunch on weekends. He offered to help Penny with the dishes and Frank with the lawn.

Bronson's intellect and physical prowess extended beyond high school as well; he excelled in everything he did. Sports, academics, and business were his passions in high school. Richard tried to keep up and though he could not match Bronson's speed or strength, being friends with him made him a better person. Frank talked to Richard's grandmother because he wanted to take the boys to a baseball game in Tampa and needed her permission to take him for the day. He heard the whole sad story of Richard Marlowe. Frank felt compelled to tell Bronson because Richard had become his best friend.

"Bronson, remember you always asking me about Richard and I always told you to ask him?"

"Yes, Dad, I did ask him, but he didn't tell me anything. He just gets quiet and walks away."

"Well, first off, he's two years older than you. He's nineteen years old. His grandmother told me."

"Nineteen? But I'm taller than him."

Frank smiled and said, "That doesn't always matter, son. He started school two years late and he got put back a year two years ago. That's why he's in a grade lower than you. He's had a rough nineteen years. His mother forgot to submit the forms for first grade so he had to wait until the next year."

"He has had it rough? Where does he live? I've never met his mom and dad or his grandmother."

Frank continued, "His father left his mother just after his birth because his mother drank too much. His grandmother told me that his mother stayed drunk and didn't even know where he was half of the time."

"Dad, he never said anything about that."

Frank thought for a bit and speculated. "He probably thought that you would not be his friend if you knew the truth."

"Where's his mom now?"

"That's why he didn't start school the next year. Drunk again, his mother received a telegram from Richard's father asking her for a divorce because he wanted to marry another woman. He witnessed his mother shoot herself in the head with an antique pistol his father owned. His grandmother said that Richard had to be hospitalized for a year because of what he saw."

"Oh no! He saw his mother shoot herself? Maybe that's why he doesn't want to talk about his life. Dad, what should I say to him?"

Frank scratched his head and said with fatherly wisdom, "You must not say anything to him about it. When he's ready to tell you, he will. Does knowing this change the way you feel about Richard?"

"No, Dad, he's my best friend."

Frank's chest heaved with pride. He held out his hand to shake his son's hand, and said, "That's my boy!"

Frank and Bronson kept what they knew about Richard to themselves and never brought up Richard's family life to him.

Bronson and Richard did everything together—they attended summer camps, went to ball games, and played video games. At the age of twenty, Richard started his junior year in high school and Bronson, his senior year. They ran into each other daily, mostly because Richard needed help understanding his studies, and Bronson was a brilliant mathematician.

During his senior year, he saw Richard in an altercation with four bullies who Bronson knew very well. Bronson knew all four boys because they were the starting offensive linemen. Richard, a skinny kid from the other side of the tracks, could take care of himself and Bronson knew it. Richard had prevailed in many fights in the past, so Bronson did not feel the need to interfere; he'd seen him fight many times. Bronson normally minded his own business, but when he came across Richard fending off four much larger boys, he sat and watched.

One of the bullies named Bo Stocker walked over to Bronson and said, "We're going to fuck this idiot up. He asked out Jo Jo's girlfriend. Are you with us?"

Bo and his bravado, as well as the others', amused Bronson because he knew what Richard brought to the table and he felt that his offensive line needed to be taken down a bit. "Oh yeah, I'm with you, Bo, but I'll put my money on the skinny kid. All four of you going to rush him or are you going at him one at a time?"

"I'll kick his ass all by myself and here's a hundred. I say he gets knocked out in one punch."

"You're on, Bo. Now go make me proud," Bronson said as he placed his own one hundred dollar bill on the bench.

Bo turned around and Bronson caught Richard's eye and winked at him. He knew better than to get involved with a fight with Richard's pride on the line. Bo walked over to Richard with a confident look and swung a mighty fist. Richard avoided the punch, and gave him a right to the solar plexus. Bo fell, holding his side and wincing in pain. One by one, the bullies went after Richard. Each of them joined Bo on the ground, holding various body parts.

Bronson saw that the rush of adrenaline dwindled in Richard, but he prepared to continue the fight. The four bullies stood up, rushed Richard, and sent him flying across the grass. Bronson, seeing the melee had escalated, came to Richard's aid and pulled each of the football players off him.

"What the fuck are you doing, Bronson?" a bloodied Bo asked.

"I'm preventing you from getting hurt because we have a game Saturday, and secondly, Richard here is like my brother. He is not to be touched again! You read me?"

"Fuck you, Bronson! Come on, guys, let's get out of here."

"Oh, Bo, I forgot to thank you for the hundred," Bronson

taunted as he placed the bill in his pocket.

Richard wiped blood from his mouth, gathered up his backpack, and said, "I could have taken them, but thank you for getting them off me. What's the hundred for?"

"Oh, that's yours. Bo told me that he'd give me a hundred dollars if you knocked him to the ground before he sent you there. I've seen you hit harder. Why did you let up?"

"School spirit. He has a game Saturday and I wanted him to be able to play without broken ribs. He's a damn good lineman. Besides, he protects you on the field."

Bronson smiled and said, "Okay, Richard, let's get to class. Are you all right?"

"Yes, just a few scrapes, I'll be fine. So long!" Richard said, and the boys went their separate ways.

During lunch, Bronson spied Richard eating alone. He walked up to him and asked, "Hey, Richard, why are you over here by yourself? Come on over and sit with me and the team."

Richard looked over to the area where the Varsity football team sat and said, "I'm fine here."

"Okay, do you mind if I sit here?" Bronson asked.

"Sure, go ahead," said Richard with a smile.

Bronson sat and, a minute later, a few of the team walked over to Richard's table and sat also. Eventually, they all joined them. He introduced Richard to the team. Bo lumbered up to the table and held out his hand in friendship. "Richard, me and the boys want to apologize to you for what happened this morning. I had some time to think about what I did and it didn't make me happy."

Richard stood up and shook each of the players' hands and they all sat, ate lunch, and gabbed about school, girls, and football.

The players liked Richard, and from that day until graduation, he never had to fend off another bully. During their time at high school, Bronson helped him with his studies and Richard helped him in the gym. A solid A student, Bronson's intelligence won him a full scholarship to any college he wanted to attend. Richard had other aspirations, but they still included college. Since the scuffle with the football team, he felt the need to get in better shape. For the next months, he practically lived at the gym, lifting weights and building his muscles to the point where no one, football player or otherwise, threatened him again. However, his primary ambition did not include lifting weights and conditioning.

He achieved success with his new body, striking good looks, flowing blond hair, and blue eyes. He wanted to be an actor and excelled in the drama department; he melted the hearts of his costars, as well as the women in the audience. But his good looks and technique failed to get him a scholarship. Richard did not have the money to further his education, although he had a few jobs, but most of the money had gone to his grandmother because she had problems with her mortgage payments. However, since his grandmother's death a few months earlier, he still had to spend everything he earned on his small apartment.

Bronson met Becky Knoll during one of Richard's performances and she instantly fell in love with him and vice-versa. They dated through his senior year. He popped the question on graduation night. Her parents scoffed at the early engagement, but softened their stance once they knew Bronson better.

Bronson graduated with honors, along with Becky, but they delayed their marriage and their entry into college for a while due to time considerations. However, they always returned to their high school to catch all of Richard's performances during his senior year.

During his two-year engagement to Becky, Bronson and Richard solidified their friendship even more. Becky adored Richard as well. Richard dated little, which perplexed Becky. She had a friend who wanted to meet him badly, so she decided to play matchmaker after a perfectly performed *King Richard*.

"You were fantastic tonight, Rick!"

Richard sadly responded, "Thanks, Becky. I really miss my grandmother out there in the audience. Hell, I miss her period."

"I know, bro. I'm sure she saw it!" Bronson added as he looked up. "Tell him, Becky!"

"Tell me what?"

"I have a friend who wants to meet you. I brought her to a few of your plays and she thinks you're hot."

Bronson interrupted. "Tell her to get in line. Half the female population of this school thinks he's hot."

"Shut up, Bronson! Richard, you'll like her, she's beautiful."

"Is she that blonde girl you came with a few weeks ago?" he asked as he wiped off his stage makeup.

"Yes, what do you think?"

"Are you joking? I'd love to meet her! I can't believe she'd want to go out with me, though. What's her name?"

Bronson rolled his eyes and stated, "Oh come on, Rick, are you serious?"

"Shut up, Bronson! She's Sally Roberts. I know she wants to go out with you. You're a hot guy!"

"I think my best man should ask her to come to our wedding," suggested Bronson.

"That's sounds great! I think I will. Is the wedding set, Becky?"

"Yes, I just have to hire a photographer, then it's all done. Now hurry up and get dressed, we're taking you out for your birthday," Becky asserted as she closed the dressing room door.

Fifteen minutes later, Richard emerged and met Bronson and Becky in the auditorium lobby.

They treated Richard to dinner at the finest and most expensive restaurant in town.

"Whoa, I can't afford this," Rick said.

"Relax! You're not paying for anything! I got this, bro!" said Bronson as they walked into the restaurant. "We've got news. I've decided to go to Florida State along with Becky. Rick, my parents have been saving for my college education since my birth, but because I got a full ride, I don't need the money. I want to give it to you so you can join us next year!"

Overwhelmed, Richard could not find the right words to thank him, but Bronson stopped him before he got the chance to form them.

"Hey, I've already talked it over with mom and dad and they agree. They do not need it and neither do I. Happy birthday, bro!"

"I don't know how to thank you, Bronson, and you too, Becky. That has been a dream of mine. Do you know they have Academy Award winner Joe Sample teaching acting at Florida State? Dammit! I have an entire year to wait for this.

When are you two going for your freshmen year?"

"Right after our wedding. We'll be there when you get there next year, but you have to get through your last year of high school first," said Becky.

"You don't have to worry about that, I got the grades," Richard proudly stated.

"Rick, I hope you don't mind if I ask a personal question?" asked Bronson.

"Sure, bro, but you already know everything about me."

Bronson took a bite of his steak and said, "Not everything. All the years we've hung out together, and I've never been to your house or met your family. You're like a member of the family over at my house."

Richard seldom talked about his parents, but he explained. "Well, you know my mom died when I turned seven, but prior to that, she told me that my father left us a few years after my birth. I lived with my grandmother up until she died a few months ago."

Bronson wondered why Richard had left out the fact that he'd seen his mother commit suicide. "Your mother, how did she die?"

Richard got quiet. "Bronson, your father told me that he told you my story many years ago. Why must I tell you now?"

"Dammit! My own father betrayed me! Okay, I'm sorry to try to pry it out of you."

"It's okay. I accepted it many years ago."

Richard turned to Becky because of the quizzical look on her face and said, "She killed herself in front of me and they locked me up for six months in a hospital to make me understand that I didn't cause my mother's death. She never got over the fact that my father left us."

Becky asked, "Wow, I'm sorry, Rick. Have you ever tried searching for your father?"

"No, I don't know where to begin. Here, I have a photo of him taken a long time ago." He reached for his wallet and pulled out the wrinkled photo.

He and Becky looked at the photo and asked, "Is that your mother in the photo?"

"No, that's his sister, according to my mother's recollection. I don't know if I really want to find him; after all, he left my mom," confessed Richard.

Becky smiled, handed the photo back to Richard, and said, "Don't worry, once you're a big star in Hollywood, he'll probably find you."

"Yeah, when do you plan on trying some real acting? You know, getting an agent and all that stuff?" Bronson asked.

"After college, I suspect. I have a lot of learning to do, and I plan to learn everything. By the way, what are your plans?"

"I want to go into business. I want to rule the world. Same old stuff." He and Becky started laughing.

Richard asked to meet Sally before the wedding and Becky liked the idea. "Maybe we can double date the weekend before the wedding. That is, if Bronson can get away."

"Hey, you don't have to tell me twice. I can study when I get to college." Bronson called the waiter to get the tab.

Richard had a great time, but felt embarrassed that Bronson always picked up the tab. Richard held two jobs, seven days a week, but his apartment took nearly all of his pay. His perpetually vacant wallet seldom left his pants pocket during the uncomfortable after-dinner conversations. He made payments on his grandmother's funeral, too, and he never missed one. A small, scarcely furnished place, his apartment embarrassed him and he did not want to bring Bronson and Becky to see it, much less Sally. A proud young man, Richard could not wait to get out of high school, join Bronson and Becky at Florida State University, and leave his hellish existence behind, hoping for a new start.

Richard loved Becky and constantly proclaimed Bronson's luck at finding such a sweet girl.

Sally and Richard went to the movies on their first date, but again, his empty wallet constantly reminded him of his shortcomings. Sally wanted popcorn and a soda, and he did not have the money. She paid for her own refreshments and Richard wondered what she thought of him not having the required funds for a simple date to the movies.

Sally did not give it a second thought and she let Richard know that night. Despite his reluctance, she insisted on going back to his apartment; considering she still lived with her parents, she had plans for the night that required them being alone.

There, they talked, kissed, and made love, a first for both

of them.

From then on, the four friends were inseparable. Becky and Bronson did not care about Richard's age. None of them drank, so they spent their days at the movies, restaurants, or parks.

Bronson and Becky's wedding day arrived. The formal affair went off without hitch. Bronson and Becky happily danced for the first time as husband and wife. Richard and Sally had fun also; Sally did not like dancing, but Richard coaxed her out a few times and, soon, she liked it.

Richard, being the true entertainer, sang a tribute to the happy couple and garnered huge applause for his golden voice.

Bronson stood and applauded the most. Later, he asked, "When did you learn to sing?"

"Hey, to be an entertainer, you have to know a little of everything. I learned last year."

Sally fell deeply in love with Richard that night as his melodic voice blasted all barriers that she set up for herself.

After the wedding, Bronson and Becky explored the Virgin Islands, Africa, and Europe on their whirlwind honeymoon. They wanted to see it all, but were eager to get back to Florida to begin their college life together.

Richard and Sally spent the time dating, furthering their burgeoning relationship.

When Becky and Bronson returned from their honeymoon, Richard announced that he and Sally planned to marry once they finished high school, much to the dismay of her parents, who did not like Richard solely because they did not believe in the entertainment industry and did not think Richard had the drive or the skills to succeed at it.

However, Richard and Sally were in love, and on her eighteenth birthday, Richard, wanting Sally's parents' approval, proved that he had acting ability by landing a national commercial for men's underwear. A risqué commercial, but Richard possessed the body and good looks to pull it off, and garnered five hundred dollars for his efforts. It did not pay much, but he looked at it as a stepping-stone to bigger and much better roles. He had begged the decision makers to allow him to do the commercial, and promised to do it at a fraction of what other actors charged.

Richard and Sally were married three years after they graduated from high school and three years into his college education with her parents' permission; by then, he'd proved to them that he could provide for their daughter. Because he attended college, they finally relented.

Bronson and Becky were into their last year of college and Richard, his third. He joined the prestigious acting club at the university. However, he soon realized that many of the other students far exceeded his abilities, even though many were the same age.

He did not tell Bronson of his worries and gladly accepted any role he could get. He no longer starred in the many college productions his class performed. He played minor roles and was used sparsely on stage. Becky, Bronson, and Sally attended every show, which gave Richard the confidence to continue. It embarrassed him at times to see his friends in the audience, when he had to wear a mask or costume that obscured his face; however, they still came. Richard delivered unnecessary excuses as to why he never played a major role. Many of the plays were the same ones from high school, but with a professional staff and extraordinarily talented cast, they seemed like different plays. Doubt blasted through his mind as to how far he can go. In high school, his performances brought rave reviews, but now relegated to a frustrated permanent understudy position, his once lofty acting ceiling dissipated into a sea of self-doubt.

Bronson lived up to all the praise heaped upon him. He did well in all his classes, but excelled in business so much so that he garnered attention from the largest financial firms in the country. He devised innovative plans that the business community had not seen before. Oblivious to what was going on, Bronson assumed that Richard had money problems because he had quit one of his jobs to go to his classes. Sally helped by getting a job as a waitress, but it did not pay that well. Regardless, Sally and Richard were deeply in love and she had a way of making him laugh when money issues cropped up.

Bronson and Becky did what they could to think up occasions that they could foot the bill so Richard and Sally would allow them to pay without the angst he felt, but Richard kept a mental tab to pay them back when he got over the hump.

The national commercial he did during high school did not

garner any more jobs, but it did get him into the most important acting classes. He tried to get an agent, but he had limited time in front of the camera or on the stage, so he had to find his own auditions.

Richard worked hard at his low-paying job and his classes; that caused him to tire easily, but he always kept his trademark smile and never allowed his misfortune to impact his friendships. However, Sally knew what really went on in his troubled world. She confided in Becky during one of their bathroom visits at one of the better restaurants in Florida.

"I know it seems like nothing is bothering him, but he has a mountain of pressure on him. He tries so hard to succeed, but he always has to take the back seat to inferior actors. Becky, I've seen him act. He is good, very good, and that's just not his wife talking," Sally said, cresting on shedding tears.

"I had no idea he had that many problems," stated Becky as she put her arms around Sally.

"Oh, he's not going to say anything. Not my Richard. He goes through life with that big smile on his face and it kills me to see him try and try and never get where he wants to be."

"Is there anything we can do to help?"

"Oh God, don't do anything! Richard is a smart guy and he can see charity a mile away. He even has an issue with you two paying for dinner every time."

"Okay, but we will not allow either of you to go hungry even if we have to go to that restaurant you work at and tip you a few hundred dollars. He will never know."

"You two are so kind! As you can see, I'm a little desperate as well. I know that we will be able to pay you two back as soon as college is over. Usually, I'm with Richard on the charity issue, but we have bills that haven't been paid in months."

"Well, you and I will have to take care of that. Listen, Bronson worships Richard and I will not have our best friends be in distress. Sally, my mind is made up; you two are our most precious friends. Allow us to help."

Sally, overwhelmed with emotion, cried and hugged Becky, then they got themselves together to go back to the table.

Becky and Bronson covertly helped the struggling couple. Graduation approached for Bronson and Becky. Both achieved many honors while at college, but Bronson excelled beyond all previous estimates with no fewer than ten offers on the table from the largest financial firms in the world.

He looked them all over; however, he did not want to work for a company that had already succeeded. He wanted a challenge, so he chose a smaller firm where he could use what he had learned to build up and mark his accomplishments. He chose Burkett Financial, a small up-and-coming firm specializing in money management, the stock market, and a vast array of moneymaking opportunities.

Bronson delivered the valedictorian speech as Richard, Sally, and Becky looked on. They were proud of Bronson as he masterfully wove his speech to touch hearts and to spur the graduates on to the next step in their lives. The graduates threw their caps in the air. Bronson walked amid them and the descending caps, high-fiving all the way to his beloved Becky, who also plowed through the chaos to meet her husband. Together, they searched for Sally and Richard, and found them still applauding.

"Congrats, buddy! Great speech!" Richard said as Sally hugged them.

Bronson and Becky removed their robes, Becky folded them up, and Bronson announced, "Mom and Dad are having a party at their house. Let's go."

Richard, having not dressed appropriately for a gala party at Bronson's well-to-do parents' mansion, felt the need to return home and dress appropriately, but Bronson dismissed the idea; he insisted Richard looked fine for what was going to be a casual party, not a formal affair.

"Nonsense, you look great! You actually think I'm wearing this suit? I have a better idea. I've changed my mind. Let's get in our shorts, have a few cocktails, and head to the beach," Bronson stated.

"You're going to miss your own party?" asked Richard, as they walked to their car.

"After thinking about it, this is my new plan. I start work in a month and I want the fun to start today." Bronson stated.

Sally looked at Richard as he pulled out a sparsely wrapped graduation present for Bronson and Becky.

Bronson opened the long cardboard tube, pulled the contents out, and unrolled it to see an original autographed poster of *Duck Soup*, the 1933 comedy by the Marx Brothers.

All four Marx brothers had signed the poster, as well as the movie's director, Leo McCarey. With Bronson being an avid Marx Brothers fan, he loved the gift, but he wondered how Richard afforded it.

"Richard, I know the value of this. Where the hell did you come up with the money to buy this?"

Becky jumped in and said, "Bronson, can't you just accept the gift without a bunch of questions?"

"It doesn't matter; this is a gift from us to you," Richard said. "You are only going to graduate once and I wanted to repay you and Becky for all the kindness you've shown us. Because of you two, I had the opportunity to go to college. You always said that you wanted a poster of this movie and I found it on the Internet. The cost isn't the issue—how much you like it is."

"I love it! I've never seen anything like this! Honey, the first thing we are doing when we move into our house is getting this framed." Bronson carefully placed the poster into its protective casing.

Later, Sally divulged to Becky what it had cost and that they'd charged it on their credit card, but she assured Becky that it would be fine. Becky noticed that the conversation veered into uncomfortable territory and changed the subject.

Despite Bronson's obvious success, a year later, a tragedy created havoc in his perfect world. His parents had flown to Cancun, Mexico for a summer vacation. A good pilot, Frank flew his jet all over the world, but a combination of bad weather and worn components on his plane caused it to crash into the Gulf of Mexico. Frank and Penny met their fate. The plane and all its contents sank to the bottom of the deepest part of the Gulf.

Richard and Sally immediately went to Bronson's aid and

mourned with them throughout his ordeal, and Bronson and Becky were thankful for their comfort.

They had a funeral with two empty coffins. Though Bronson, sitting in the family pew, knew that they were empty, he believed that his parents were there. Richard noted that Bronson lost a lot of himself that day, and thereafter. Sitting in a pew a few rows back, Richard stared at the man who had a great role in shaping his life, and felt powerless as to how to make things better.

Easing his pain proved difficult, so Richard allowed Bronson to feel it and all the misery associated with such a loss. Richard had already gone through it with the passing of his mother and grandmother, and he'd never known his father, but he still remembered how he felt when told why he'd father left him and his mother.

A reception held at the family home did not help ease Bronson's heartache. Many tried to console him, but Richard did not join them because he knew that Bronson wanted to get away to a place where he did not have to confront such sadness. Richard waited until all had their time with Bronson and Becky, then he approached with Sally firmly holding his hand.

They sat next to the couple and suggested that they all go to the beach the next day to celebrate his parents' lives together.

Bronson, teary-eyed, responded, "Yes, I'd like that."

They met at his parents' beach house in Daytona Beach and talked all day about what had happened.

Later, Richard stated, "He really needed this, Becky. I've never seen him so hurt and confused."

"I know, I'll let him work it out," Becky responded.

Richard and Sally stayed the night, and a few nights afterward. By the end of the week, Bronson smiled and laughed more than he cried, to the great relief of Becky, Richard, and Sally.

Bronson was more than successful at his job as a senior vice president of Burkett Financial, bringing in more than his hefty seven-figure salary and living large. His wealth exploded when he took control of all his parents' assets, including four homes in various parts of the country, four expensive cars, and a lump sum of twenty million dollars in cash and securities. Regardless of Bronson's exorbitant wealth, Richard and Sally accepted no gifts. Richard wanted to get his acting career started immediately and went on countless auditions trying to get a foothold in the industry, but he found very few interested in making his dream a reality. Still, he did not allow his wife to notice his frustration, or his friends, but Bronson knew.

He easily saw from his mannerisms the frustration and hurt. Richard's long laughs became shorter; his jokes lessened the tension, but his voice held less verve because his desire to be the life of the party waned.

However, tragedy struck again. A drunk driver ran Sally off the road, tragically killing her when her car struck a tree. The police officer at the crash site identified Sally as the victim after looking through her purse and finding her driver's license. He called into his headquarters and, through records, found out that she was Richard's wife. The captain called him.

"Mr. Marlowe, this is Captain John Maris of the Daytona Police Department. It's my sad duty to inform you that your wife, Sally, was killed by a drunk driver."

"What? Sally is dead? Where is she?" The captain heard that Richard was hurt badly from his broken voice.

"She is being transported to the morgue as we speak. If it's any consolation, Mr. Marlowe, your wife did not suffer. She died on impact." The captain heard nothing else and asked, "Mr. Marlowe, are you there?"

Richard hung up the phone and sat back in his chair, confused as to what to do and who to call.

Chapter Two

Richard's Fall

Richard immediately sank into a deep depression that no amount of friendship or words could shake him out of. His world revolved around Sally, and the depths of his despair crossed new barriers. She'd inspired him to continue in his pursuits, and was his rock when he failed. When he saw her face and felt her touch, he considered his life a success.

Angered, he let out all of his frustrations and deeply hidden thoughts. He screamed at whoever had the ill luck of being in front of him. Bronson and Becky, the two who had been his saviors on many occasions, did not escape his anger and grief. Richard went on irrational rants, refusing to accept that his loving wife had died.

He refused to do anything with regard to her funeral and alienated himself from everyone who meant anything to him. The loss of Sally propelled him into a depression that caused Bronson to have him committed for his own safety. Richard did not attend Sally's funeral because he had to be strapped onto a bed for his own protection in a mental hospital.

Bronson visited him several times during that year and, each time, Richard refused to see his lifelong friend. Bronson paid for his care. He constantly went there hoping to talk to him, but had to watch him through one-way mirrors because Richard did not want to see anyone.

Bronson's business life flourished; as the new CEO of a billion-dollar company, his salary reached eight figures with enough perks to set him up for life. The more money he spent, the greater wealth he acquired, and soon he became the richest man in the state. He gained everything he ever wanted, yet remained unhappy while his best friend was locked up in a mental hospital.

Time, however, had a way of healing wounds; soon, Richard relented and allowed Bronson, and later Becky, to visit him. Richard lost a year of his life grieving for his beloved wife, appearing to talk to her every day during his walks in the park-like setting of the hospital grounds.

Bronson and Richard walked among the tall trees and the well-manicured grounds to a bench where they talked for hours. With each visit, Richard appeared to get better, and talked about acting and Bronson's successes in the business world.

"Rick, are you ready to talk about Sally?" Bronson asked during one of Richard's better days.

"I am, Bronson. I know that she died and I must say that the last year has been confusing to me. I remember very little of it, but I think something happened to make me realize that she died," Richard confessed as he looked toward the hospital.

"What happened?" Bronson looked intently at Richard.

Richard turned to him with a tear rolling down his cheek and said, "Sally stopped talking to me in my dreams yesterday. I talked to her daily and heard her responses, but now, she does not respond. I imagined she said goodbye to me, or my mind told me to accept what fate brought to me. She's gone, Bronson."

Not knowing what to say, he just listened in hopes that Richard could let out more of the pain and remove his unfounded guilt forever. That day, Richard cracked a smile that Bronson had not seen in the year and a half since his wife's death. A stray kitten wandered near the two, playing with a blade of grass. It seemed trivial at the time, but a very important step for a man he considered a brother. Sadly, his many improvements did not guarantee his release from the hospital because of setbacks, which occurred during Sally's birthday, their wedding date, and holidays.

Richard never allowed his mind to venture off toward insanity while Becky or Bronson visited him. Slowly he gained back control of his mind. Richard had long lost everything—his home, his money, and he'd abandoned his car. A roadblock to his release existed because of Richard's unwillingness to accept Bronson's kind offerings. His mother and grandmother instilled in Richard that proud mentality, *"Make your own path."* They drilled that into his mind so deeply that no amount of medication could erase it. They told him that a truly successful man did not rely on or accept outside help from others to achieve their goals. *"The dignity of a man is measured through years of hard work and dedication to achieve a successful result. Only then can he look back and feel pride in what he has accomplished."* The words stated often by his grandmother rang in his ears.

Richard had heard that saying many times throughout his life and it remained with him. More importantly, he still believed it.

However, Bronson held something back. A production company had called him and relayed an interest in making his great-grandmother's book, which his mother left to him, into a movie. Bronson did not sign the contract until his doctors released Richard from the hospital. He added a clause in it to allow Richard to play a major role in it and, thus, create his own success.

He thought back to when his mother told him about the book and how others assisted her in writing it. She did not know what happened to the Premingers after they embarked on their final voyage. So she wrote the book as a non-fiction account of her parents' exploits, but with a fictitious ending added to please her personally. His father's grandmother did not like the thought of them dying at sea and formulated a scenario where they made it to an uncharted island and lived the rest of their lives in tropical bliss. Much of the story had not happened as written, but the story mystified Bronson by its colorful depiction, and its overall happy ending. However, deep in his father's heart, he knew that his grandmother speculated that they suffered an unimaginably painful death.

Months went by, during which Bronson found out something that angered him beyond words. The hospital fixed the books and gave wrong reports on Richard. Unwilling to allow Richard to leave and give up all the money Bronson paid for Richard's care, they purposely misdiagnosed Richard's problems and lied on progress reports. Richard had actually made huge strides in his recovery, but the doctors at the hospital prescribed drugs that gave an impression that Richard had made no progress. One doctor objected to the practices and the Board dismissed him immediately without cause. He knew why the hospital executives fired him, but he'd signed a form preventing him from disclosing staff conferences. Bronson had no such agreement. He found out through sources what the hospital did and confronted the owner. He walked into the grand office, threw a large file on his desk, and asked him to explain his hospital's practices.

"What is this?" the owner asked.

Bronson, angered beyond measure, stated, "This is bullshit! That's what this is. Your hospital has drugged my friend, Richard Marlowe, to keep him here. I have ways of finding information. It's what I do best. Then I read this whole load of crap. Doctors' assessments, drugs issued, and a quaint little email from you insisting that Richard appear sicker than the doctor's diagnosis. I noticed your reply when the doctors resisted. You wrote that the hospital needed the money and ordered them to continue to prescribe mind-altering drugs to keep him in a semi-conscious state!"

"You have it all wrong, Mr. Worthington, I assure you! I'd never be a party to that kind of deception," the owner stated angrily.

Bronson asked him to read a certain part of the file. The owner put on his glasses and turned to the specified page; he read a report written by the fired doctor. The owner's hands shook as he turned the page. He read the two pages, removed his glasses, placed them gently on the desk, closed the file, and stared at Bronson.

"What do you want?" He knew that he and his hospital were caught in a bevy of crimes, not only criminal, but moral as well.

"I want you to resign your position. I want an outside forensic accountant to conduct an audit of the practices offered here. I want that accountant to see what I have seen, and then I want the state of Florida to indict you and send you to prison for the rest of your life."

The owner, who equaled Bronson in wealth, took a devious and troubling tone and threatened, "You may want to rethink your desires. I know people who can make your life very difficult."

"What are you asserting?"

"Should you go public with this information, you and your wife will suffer great difficulties," he continued.

"Are you threatening my life and my wife's life?" he asked, getting increasingly irate.

"Well, it may come to that. It depends on your ability to see the big picture. Mr. Worthington, you are an amazingly successful executive. Surely you know that these kinds of things happen in the throes of profit making. It's all a part of success."

Bronson stepped back a few steps and opened his shirt to show a listening device taped to his chest, placed there by the federal authorities. Five FBI agents blasted through the doors and arrested the whimpering millionaire.

As the man walked away in handcuffs, Bronson stared him straight in the eye and said, "Not all of us have to sacrifice our morals for a buck. Some of us succeed because of our morals. I hope you see the big picture where you're going."

The hospital's Board of Trustees immediately took over operational control of the hospital. The doctors who assisted in the conspiracy confessed and immediately found themselves arrested, locked up, and stripped of their credentials.

Richard, a drug-dependent shadow of his former self, recovered from chemical dependency as Becky and Bronson held his hand for the entire horrifying episode. They saw Richard at his worst. However, they knew that the drugs played havoc on him, which caused Richard to scream violently at them.

A few days had passed and Richard recovered quickly. Because of the owner's efforts to keep him there, it took a little longer for him to recover completely, but all were relieved to find out that Richard had no lasting effects.

Another month passed, and Richard made great strides in returning to his old self without the side effects of his drug-induced paranoia.

All totaled, Richard spent two long years in the hospital, but was released and ready to go home, although he had no home. Regardless of his deep-seeded views on personal responsibility and wanting to do things on his own, he was destitute with nothing. After many arguments on the subject, he finally relented and graciously accepted Bronson's offer to live with them in their palatial estate. He justified Bronson's offer by understanding that Bronson was the closest person he had to family, and that fact eased his internal pressure to do things on his own.

The next year brought joy to all of them and Bronson, who still had not signed the movie contract, wanted to get Richard interested in being an actor again. His previous mental episode completely behind him, he visited Sally's grave and placed flowers in the empty vase attached to her monument.

Richard accepted Sally's death and he vowed to continue with his life. For the first time, Richard accepted the generosity of his lifelong friend and allowed himself to have other people's money tend to his needs.

"I apologize for this, Richard. The hospital sent this over to my house just after your release and my staff stored it, not knowing what to do with it. They forgot that they had it until today" Bronson said as he handed Richard a packet with all his belongings in it.

Richard opened it up and took his wallet, his wedding ring, and an old photo his mother gave him a long time ago, the cherished lone photo of his father that he'd showed to Bronson years earlier.

"I see you still have it," Bronson stated.

"I don't think I could ever throw this out. It's the only thing I have to remind me of my father and my mother. When I see this, I can see her face in my mind. This is my most important possession," Richard stated as he carefully placed it back in his wallet.

"I thought you said that the photo depicted your father and his sister?"

"It is, but my mother gave it to me. Other than my life, it's the only thing she gave me that has lasted through the years. I still remember the day she gave it to me and asked me to keep it safe. I still do not know why she felt so strongly about it."

"Maybe she wanted you to remember your father with hopes that one day you may find him"

"Possibly, but I don't care if I ever find him. I kept this because she gave it to me. It allows me to remember her."

"Then I'm happy you got it back. I've already scolded my staff for forgetting about the delivery."

"It's okay as long as I have it. I don't know what I would have done without you and Becky."

"It's okay. If the situation was reversed, you'd be there for us."

Richard, thankful that he had Bronson and Becky as friends, had a request of them. "I want to get on with my life. I wanted to be an actor once, but I have to relearn the craft. Do I have your support for my efforts to get back to it?"

Bronson smiled and accepted anything he wanted to do, even going so far as to offer him a job in his firm, which Richard gladly accepted. He did not get a high profile position and it did not pay much, but it gave Richard his dignity back. While he worked in the mailroom, he had the opportunity to go to night school to regain his acting abilities. Richard retained his natural good looks and his body returned to fine form utilizing Bronson's extensive weight and exercise room. He practiced the lines his teachers gave him with some of his coworkers. They liked him and supported his efforts, and offered their help in preparing for every audition he went on.

Bronson wanted to find him an agent, but Becky convinced him to allow Richard the freedom of doing things on his own. Richard needed that to feel better about the accomplishment.

The time came when Bronson signed the movie contract, relinquishing the movie rights to his great grandmother's book with the caveat that Richard could audition for the Bronson Preminger part. He made it clear in the contract that Richard had to win the role on his own and not have it given to him because Bronson was his best friend. Bronson respected the director's decision, whatever the outcome.

One night after class, Bronson told him about the movie and his resolve to get him to audition for it. Ecstatic about the role, Richard gladly accepted Bronson's gift, but he did it with the provision that Bronson not ask to have him get the part without an audition.

Richard practiced day and night and studiously went to classes. Months later, the casting director contacted Richard to ask him to come to Hollywood and audition. The movie had a multi-million dollar budget. They wanted top tier stars for all the prominent roles, but Richard only cared about one. Rumors indicated that a very well known and accomplished actress intrigued the casting director.

Weeks later, Bronson, Becky, and Richard chartered a flight to Hollywood. Bronson owned a beach house in nearby Manhattan Beach; they lived there while in California.

Bronson had an office in Beverly Hills and decided to pop in for a surprise visit, but the rest of the time, they stayed on the beach playing volleyball and talking. Richard spent his time reading Bronson's book. Late the next afternoon, Bronson ran to him with news about the movie.

"I just found out who will be playing Catherine."

"Well, who is it?" asked Richard.

"I don't want you get crazy, but it's Willow Barrett!"

Becky jumped up and asked excitedly, "Are you serious? I love her! Bronson, please tell me that we're allowed on the set. I want to meet her."

Excited, Richard said, "Wow! That's unbelievable!"

Willow Barrett had won two Academy Awards before she turned twenty and the film industry considered her the number one actress; she'd starred in multiple mega-hits.

Willow Barrett had begun her acting career at a very young age. She grew up with millionaire parents and had the best acting coaches in the world while her parents' money backed her every step of the way. Many a leading man had told the tabloids about her intolerance of amateur actors who made mistakes in filming and the difficulty they had working with her. Her irrational rants on set were legendary and caused many retakes. Even the most seasoned actors felt her wrath trying to get through a difficult scene.

Nervous, the casting director, George Sanders, informed Richard that he'd won an audition with her and director Ben Yaro.

Richard had a week to think about the role; she postponed her audition with him because she had promotional dates in San Francisco. That elated Richard because it gave him additional time to prepare. He did not want to give her the chance to complain about his performance, so he practiced daily with Bronson and Becky assisting him.

The morning of the audition, Bronson could see the agitation in Richard. He nervously read the tattered script again, even though he remembered the entire thing. He wanted to impress the director by not needing the script.

He arrived at the studio with ten minutes to spare. The director's assistant told him wait in a room full of potential actors who also vied for the role, many of whom he recognized. Richard knew the odds of a completely unknown actor winning a major role in a Willow Barrett film. Every actor worth his salt wanted the coveted role.

Richard sat patiently while all the others read the scenes out loud, trying to capture the essence of the role.

Being the former rights holder, Bronson and Becky looked in on the auditions as credentialed guests of the studio. They met the director and some of the actors who'd won lesser roles, and kept quiet during the audition process.

One by one, the actors paraded in and read their lines. Obviously, Richard had an uphill battle because they all far exceeded his talent.

The director looked to George Sanders and said, "This is a good group of actors."

"Yes, but there are a few more waiting outside. Some good ones."

With a furrowed brow and an obviously angered tone, the director responded, "George, I think we have what we need already. I can't be here all day looking at actors when I already think we have the ones we want. I love Jacob Marsten's reading. He's perfect for the lead role of Bronson."

Willow spoke up and said, "Yes, I vote for Jacob as well. He was great."

The casting director said, "Yes, I agree, he is perfect, but I think it's the right thing to do for us to hear them all before we make a definitive decision."

"I don't know about you, but I have things to do. I don't see the need to hear more actors when all of us agree that Jacob's reading was the best."

George countered. "How do we know his is the best when we have more actors waiting?"

"Who else do we have? It won't make any difference in my decision and, remember, it is my decision as to who gets the role. Your job is to bring them before me and you've done a fantastic job in your selection process."

"Listen, we only have three more in the waiting room and

I think it's unprofessional to leave them out there. One of them has to audition or we're in breach of the contract we signed with the Worthingtons," the casting director informed the director.

"Who the hell are the Worthingtons?" asked the agitated director.

"This film is based on their family's history and they are right up there. You met them earlier, remember?"

The director looked behind them. He remembered them, although, he had not realized that they were the real family members, "Okay, three more and that's it." He looked to Willow Barrett. "How are you holding up?"

Willow Barrett had wanted to leave hours earlier, and angrily protested every scene with a new actor. "Are you serious? I've been here for six fucking hours! Four of these actors are perfect for this role. How many do you need?"

The director said, "Just a few more and we'll let you go. I'll make them go fast. We'll have you out of here in twenty minutes."

"Okay, but hurry up. I have a lunch date with friends on Rodeo and I don't want to be late," she explained as she barked orders to one of her assistants.

As it happened, Richard auditioned last. The previous two were in the room auditioning for mere minutes and complained loudly when they returned to gather their things. One guy stopped and said to Richard, "They already gave the role to someone. I read, but that bitch Willow Barrett cut it short. What made me want to be in a Willow Barrett movie?" he rhetorically asked himself.

Seeing the disgusted looks of the failed actors made Richard more nervous. He walked into the lion's den without a script, knowing that he would not get the role.

"Where's your script, son?" the weary director asked.

"I don't need it. Besides, how can you get a proper read on an actor when he's constantly looking at a pile of paper?"

The director's eyes opened wide as he looked upon the nervous but confident actor. "I'm impressed that you already know the script, Mr. Marlowe."

"I feel the story is important, so I need to treat it as such and come prepared."

The director smiled and looked at the casting director in a

favorable light, "Are you prepared to offer any excerpt or just the text provided?"

"I have memorized the entire script. Please give me the situation and the scene and I will respond as Bronson Preminger." Richard noticed that the director moved his seat closer to him, indicating that he was thoroughly intrigued by his confidence level. The director called Willow in to deliver her lines so Richard could react.

A distracted Willow read her lines in a monotone that indicated she really did not want to be there. She read without an artistic flair, and that irritated Richard.

He stopped her mid-line. "Why are you doing this? You are a professional actress with major awards, and you're walking through this as if it doesn't matter. It matters to me, dammit! Now act!"

Willow Barrett took exception to Richard's excoriating words, threw her script in his face, and walked out, but not without getting the last word in. "I already got the part, asshole! You didn't! Fucking amateurs! I'm out of here! Call me when you decide who gets the part. This idiot will not. Do you understand me?"

"You can't leave now!" the director pleaded.

"I've got a headache and I don't know why, so I'm leaving," she said without waiting for a reply.

"That will be all, Mr. Marlowe. We will call with our decision," he said.

"But I didn't get to read. Who is running this audition? You or her? I'd like to stay and read without her. I know her lines, as well as mine."

"The audition is over, Mr. Marlowe!" The director stood up and stormed out.

The casting director stayed and allowed him to continue. Richard blew him away.

Bronson and Becky, still watching from the back of the room, applauded Richard's efforts. Becky said, "I know he is our friend, but he is as good as I've ever seen him. I actually believe he is Bronson."

"Yes, he is that good. It doesn't appear that the director and Willow agree, though."

Becky asked, "This is your family's story. Don't you have any say in the matter?"

"No, I sold the rights to the story and, even if I did have a say, do you honestly think Richard would appreciate me getting him the part simply because I said so?"

"No, I guess not, but after seeing this, he should get it just using his talent alone."

"I agree. Look at him! Reading his heart out and the director isn't even here to see it, and that spoiled Willow! Wow, I don't know how she got as far as she did with that attitude."

"I know. He is so great!"

"I will be right back," George said. "I want you to continue." He stood up and walked out of the room.

Becky said, "Look, now he's reading for no one. The casting director left, but he's still reading both parts."

Meanwhile, in the film editing room, George found the director going over some film of the other auditions. "Listen, Ben, I know this guy pissed you off, but you have to see this," the casting director said.

"I'm busy, George. Why are you fighting me on this?"

George turned a volume knob that allowed the director to hear Richard still reading his lines in the sound room, "This is why I'm fighting you. This guy is who we need on this project. He's a handsome man and he's got the chops, and we both agree he can deliver a line. Come back in, Ben. Humor me."

The director was hesitant to return, but finally complied as a courtesy to the award-winning casting director. When he reentered the room, he heard Richard talking, and using his hands and body to add definitive action to his words. As the casting director looked on, it was obvious to him that the director was unimpressed with Richard's performance.

"Mr. Marlowe, are you finished?" the director spouted.

He finished the scene, then stated, "Yes, I'm done."

The director said, "Okay, now leave! We will not be calling you!"

George stepped up and angrily asked, "You're joking, right? You're just going to blow off such a fine performance like it was a hack just reading words?"

"George, I'm getting really tired of your persistence."

"I have cast most of this studio's biggest hits. You don't want Marlowe, fine! I'll find a part for him and you'll be the guy who passed him up because of your precious time and an enormous fear of a young, egotistic actress that you secretly abhor."

"George, just let it go already. I don't dislike Willow Barrett."

"Bullshit, Ben! This is George you're talking to! Not some PR executive." He turned to Richard, who'd heard every word of George's admonishment to the director, and stated, "Meet me in my office after lunch. We have other projects that we need to cast. That was one of the finest performances I've ever witnessed."

George Sanders had an innate ability to find the perfect actor for any role. An ex-director, he knew talent and thought Richard had an extraordinary amount of it, though very minor parts of his performance needed tweaking.

"You are an impressive actor, Mr. Marlowe. I want to add you to my database. Are you in the union?"

"No, but I'm willing to join."

George looked him over and stated, "You realize it's not cheap to join the Screen Actors Guild?"

Richard knew about SAG, but had never looked into joining. "How much is it?"

"Ten thousand dollars a year."

"I don't have that much money, but I have friends who may loan it to me. I'll have to ask."

"Well, if you want to make it here, you had better find out. Most major productions only use SAG actors, and this is one of them." George handed Richard a form to fill out. "I need some head shots and a list of your abilities, such as what stunts you can do or if you can ride a horse. Take this with you. Once you've completed it, bring it back to me. Better yet, call me first and they will allow you into the studio if you have an appointment."

Richard left the studio with Bronson and Becky, and they peppered him with questions about what was said.

"Well, how do you think you did?"

"Apparently not good enough. I think that they are taking Jacob Marsten, but the casting director wants me to see him after lunch. I think I'm just going to stay around here until then. You two can go, I'll take a taxi back."

Becky said, "Okay, keep your head up. You did great today and, if that director didn't see it, then he's no director."

"Yes, Richard, we are going back home. Give me a call if you want a ride back."

"It's not that far. I can take a cab. I should be back in two or three hours. Thanks for coming and offering support."

"No problem, Richard. We'll see you later."

Richard nervously walked around the studio and saw all the extras and costumed performers out taking a smoke break or grabbing a quick snack from the studio commissary. The minutes went by very slow for him.

It was one o'clock in the afternoon when Richard stepped into George's office and was greeted by his secretary.

"Hello, I'm Richard Marlowe. I have an appointment to see Mr. Sanders."

"Yes, Mr. Sanders is expecting you. Go right in. Mr. Sanders will be right with you."

Richard walked into the empty office and sat down. Soon, George walked in and greeted him.

"Hello, Richard. I want to put you in my files."

"Mr. Sanders, what went wrong for me in that audition? What do you think my chances are?"

"Let me be honest with you. You and I both showed up the director and the major star of the movie. I doubt very seriously that you will ever work with either again. They have very long memories. Regardless of how well you did, they will not select you. I, though, think you have a lot of potential, but I can't guarantee anything. You see those cabinets? Those are filled with files of thousands of actors who have done more than a few commercials. A few have won Academy Awards and still can't get work."

"It certainly looks bleak for me," Richard lamented.

"It's bleak for them as well. This is a tough business, but I think I'll see you in something eventually. However, that 'eventually' could take many years."

Richard appreciated George's interest in him, but left dejected with the picture of all those files in his mind. He had nothing. The car he used to get to and from the studio belonged to Bronson. His wardrobe, a small amount of spending money, and his house, all supplied by Bronson. The charity bothered him greatly, however, over the years, he had learned to accept help when it was offered. He always intended to pay them back with interest to help him cope with accepting assistance.

Richard had taken a leave of absence from his job, so he spent a few extra days on the West Coast. He sensed that something mystical forced him to stay. Bronson had no issue with staying for another week, but not any longer than that, due to obligations back in Florida.

Richard told him about his strange feelings. "I can't explain it, Bronson. It's as if I'm fated to be here. Something is making me want to stay."

"It's probably because it's the movie capital of the world and it's your passion for all things acting that's making you feel that way," Bronson theorized.

"No, it's not that. Hell, I've lived in Florida all my life and love it there. Something is calling me here. I feel like, if I leave, I'm going against some twist of fate."

"Well, I have to go back next week. You're welcome to stay here as long as you want, but I'll have to fire you," Bronson said, then laughed loudly.

Richard laughed as well and said, "I bet you've been waiting to fire my ass for a long time."

Richard didn't mention SAG or the union dues because he had serious doubts about the role, and from what George told him, it might be years before he got another call, so he had plenty of time to join the union.

"Well, did you get the part or not?" Bronson asked suddenly. "We thought that you were great."

"I don't think I did, according to the casting director. Perhaps I will go back with you." He grabbed his head as if in pain.

"What's wrong, Rick?" Bronson asked, concerned.

"That's what I've been talking about. I get these sudden headaches when I talk about leaving here. It's the strangest feeling. My head just pounds. It feels like it's going to explode." Richard rubbed his eyes.

"Interesting. Maybe you should see a doctor."

"No, I'll be fine. It only happens occasionally."

Bronson, Becky, and Richard hired a limousine and hit the town that night. Stopping at all the hot spots, Becky noted that Richard got a lot of attention from some of the hotter women in the clubs. He danced with a few of them and talked to all of them, but did not seem to want to get to know them better.

"Why are you blowing off all these hot women?" asked Bronson.

"I don't know, Bronson. I came here to get a job and it does not look good. I really wanted this gig. I should find out something tomorrow. I can't focus until then. Those girls better watch out when I get this off my mind," Richard proudly asserted.

They climbed back into the limousine and went home to Manhattan Beach. They talked all the way back about Richard's possible role in the and about Bronson's ancestors, whose story the book told. They discussed Bronson Preminger, and his service in the Navy, and what Chelsea had told him about the old times. They had not been born when the Premingers disappeared at sea, so some of their extraordinary stories Bronson remembered from the book.

Richard had read the book ten times trying to capture Bronson Preminger's persona. In the end, Richard knew more about Bronson's family than Bronson did. More than that, Richard could voice the original Bronson perfectly because he had seen videos of the happy couple.

Becky and Bronson listened as Richard mimicked Bronson Preminger, talking about the sea and his wife Catherine. However, he could not hold the voice for very long because he had been drinking all night and wanted to lighten the mood with jokes. He'd returned to his old self after years of turmoil. Even if Richard did not get the role, Bronson convinced him that other opportunities existed for him. Richard had regained his confidence and Bronson credited the trip to California.

The next day, Bronson woke up and looked out the window to see Richard in a chair on the beach. He got dressed and went outside. As he approached, he saw Richard reading a letter that he let fall on the beach. The wind kicked it to Bronson's feet; he picked it and read it. Richard officially had not gotten the part. Bronson walked up behind him.

Richard turned around. "Oh, I see you've read it. Big joke, eh?" he muttered solemnly.

"Hey, you tried. This won't be the first time you get rejected, buddy. There are many opportunities out there.

You're a fine actor, and I'm not saying that because you're my friend. You've got to trust me on that."

"I do, and you're right. I'll succeed. I think I'm ready to go home now."

"I'll have Marty get the plane ready and we'll be there for dinner," Bronson asserted. He called his pilot, and he'd already fueled it up and done the flight line. Bronson went back to the house to tell Becky; Richard stayed in the chair contemplating his future as he watched the waves come in and go out.

He'd packed his suitcase when he got the letter early that morning, and made his decision immediately upon reading it.

They loaded everything in the car, but Richard's headache returned. He hid the pain from the others, enduring it and waiting for it to subside. However, not only did it not leave, it got more intense as they approached the airport. Still, Richard held on and acted normal so the pain would not elevate Bronson or Becky's concern.

They walked out onto the tarmac toward Bronson's chartered jet. Richard suddenly collapsed, unconscious on the warm concrete.

Bronson turned him over and slapped Richard's face. "Richard! Richard! Wake up, buddy!"

Becky asked in broken words, "Is he breathing?"

Bronson replied, "Yes, he is, and his heart is beating."

Becky panicked and screamed, "Someone help! Please help! Hurry!"

Marty said, "The airport paramedics are on their way. He looks pale. How did he get that cut on his head?"

Bronson said, "He must have hit his head when he fell. Becky, you have anything to stop his bleeding?"

"No, take off your shirt, Bronson! Hurry, he's bleeding badly!"

Bronson ripped off his shirt, not stopping to unbutton it, and pressed it hard on Richard's head.

Bronson tried to revive him again, but to no avail. The airport medical team arrived and took over trying to wake Richard, but they too failed. They placed him in a medical helicopter and flew him to the nearest hospital. Bronson and Becky drove there. Becky cried profusely, thinking that Richard had died.

Arriving at the hospital, Becky and Bronson ran through

the lobby to the receptionist desk and frantically asked for the location of Richard's room. After they were told, they hurried to the elevator and punched the fourth floor button. They arrived at Richard's room, winded, to see him sitting up in bed and joking with the doctors.

"Oh, hi, guys." Richard gave a wave. "I just told the doc about the girls in Florida."

"What the hell is going on? How is he, Doctor?" asked Becky.

"Oh, he's fine. Just a little dehydrated, that's all. We can release him tomorrow."

Becky walked up to a smiling Richard and punched him as hard as she could in the shoulder. "You scared the shit out of me!" she screamed.

She hugged him tightly and whispered, "Thank God you're still with us." She looked back to Bronson. "Bronson cried."

"Really, Bronson? You cried?"

Bronson smiled and joked, "I think my wife has betrayed me!"

"He will have to stay here overnight for observation, but he will be fine," the doctor interrupted. "As far as his head hurting every time he talks about leaving, I have no clue. It could be psychosomatic or just a weird coincidence."

Bronson said, "Well, I have a board meeting tomorrow, so I have to leave. You want to stay here or go with me, Becky? I'll be back the next day after the meeting."

"No way! I'm staying. That's too much flying for me!" Becky confirmed.

"Okay, I'm going back, but I'll be here before you get out, buddy," Bronson stated.

"Take your time," Richard said. He smiled at Becky. "Take all the time you need, bro."

"Easy, hot shot! That's my wife you're talking to," said Bronson as he took his wife's arm. "I'll be back tomorrow morning."

Becky and Richard laughed at Bronson's bad attempt at acting jealous because they knew Bronson trusted them implicitly.

Chapter Three

Mysterious Happenings

Richard stayed in the hospital for the next two days; he contracted a mild case of pneumonia and the doctor made him stay for observation.

Bronson returned the next day, but turbulence and a layover in Denver made him tired, so he went to sleep. While Bronson slept, Becky went to pick up Richard from the hospital and wanted to stop for lunch. Richard picked a small Italian restaurant on Rodeo Drive. Becky thought it strange that he wanted to go to an Italian restaurant because he never ate Italian.

They sat at the outside café and ordered their food. He looked behind him as the waiter seated three patrons, and two were very familiar—the director of the movie that he'd auditioned for just days earlier, Willow Barrett, and an elderly well-dressed man whom he'd never met.

Richard wanted to apologize for his behavior at the audition, but Becky tried to stop him, thinking that they were going to get agitated with him all over again.

Determined, Richard approached the table. Willow Barrett was wearing large dark sunglasses, jeans, and a slinky white shirt. The director, who seemed to be stuck in the 1960s, tugged on his sloppy clothes and talked about the movie.

Willow looked up and said, "Oh! God! It's him again! I feel another headache coming on."

"I just wanted to apologize for my behavior a few days ago. I acted like an ass and I'm sorry."

The elderly man stood up and extended his hand. Richard shook it.

"Who is this young man?" he asked.

The director, obviously still angry about their last encounter, said, "Richard Marlowe is the stooge who tried to upstage me and Willow, that amateur who disrupted the auditions a few days ago. Bounce yourself back over to your table, asshole."

Richard, embarrassed at the director's remarks, started to walk back to his table, but the elderly man stopped him. "Where are you from, Mr. Marlowe?"

"I'm from Florida. I just came out here to audition for the movie."

"*The Isle of Ages*?" he asked, seemingly excited.

"Yes," Richard confirmed.

"Interesting! How old are you?"

"I'm twenty-eight...well, I must get back to my table. It's nice meeting you, Mr.—"

"I'm Peter Nance. It's nice to meet you, young man."

Richard walked back to Becky. She asked him what they said and caught Peter Nance staring at Richard.

"Why is that old guy staring at you?"

Richard looked back over to the table and saw the old man in a heated conversation with the director and Willow Barrett. "I don't know; he's a weird guy. Kept asking questions."

"I bet he's gay and he tried to pick you up. You are a hottie, after all."

"Oh please, Becky! Now you think guys are hitting on me, very old guys!"

"You know where we are, don't you? He could just be a very old gay guy."

"I think he may be associated with the movie somehow, or maybe he's the guy playing an elderly Bronson Preminger."

Richard spied Willow looking at him and quickly turned away. He tried to eavesdrop, but could not hear with all the other patrons talking at once. Richard and Becky finished eating and paid their bill.

He wanted to stay longer, but the waiter informed them that he had many people in line waiting for a table, so they left. All the time, the elderly man watched them as they walked toward their car.

"Wow, that guy gives me the creeps!" Richard said as he climbed into the passenger seat. They arrived back at the house to find Bronson on the beach. They went over to him and Becky gently placed her hands over his eyes.

"Hey, baby! You feel better?"

Richard followed suit. "Hey, baby! You feel better?"

"Wow, you have soft hands there, partner. Much softer that my wife's."

Becky slugged him in the shoulder.

Richard plopped on the sand next to him.

Bronson handed a note to Richard. "A messenger sent this over just now."

"Who's it from?" asked Becky, eager to know what it said.

"It's from that casting director, George Sanders. He wants me to come to his office tomorrow afternoon. Wow! Maybe he has something for me!" Richard stated excitedly.

They stayed on the beach the rest of the slightly overcast day. Thrilled, Richard did not want to do anything but relax by the water with his friends. He felt grounded by the water. He did not want to get his hopes up, but Bronson and Becky agreed that a letter like that could only mean one thing—Richard had won the role in his first big-budget movie. His life-long dream.

They drank a few beers and, when night fell, they lit a small fire on the beach and watched the surf lick the sand. A few neighbors arrived and joined the impromptu party. One brought his guitar, and a few others had instruments as well. They provided the melodies as the rest of the group sang songs and toasted Richard's impending stardom. He cautioned his friends that it might just be another audition, and he harnessed his excitement.

After the beach celebration, they walked back to the house slightly inebriated and went to their respective rooms to sleep, but no amount of alcohol settled Richard's nerves.

He lay on the bed and tried to sleep with a myriad of scenarios dancing in his mind, ranging from Academy Award possibilities to a minor role in another commercial. However, the majority of his thoughts centered on the potential role of a lifetime. The one that marked his abilities and would be talked about by the greats of the cinema. Richard finally could start paying back Bronson for all his friendship and kindness over the years.

Tossing and turning all night, he dreamt of the process. Being on set and listening to a barking director, and multiple takes until he got the perfect shot. Then there were the parties, fan adulation, getting an agent...

He woke up in a cold sweat as he remembered a very important point that the casting director had said. Richard did not belong to the Screen Actors Guild and forgot to ask Bronson to loan him the money to join. He couldn't wait until morning to ask; he put on his robe, went to the master bedroom, and knocked on the door as quietly as he could, hoping not to wake Becky.

A groggy and still somewhat inebriated Bronson opened the door, scratching his head. "What time is it?"

"It's about three o'clock. Bronson, I forgot to ask you. I need to borrow five thousand dollars to join the Guild. I forgot all about it!"

"Five grand to join a union?" Bronson asked.

"Yes, George told me I need to join if I hoped to work in this town."

"Okay, but I have to get some sleep. We have to fly back to Florida early tomorrow because my senior VP just died. I'll leave it on the table. I think I have the cash here. Now, let me get back to bed. I don't want to still be drunk when I get to Florida. You can stay in the house while we're gone. Okay?"

"Sure, thanks, buddy. Oh, and by the way, if an idiot knocks on your door at three in the morning, make sure you have pants on."

Bronson looked down and said, "Oh shit! Noted!" He closed the door.

Richard went back to his room and tried to get some sleep.

Morning came, and it appeared that Bronson and Becky had already left the house. He went to the table to get the money. It seemed that Bronson, in his semi-conscious state, had forgotten to leave it.

He still made his appointment, but hoped that the casting

director gave him more time.

The urgency of George's words in his letter seemed to indicate that whatever project he wanted to speak to Richard about would probably start soon.

He arrived on time and walked confidently into George's outer office and his secretary informed him that Mister Sanders had met with some movie executives and that he would see him soon.

Nervously, he read magazines and periodically glanced at George's closed door. Fifteen minutes later, the door opened, three people shook George's hand, and left. He called Richard into his office and sat in front of the large shelf full of files.

George perused Richard's file, and asked, "So, are you ready to be famous?"

Richard took a deep breath and said, "I've been ready for it my entire life."

George smiled. "Let me get to it. You know the movie that you auditioned for?"

"Yes, of course."

"Well, it appears the executive producer took a liking to you and overruled the director. He wants you to play the part of Bronson Preminger. The angry director said things that are not supposed to be said to an executive producer and he fired him on the spot. The new director is Gary Norman. I bet you've heard of him, right?"

"Are you joking? Gary Norman? He's the best young director in the business. Three Academy Awards already and he isn't even forty years old. Wow, I don't know what to say."

"Say yes! We'll have a contract ready for your agent. Have you got one yet?"

"No, I haven't, nor have I joined the Guild yet. My friend, who is a relative of Bronson Preminger, is going to lend me the money when he comes back from Florida."

"Well, we have plenty of time. Production won't start for another month or so. In the meantime, you need to get an agent." The phone rang and George answered it. "Okay, sir, I understand," he said. "He's in my office right now, I'll be sure to tell him." George said goodbye and hung up. "Here, contact this agency. They already know to expect your call.

As for the money to join the union, you are a member in good standing as of five minutes ago."

Richard thought that Bronson had maybe remembered that he had not left the money and had wired it to SAG, but felt perplexed as to how whoever had called George knew that he needed an agent. Richard did not ask questions. George handed him a piece of paper with the agency's name. He shook George's hand, then stared at the piece of paper. Excited, he visited the agency unannounced instead of calling.

On such a beautiful Southern California day, he decided to leisurely walk the distance rather than sacrifice his parking space. He confidently strolled into the agency's huge building, not really wanting to talk to anyone. He just wanted to be inside with a legitimate reason to be there. He stopped in the lobby, sat in one of the plush chairs, and daydreamed.

The guard noticed his strange behavior and confronted him. "Are you supposed to be here, son?"

"Well, no! I mean, not yet. This is the agency that's going to represent me soon," Richard stated with pride.

"Do you have an appointment?"

"No, not yet, because I haven't called them to set one up, but they are expecting my call," he explained.

"Do you have a name?"

"Yes, I'm Richard Marlowe."

The guard smiled. "No, I mean who are you here to see?"

Richard retrieved the now crumpled piece of paper and handed it to the guard.

"Jonas Green." He handed it back. "Wait here."

"No, wait, I haven't called him yet!"

The guard did not hear his plea and called on the phone, "Mister Green, there's a gentleman named Richard Marlowe here to see you."

As Richard stood up, ready to leave, a man came off the elevator and introduced himself. "Richard Marlowe?" he asked with a smile, a Bluetooth hanging on his ear.

"Yes, I'm Richard," he responded sheepishly.

"I expected a phone call, not a visit," he said with a welcoming handshake.

"I decided to see your building, but did not expect to see you. I'll leave if you're busy."

"Nonsense! Come up to my office and we'll talk. I hear

that you've been cast as a lead character in a major picture."

They went upstairs and Richard felt instantly at ease with Jonas. They talked for an hour and went over all the technical details, including his fees and what he would do for Richard.

After the meeting, Richard left the office building brimming with pride. He could not wait to tell Bronson all that had happened. He called him during his walk back to his car. Bronson wanted to hear all the details and Richard happily relayed everything he knew. The half-hour walk seemed to take seconds as he excitedly talked to his friend.

"Oh, dammit! I nearly forgot to thank you for sending the money for my union dues. I really appreciate it, buddy."

"Shit! I forgot all about that, Richard. I had other things on my mind and it completely slipped through. I can get it to you in minutes!" Bronson explained.

"You didn't send it?" he asked.

"No, I forgot to leave it on the table, and I didn't tell Becky about it either. I'm so sorry, Rick!"

Richard opened his car door and got in. "Well, if you didn't pay it, who did?"

"I just know I didn't. Look, I've just directed my secretary to wire you twenty-five grand. You'll need new clothes and some spending money."

"You don't have to do that, Bronson, I have a little money."

"Hey, we just want tickets to the premiere. Rick, do my ancestors proud. I know that I'm proud to have my best friend play Bronson Preminger."

"I know this is going to sound corny, so I don't want you to take it the wrong way, but I love you. You and Becky have been my family for so long and I want to tell you how much you two mean to me."

"Well, we pretty much think the same way about you, superstar. Hey, we're flying back to LA in a week or so. We have to attend the funeral of my VP and then we'll be heading out. We want an invite to watch them film the movie."

"You got it, Bronson. I can't wait to see you. Tell Becky I love her and have a safe trip."

A week later, Richard found himself in the massive mansion of director Gary Norman with the rest of the cast going
over the first read-through of the script. He saw and met the
entire cast at the meeting, including an agitated Willow Barrett, who still appeared to have a grudge against him. They
practiced their lines as the director told them how the scenes
developed. Willow gave Richard some nasty looks as he read
with her. Even in her fits of rage, Richard saw a stunningly
beautiful woman with long blonde hair and a face that melted
a man's will to dream of other women.

Her classic look and heart-shaped face demanded to be
gazed at and adored, and her bright blue eyes twinkled in
the slightest of light. Richard could not turn away when she
looked at him, and settled on staring, which made her uncomfortable and caused her to turn away. Even her poor attitude toward him did not diminish her glamorous façade. He
wanted to play opposite her, but also wanted her to keep her
mouth shut during breaks because some of the words coming out of her mouth dimmed her beauty.

She walked through her lines with Richard, not wanting
to put her full effort into it, especially when the scene called
for them to kiss. The director admonished her. She feigned
another headache as she cut the session short and asked to
leave.

Richard also had a headache, but he did not want leave
such an important first meeting with the director, so he with-
stood the pain and continued being involved for another
three hours.

Later, he and many of the actors who'd attended the
meeting went to one of LA's hottest nightspots. They had a
long table in a secluded room off the main dance floor. The
room had a clear view of everything in the nightclub, as well
as a small television screen in the wall. The loudness in the
club made it difficult to hear what the reporter said on the
sudden breaking news report. However, Richard took sharp
notice when he saw a photo of Bronson on the screen. He
ran to the television and turned the volume up full blast,
much to the dismay of his fellow actors, who wanted to hear
the music rather than the account of a rich CEO's plane
crashing in the San Bernardino Mountains near Beverly Hills.

"Shut up!" he screamed at his new friends.

The news broadcast reported that four people had perished in the fiery crash.

A very distraught Richard ran out of the bar without paying his tab, fumbled with trying to get his key into the door lock, got in his car, and recklessly drove to the crash site, all the while ignoring all street signs and taking serious chances while crossing the lines. He straddled hard curves too fast, not caring if other cars approached. He yelled, trying to convince himself that it wasn't real. He could not stop the tears rolling down his face when he saw the first police cruiser with its lights flickering feverishly, indicating that it was all true. He saw that the police had blocked the road and had thoughts of busting through the roadblock, but thought better of it.

He parked his car in the middle of the highway with the engine running and hiked through the dense, thorny underbrush. He did not care about the sharp thorns because the pain he felt in his heart dug deeper than any thorn could. Relentlessly, he ran through the dense thicket until he saw bright lights and a strong police presence. The overpowering odor of burnt jet fuel filled his nose. Bright yellow crime tape circled all the way around the wreckage, but that did not stop him. The police officers saw him as he rushed toward the perimeter tape and stopped him. He stood there watching the remnants of the plane burn. Two officers demanded that he step away from the still dangerous scene.

They grabbed his arms and he shrugged them off, still mesmerized by the smoldering plane. The officers saw that Richard had rage in his eyes and, when they tried to subdue him, he lashed out in an unhinged hatred and swung at anyone who impeded his progression to Bronson's plane, connecting with several police officers. Richard's adrenaline flow was at a fever pitch and he easily broke through the ranks of the barrier-enforcing officers. They brought out their Tasers and fired at him, striking him multiple times. Richard fell, not twitching, and numb to the Taser's effects. He just lay there perfectly still on the scorched earth. He nonchalantly pulled the Taser's prongs out of his chest and arms, threw them aside, and looked up at the stars. He lay so still and quiet, the officers thought they might have killed him.

"Mister, are you okay?" they asked.

Richard did not respond because of the shock that his only friends were among the burnt cinders of Bronson's plane.
They approached him with great caution and handcuffed him.
He sat up and watched the fire department extinguish the
final cinders, leaving clouds of black smoke ascending to the
heavens.

Next came the task of sifting through the still hot rubble
to find the four bodies. The medics treated Richard's deep
cuts, though the handcuffs confused them.

"Was this man on the plane?"

The lead officer said, "No, I think he's a friend of one of
the victims. He came in here fists a-blazing and we had to
control him. What makes you think he was on the plane?"

"Well, look at him. He has multiple injuries with all the
blood on his face, arms, and legs. Can you remove the handcuffs? They're creating cuts on his wrists."

"I think so, but be careful. This guy is as strong as an ox."

"I think he'll be okay. To tell you the truth, that catatonic
look on his face has me more concerned than all his other
injuries."

They placed Richard, incoherent and unresponsive, on a
gurney and loaded him into the back of the ambulance.
However, before they left the scene, they also loaded the
remnants of four bodies in thick black bags on a single gurney and rolled it in next to Richard.

The sirens blared as they left the crash site. The very
rough road bounced them around quite a bit. Richard could
not take his eyes off the body bags. The ambulance hit a
large rut, which loosened the straps holding the body bags.
One of the bags fell to the floor and opened enough to allow
an unburnt female hand with perfectly polished nails and a
very familiar wedding ring affixed permanently to her finger
to fall out. The sight of Becky's hand enraged him to the
point that sheer adrenaline allowed him to rip his bonds
apart. One strap remained intact when the medic turned and
shot him with a powerful sedative.

Richard woke up at the hospital with a doctor and nurse
examining him. He had bandages all over his body and ques-

tioned the doctors as to whether or not he'd dreamt the horrific crash that killed Bronson and Becky.

The doctor welcomed him back and injected him with another sedative because his blood pressure skyrocketed to
unsafe levels. He calmed down a few minutes later and con-
versed with the doctor in a garbled voice. The nurse stated,
"I'm sorry, Mister Marlowe, but you did not dream about the
plane crash. I understand you had friends on the plane?"

"Yes, I did! Where are they?" a weary Richard asked.

"I'm really sorry. Mr. and Mrs. Worthington, along with
the two pilots, died on impact. The impact ejected Mrs.
Worthington from the plane. They're in the morgue. The fire
didn't reach her broken body."

"Becky! Her name is Becky!" He started to take his bandages off and the nurse pleaded with him not to.

"I understand that you're an actor, Mister Marlowe. I just
want to tell you that all of your facial injuries are just
scratches. In a month or so, they will be completely gone."

"No, I'm not an actor, nor will I ever be. I want to go
back home with my friends."

"See all the flowers and balloons? You must have some
friends in big places. Most of these flowers came from the
studio and these came from Willow Barrett herself."

Richard complied with the nurse's wishes and left the
bandages on. He saw the card from Willow and said, "No, it's
not from her. Her assistant must have written it because Willow is left-handed and a right-handed person wrote this."

He did not allow visitors during his time in the hospital,
and when the time came, they released him quietly, in the
dark of night. He went back to Bronson's Manhattan Beach
home and arranged for their bodies to be delivered to their
families.

Richard still could not calm his nerves a week later, reliv-
ing the horrific scene in his mind over and over again. The
slightest sound reminded him of their voices, their laughs,
and their unyielding happiness for his future. He seldom ate
and his once perfectly kempt appearance now suffered. He
did not bathe, shave, or care how he looked or smelled. His
long, disheveled hair seldom saw a comb or brush, and he
allowed it to be what it was. His nose could not smell the
sweet aromas of the seawater crashing on the surf, nor did

he want to hear the pleasantries of children playing on the beach in front of Bronson's lavish estate. Everything in the home had its story and he knew them all because they all had history with Bronson and Becky.

Richard quit acting and followed his friends' bodies back to Florida. There, he would try to rebuild what was left of his world and try to make a life for himself. His phone's mailbox filled quickly because the studio, director, Jonas, and even George tried to contact him.

Their funeral was to be his last act of sanity, and he struggled to hold it together for that. After that, he had nothing to live for other than remembering how close he came to paying back the kindness that Bronson and Becky bestowed upon him. As he boarded the plane, a splitting pain seared through his head, but unlike the pains he had experienced before, he ignored it. He looked out the window to see the luggage handlers loading the coffins onto the plane. Four hours of intense pain later, the plane landed in Florida. He met some of Bronson and Becky's relatives and relinquished control of the bodies to them.

The plane left the tarmac and the sad family members left as a small sprinkle of rain fell. He stood on the tarmac alone, not knowing where to go. He had no home other than Bronson's on the beach.

He looked all around and felt confused as to which way to walk because every road seemed tangled with remembrances in one form or another. Tears flowed without cause for most of the days following that day on the tarmac, and stopping them proved hopeless. Richard had sunk deep into a dark depression where his mind was no longer controlled with what was good and healthy. He felt like an empty vase once filled with brightly-colored aromatic flowers that were days away from reaching their peak beauty that had gone to a deep despair. He sensed that, not only did the flowers not peak, they withered and died and were left for the wind to remove the remnants. There was no one left to replenish the splendor of the bouquet, nor enough water to allow the flowers to live a promised lifetime.

A week later, the somber funeral took place. Richard, dressed in his finest suit, delivered the heartfelt eulogy over the flower-draped caskets with not a dry eye in the house. In an eloquent address, he told them what Bronson and Becky had meant to him over the years, and what their deaths had done to him. He kissed the coffin of each, then sat and cried openly. Richard had a lot of practice grieving. Everyone in his life had left him.

After he saw them lowered into the ground, he left the cemetery, not talking to anyone. He went back to Bronson's coastal home and brought three chairs, a small glass table, and a bottle of Bronson's most expensive champagne out on the beach directly in front of the house. He placed three crystal stem glasses on the table and filled each one. He did not bother to change out of his suit, but he did remove his shoes and socks and rolled up his pant legs. He toasted his friends and talked as if they were there beside him, laughing at his jokes and making plans for their future.

Right in the middle of a story, Gary Norman called him. He glared at the phone as it vibrated on the glass table.

"Can't you see that I'm talking to my friends?" he screamed at the ringing phone. He grabbed it and threw it into the ocean, then calmly returned to his imaginary friends and finished his funny story. However, only he laughed. "What? It's not funny, guys?"

Reality set in after a neighboring couple who walked on the beach spied him talking to himself.

"Are you okay, son?" the old man asked.

Richard ignored the couple, so they asked him louder and Richard lashed out. "Get the fuck away from me, you old crows!"

Insulted, the elderly couple walked away.

The interruption caused him to step back. He looked at the empty chairs and the two full wine glasses, and destroyed them. He took the bottle toward the house, but returned as a spark of his old self came back for a moment at seeing children playing on the beach. He took off his shirt and returned to the table. He got down on his knees, searched out the broken glass, and piled it on his shirt. He cried once more as he sifted through the warm, white sand until he found it all. He placed the shirt with the shards of glass piled up on the table and saw what his mind thought. "A pipedream. Just a pile of shattered dreams as fragile as crystal and wiped off the face of the earth as easily as it came. I miss you guys."

He realized he must have looked like an idiot talking to non-existent people. He chose to accept Bronson and Becky's deaths after many more bottles of champagne and, when he'd had enough, he fell onto the bed with his suit still on and slept. He never thought about the fact that he had a binding contract to perform in the movie. He just thought that the producer would replace him, although he hoped that they did not want to sue him for breach of contract.

Three years went by and he heard nothing; he did not know whether or not the studio produced the movie without him. He had other more serious problems. Bronson's house finally had a buyer and Bronson's sister-in-law told him that he had to leave. He'd spent three years living off the money Bronson gave him years ago, but with the fund nearly depleted, he had no way of earning more. Getting a job was impossible because he did not have any skills other than acting and also lacked the desire to do that.

Richard lived a solitary life. When he needed food, he walked to the nearest store. He was unrecognizable to the people who'd known him before Bronson's tragic death because of his long hair and beard to his chest. Many people tossed him coins, thinking he was homeless. He gladly accepted the money, thinking that he may need it. He fought hard to get out of his depression, but Bronson's and Becky's deaths still haunted his thoughts. If that wasn't bad enough, other equally harsh thoughts came back to him as well, furthering his depression and making it more difficult for him to cope with the added pressures of life.

Bronson's sister-in-law hated throwing Richard out of the house, knowing how much her brother had liked him, but greed won out. The house sold for twelve million dollars, yet Richard got nothing for its upkeep for the past three years. He spent his last few weeks packing his stuff in his car, which doubled as his home. He had a thousand dollars left.

He moved from Florida to a quaint little town called Mystic Harbor in Connecticut. He arrived in the summer and tried to find a job in construction or at a fast food restaurant, but found nothing. With the winter months quickly approaching, he needed to find a warm place to stay.

His car ran out of gas in a remote part of town. With the car hidden, he ventured out to find work. The high cost of food made short work of his last hundred dollars.

Winter struck hard in Connecticut that year.

With the trees bare of leaves, snow measuring over four feet slightly covered his car, but it was still in plain sight of passersby. People knew Richard lived in the car, though no one knew his name, nor did anyone care to ask. Countless blankets covered him at night, but still the cold air found him in his car cocoon, and no one appeared to want to help him. He got a name for himself around town as The Vagabond. Soon, he stayed in his car and no longer attempted to get a job. His money had run out long ago, and he had to panhandle to get nickels together to buy something to fill his stomach. He noticed the Christmas season in town when the glistening streets lit up with red and green lights and the folks walked along the main street with gifts and packages.

This time of year, the Salvation Army set up their buckets right where he usually stood to beg for nickels. For all their charitable activity, they bounced him away because of the smell emanating from him. He felt as if Christmas did not apply to him because people stared at him disapprovingly, as if they had never seen a homeless man before.

Months later, the snow melted and the springtime buds returned to the trees around him. He barely made it through the harsh winter, and things got much worse when he left his car to go begging on his favorite street one day. He received a few quarters and immediately bought what he could, but when he went back to his car, someone had taken it.

He found out that the police had towed it away with all his belongings inside.

He looked to the sky and asked what he'd done to deserve such a life. With his car gone, he had nothing but his health, and felt that failing as well. Still a very young man of thirty-one, Richard's lack of personal hygiene and a good razor made him look twenty years older and even more unemployable.

The rain started. He leaned against a wall; his legs weakened and he fell to the sidewalk. People walked by him, but did not want to get involved with someone so obviously troubled. Some of the younger kids attacked him, but others were quite friendly. He remembered a young girl walking with her parents who broke free from them, ran to Richard, and gave him a five-dollar bill. Richard feared at first that she wanted to attack him and cowered as the rain drenched his clothes.

"Here, mister, this is for you," she said as she handed him the bill, then ran back to her parents as they hurried toward her. She was fifteen, but still too young to understand the horrors of life, and also too young to realize potential dangers. By the way he looked and his strange mannerisms, her parents viewed Richard as one of those potential dangers. They scolded the girl for approaching him, then took her by the hand and led her away, but in his deplorable state of mind, he remembered her face as a kind one. He noticed the girl a few more times over the next days and weeks, and each time, she stopped to say hello to him. She did not always have money; however, that was not the reason he looked forward to seeing her.

On one of her visits, he asked her name.

The girl gave him a quarter and said, "I'm Tess Walker. What's your name, mister?"

Richard paused because it had been years since he'd uttered his name or heard it from another's lips. "Richard. My name is Richard. How old are you, Tess?"

Tess smiled. "I'm fifteen. Where do you live?"

"I live here and there. It's getting late, you should be home. Thank you for the quarter."

A strange man approached him on a chilly mid-spring night. Richard did not know him, nor did he see his face. Oblivious and sound asleep when the man approached, he felt nothing as the man placed a note and an envelope in his tattered jacket and vanished.

Richard did not find the note until a week later. It stated, *"Your destiny awaits, Richard."* The envelope contained a one-way plane ticket to California and five crisp one hundred dollar bills.

Richard looked around to make sure no one saw that he

had money, then read the short note again and counted the money over and over, thinking that he must be dreaming. Although usually his dreams included money, food, and warmth, his hands held real money and a real plane ticket. He checked the date on the first class ticket. The flight departed in three short days. He held nothing dear in Connecticut, so he ventured a guess that it could not get any worse in California. He needed to buy new clothes and get himself cleaned up for his flight.

Chapter Four

Richard's Last Destiny

He had to eat first. However, he smelled bad, so he waited until the most of the patrons left the fast food restaurant; he did not want to offend them while they ate. He walked in as fast as he could, bought a few burgers, walked outside, found a secluded spot, and devoured them in less than a minute. However, he ate it so fast that he threw up most of it. Finding someone to take him in and allow him to shower and shave proved more difficult. No one wanted him in their establishment, either to sell him food or to sell him clothes.

He braved the sneers and stares and bought a bar of soap and a razor, walked to the water's edge, stripped to his underwear near the water, lathered up, then jumped in the cold water and rinsed off the soap. He did it a few times to get all the dirt and grime off him. He did not have a mirror, so he shaved blind and felt for smoothness.

He dried off with a roll of paper towels, but he had a dilemma. He did not want to put his smelly clothes back on, so he simply picked a guy who walked by who had a similar size and offered him a hundred dollars for his shirt and another hundred for the guy's pants. The man agreed, but stripping to his underwear on the beach didn't appeal to him, so he went home, grabbed clothes, and brought them to the beach while Richard hid behind some rocks. They made the exchange.

The garments did not fit well, but they allowed Richard to step into a store without being thrown out to purchase better fitting clothes. He had no problem spending the money because he liked walking around the town without mothers hurrying their children away from him and teenagers throwing stuff at him. The people who crossed his path did not recognize him. He felt as if he belonged once more. For the first time in years, he felt human, and possibilities stirred in his mind—a feeling he had not experienced since Bronson's and Becky's deaths.

He purchased more new clothes, a leather shoulder bag, and replaced his torn wallet. He gently took out the tattered photo of his father and placed it in his new wallet. He needed a haircut to complete his reemergence into society. He had a full head of hair, but much of it flowed past his shoulders. He entered the barbershop expecting the people there to notice him, but it pleased him that they did not recognize him.

The stylist shampooed and cut his hair. While the stylist finished his new look, he wondered who and why the generous soul had given him the money and the ticket, and what the future held for him once he got to California. Due to his dire situation, his memory suffered. He remembered little of what he'd done in California, but the searing memory of his lost friends still festered in his mind. The mere mention of the state brought it all back vividly.

The days seemed longer in anticipation of his flight. He used the rest of his money to catch a cab to the airport. On the long ride to JFK Airport, he thought more and more about the reasons that someone wanted him in Southern California, but couldn't think of a single one until the plane taxied toward the runway.

"Oh damn! The contract!" he whispered to himself. "They want me in California to arrest me for breach of contract. What did the note say? My destiny lies in California? Or something like that."

He surprised himself by forgetting his breach of contract issues, but he considered his homeless situation. His life had been preoccupied with staying alive and feeding himself instead of thinking about contracts and such. For the years since Bronson's and Becky's deaths, he'd tried hard to forget about the trivial things in the last couple years of his traumatic existence. At that point in his life, acting and the dreams of his past were secondary to the point where forgetting seemed to be one of the best blessings life gave to him.

He could not get off the plane. He walked toward the exit, but the flight attendant abruptly stopped him and ordered him back to his seat. The plane departed, and throughout the trip, he planned to evade the authorities once they landed.

The plane touched down at the Burbank airport. He waited for all the passengers to disembark before he grabbed his leather bag and made his way toward the exit. He hoped that he could veer away from where the passengers entered the terminal and find another entrance, but security personnel prevented him. Entering the terminal, he did not see anyone who appeared to be waiting for him, so he nonchalantly walked among the other passengers.

Richard used the escalator and saw what appeared to be a limousine driver holding up a placard with his name on it. The man did not seem threatening, so he went up to him and revealed his identity.

"Hello, Mister Marlowe, I see you haven't retrieved your luggage yet. You want me to get it for you?"

Richard looked around, did not see any other people behind him, and said, "No, I don't have any checked luggage."

"Very well. Follow me. The car is just outside the door."

"Where are you taking me, sir?"

"I'm taking you to the Ritz-Carlton. I'm instructed to get you checked in and someone will contact you later on in the day," he explained.

The driver did as instructed and drove the short way to the hotel. Richard had a reservation in the Presidential Suite. Many thoughts coursed through his mind, but no bad ones this time.

The bellhop showed him to his room and directed him to the closet, filled with the finest clothes and shoes money could buy. He pulled out his last twenty-dollar bill and handed it to the bellhop, who handed it right back and said, "It's all taken care of, Mister Marlowe."

In disbelief of all that had happened to him, Richard awaited his benefactor's call. A few hours later, the phone rang and a man whose voice he did not recognize welcomed him to Los Angeles. They talked for a bit, and the man asked him to meet him at the bar at seven-thirty where he would deliver an explanation as to why he'd summoned Richard to California.

Seven-thirty came around. Richard walked to the bar in the lobby. There were not many people there, and no one seemed interested in talking to him, so he sat at the bar and waited for his benefactor to arrive. He ordered a beer and, as he sipped it, he saw an elderly man in a wheelchair who seemed familiar.

The old man raised his hand and Richard walked over.

He held out his hand and said, "It's great to see you again, Mister Marlowe. Please have a seat next to me."

Richard picked up his beer from the bar and walked to the nearby table next to him. "Who are you, sir? Have we met before?"

"We most certainly have met. In fact, we've met a few times in the past. I'm Peter Nance. I met with Ben Yaro and Willow Barrett at the outdoor café when you came over and apologized to them. Remember now?" The old man sipped his vodka tonic.

"Oh, yes! I think I remember that meeting, but I'm sorry to say that I don't remember you."

"Well, I'm the executive producer of *The Isle of the Ages,* and also the sole investor in the project."

"So you're the man who pulls all the strings?" he asked.

"I am. I saw your audition on tape and I must say that it impressed me, despite what that idiot Yaro said, or the spoiled Willow Barrett. I fired him the next day and hired a much better director, Gary Norman. I'm sure you've heard of him, though. Willow Barrett is still the star of the picture."

"Sure, I've heard of him, and met him a long time ago. I remember him being a very friendly guy. I have to confess that I have not seen the movie yet. How did it turn out?" He ordered another beer.

Peter noticed a photo prominently displayed when Richard opened his wallet to pay for his beer.

"Who's that?" Peter pointed at the photo.

"Oh, that's my father and his sister, taken way back. It's the only picture I have of him," Richard explained as he closed his wallet and returned it to his rear pocket.

"He's a good-looking man. Looks a lot like you!"

"Yes, everyone says that. Now, how did the movie do at the box-office?" Richard asked.

"That's because we never started it. I didn't allow the filming to begin until we found you. It took me four years to do that. When you don't want to be found, you certainly can hide. I want you to do this picture, Richard. In fact, I need you to do this picture. You'll understand more later, but for now, please tell me that you will do it." His eyes twinkled as tears welled up.

Richard, not wanting to hurt the old man's feelings, informed him he had not acted in years and also, he did not know if he still could be believable. It amazed Richard that Nance had held the movie up for four years waiting for a relatively unknown actor to reemerge from the shadows.

"Why wait for me? There are very talented actors out there who are far better than I am."

"Have you been experiencing odd headaches at seemingly particular times?"

"Yes, I had them a long time ago, but they went away once I went back to Florida. Why do you ask?"

"Oh, I'm just curious. Getting back to your question, there is only one man who can play this role. That man is you. And the reason why I waited? Well, let's just say that I'm fulfilling a prophecy." He took the last sip of his drink and called for his assistant to push his wheelchair out of the bar.

"A what? A prophecy? What does that mean?"

"It's your destiny to become an actor, isn't it?"

"Well, yes, of course, I always thought that..."

The man held up his hand to stop him from talking and grabbed his hat. "Well, I'm trying to make your dream happen. If all goes according to plan, then all your questions will be answered and, perhaps, questions will be answered that you have not even asked. The driver will take you to see Gary Norman at eight o'clock tomorrow morning. Don't be late. He doesn't like tardiness on his productions." With that said, he instructed his assistant to push him out the door. He didn't look back, but Richard saw him wipe his eyes as he left.

That night, he slept well; he looked forward to seeing Gary Norman again, and the cast he left hanging just before Bronson's and Becky's deaths. Much of the cast he did not remember, but Willow held a special place in his mind for good and bad reasons.

Richard delivered heartfelt apologies to the entire cast before he uttered his first line. Honest and forthright, he explained why he'd left, and talked of the death of his best friends. He told them the sad story of his homelessness and the hardships of living on the streets. No one said a word.

Even Willow, who always had something bad to say about anyone, kept her mouth shut and allowed Richard to release some inner demons.

After his explanation, no one seemed to care about the four-year delay in the production, mostly because they'd all found jobs on other movies while they waited for Richard to return.

Gary Norman liked to act out scenes on stage, so he had a stage built in his massive theater room. He watched the actors in their raw state with no props or scenery to distract them. Alone, they held their scripts and talked to each other, but later, they ran through their lines, utilizing their acting gifts to make their words come alive with drama and grit.

The young director filmed each reading to show the actors how inflection and mannerisms completely changed the perception the way a person was depicted. He had a hard time trying to explain in words why he performed this procedure, but it appeared to have worked well for the three-time Oscar winner. Parts of these sessions actually made it to feature films he directed. All the actors had their turns, with the exception of Richard and Willow. She steadfastly refused to rehearse that way and exempted herself from the exercise. Most thought her anxiety heightened because of the scene where she had to passionately kiss Richard because she resented intimate scenes with a man she did not like or respect as an actor.

She called for the director to replace Richard with a more seasoned and established actor. For such an important role, she assessed that Richard's amateurish portrayal lacked authenticity. Willow had no issues with telling the director how she felt about Richard, even with him standing right beside her, seething with anger, listening to her hateful rants. He kept his anger to himself, but her attitude toward him made it difficult for him to act like a loving husband.

One week before filming started in Tahiti, Norman gathered his actors and staff together for a meeting in a local small theater with a large stage.

"Okay, everyone, gather around. I want to talk to you before filming begins. Everyone have their scripts?"

The group nodded that they did.

"I want to do a read-through one more time."

Willow, irritated, asked, "Again? How many times do we have to do this? I know my lines!"

Norman was tired of her prima donna attitude and said, "Shut up, Willow! I'm the boss here! Not you! On this film, you do as I say."

The cast and Willow were stunned at Norman's admonishment. Willow was not used to being talked to that way and sat mortified as Norman continued.

"Listen, Mr. Nance has put up a lot of money on this film and I want to have as few takes as possible. Every one of you are professionals, and I expect you will act as such."

Willow spoke up again and said, "All but Marlowe, that is."

"Enough, Willow! If you don't want to be here, then leave now! You were there when he read. You know he has talent, so knock the personal insults off."

Peter Nance, the executive producer and the man responsible for getting the film made, observed with great interest from a darkened corner of the theater.

Norman ran through the first scene with all the principal actors, and each delivered their lines to perfection, which impressed both the director and Nance.

When Peter saw them act on the stage, much of his past came back to him. He loved seeing them interact in the raw setting of the stage rather than on a movie screen. But even with a small audience, Willow refused to kiss Richard.

"What's with you, Willow? The scene calls for you to kiss Bronson."

"This is just a rehearsal! There are no cameras here. Why should I kiss him now?"

"Because it says so in the fucking script! Why are you being so difficult? I've worked with you on three pictures and you were never this difficult. Why start now?"

"When I'm around Marlowe, I get a painful headache. I don't know why. I can just imagine how I will feel if I kiss him."

Exasperated, Norman asked, "Did you read the book, Willow?"

"Of course I did."

"Did you read the script?"

"Yes!"

"Good, then you know that you have to kiss Richard

nearly fifty times during this movie. Am I going to get this throughout filming?"

"I can't help feeling the way I do. My head actually hurts when I'm around him! Why don't you believe me?"

"Because it's ridiculous, that's why. Okay, the two of you follow me to the office."

Peter slowly strolled down the aisle, walking with two canes, and called Norman over. None of the cast heard the conversation.

After the conversation, Norman motioned for his two stars to follow him. Norman invited Peter Nance to attend the meeting as well, given that delays could cost him millions. Peter's assistant walked up with his wheelchair and followed Gary, Richard, and Willow to the theater's backstage office.

When all were present and seated, Norman directed his anger toward Willow.

"This problem between you two has to be resolved here and now. I will not start filming knowing that I will have to cut scene after scene because of your petty bullshit, Willow. You are contracted for this film...twenty million dollars Mr. Nance here doled out for your talent, and I expect for you to be a professional and show us that we are not wasting his money! We start filming next week. Mister Nance has already paid a lot of money to rent an entire island, and we haven't gotten past the fact that you have an issue with kissing Richard. I want to know why, and don't give me that creative differences crap!"

Willow seemed overwhelmed and started to cry. "I'm sorry, but every time I draw near Richard, I get a massive headache and it hurts."

Richard opened up and confessed that he also had a severe pain when that important scene came about, but he endured it for the sake of the film.

Willow looked at Richard with tears in her eyes and said, "Oh, Bronson, it hurts, it hurts."

The director looked at Willow, even angrier. "You're acting right now, aren't you? You called him Bronson!"

Willow looked around, saw Peter Nance rise from his wheelchair and to his feet, and Richard open his eyes wide. "I didn't say Bronson, did I?"

Everyone nodded their heads in unison, and she began

crying again.

Richard thought that Willow might be having a nervous breakdown and stopped the director from berating her further. "Can't you see that she is hurting? I don't think that you yelling at her is helping." Richard made a point to walk over and hug her, despite his head pounding feverishly.

Willow felt surprisingly safe in Richard's arms. Willow embraced him, despite the searing pain that shot through her head. It was obvious that the director's harsh words hit their mark.

The embrace continued longer than any in the room thought it should. She stopped crying, looked into Richard's eyes, and saw a completely different man. He moved an errant lock of hair from her eyes and wiped the last tear from her cheek. She felt the gentleness of his warm touch. She suddenly found that her fears were unfounded. At that particular moment, she moved in to accept Richard's kiss, but the moment was not right and she stopped her lips from reaching out to his.

She felt confused as to why she'd felt that sudden urge. She ended the embrace, sat back down, and said, "I want to do the scene here and now. Fuck the headaches and my idiotic issues. I can kiss him now and throughout the film. You will have no more issues with me, Gary."

Willow experienced emotions that acting could not depict. She entered the throes of an emotional event that she could not explain, though she wanted to experience her confusion further, return to Richard's arms, and stare into his blue eyes.

Peter Nance usually showed little emotion, but he mustered a smile at the two actors' interaction. He remained standing. "Gary, can I have some time to talk to them alone?"

Although hesitant to leave, he relented if it meant that he had an easier time with the actors once the filming started.

Norman left and closed the door behind him.

Richard, Willow, and Nance were the lone occupants of the room.

"I'd like to do an experiment. Richard, I want you to enter the Bronson character for a moment, and I want Willow to be Catherine. Both of you have taken off from the dock, with Brooke and her husband Murray waving goodbye to you two for the last time. Do you remember the lines?"

Richard nodded.

Willow, wiping her eyes, said that she knew hers as well.

Richard asked, "Why are we doing this now? The director isn't here to critique it. Are we saying these lines just for your benefit?"

Nance slowly walked to Richard and placed his hand on his shoulder. "That is exactly why I'm asking you to do this. I need one more trigger."

"Trigger? What the hell does that mean?" Richard asked.

"Well, I should have said indicator. If I'm correct, then I have the most fantastic story to tell you. If I'm not, then this will help both of you interact well together to ensure a fantastic movie. Can you two trust me for a few lines?"

Willow stopped crying. "I will. I want this movie to be my best ever."

Peter kissed her on the head, thanked her, and had one more request. "I want you two to really feel that you are on the boat and are in love. I want you two to make me believe that you are Bronson and Catherine for the next few minutes, and that means movie quality acting."

Richard said, "I can do that!"

"I can do that as well," stated Willow.

"Well, this table is the 'Sailing into Our Sunset' boat and you are about to embark on what you think is your final voyage," said Peter, setting the scene.

Bronson and Willow climbed up onto the long table and held each other as Bronson steered the boat from the harbor and Catherine looked back and waved to her daughter. They delivered the well-written dialogue from memory.

Catherine:
Oh, Bronson, do you think we should do what we planned?
Bronson:
It's all changed now, sweetheart. I know you want to see our grandchild. I think we should just go out for a week and return. Hey, it's our anniversary! We deserve this.
Catherine:
I do love you, Bronson. I hope my condition holds off until the baby is born.
Bronson: (bends over and kisses Catherine)

It will, my dear.
Catherine:
I love you!
Bronson:
I love you too! Our wake is our past, our sails are full, and the horizon awaits.

Once Richard said his final line, Willow broke character, recoiled, and climbed off the table. She had a scared look on her face, but she could not explain her angst.

"That last line he delivered is not in the script." She cowered in her chair, deathly silent, shaking with an unknown fear.

Peter clapped his hands together and whispered to himself, "Bingo!"

He called for Willow to return to the table and asked Richard to step down and sit. Peter sat at the head. He implored Willow to join them. She reached into her purse and retrieved a photo of her mother. The worn photo of her long-deceased mother soothed her when fear gripped her. Her heart pounded as her hands shook. She stared at the photo for a few minutes until calm came to her and, instantly, the shaking stopped.

Peter smiled. "My dear friends, I have a story to tell you that will fascinate and possibly scare you. You see Richard, I wrote *An Isle for the Ages*."

"No, you didn't! The great-grandmother of my best friend, Bronson Worthington, wrote it," Richard corrected.

"It's true, her name is on the book, but I ghostwrote it. I took what she outlined and expanded it into the fanciful journey it turned out to be. I knew Bronson Worthington's great-grandmother Brooke very well. In fact, I knew Bronson and Catherine as well," Peter confessed.

Richard did not believe the old man. "That's impossible! Bronson and Catherine died over ninety years ago and you don't look a day over eighty."

"I know the math, but it happened to me, and it happened to Bronson and Catherine as well. Suppose I told you that Bronson and Catherine are still alive?"

"Pardon me, Mr. Nance, but you're delusional!"

"I'd have to agree with Willow; if they were alive, they'd

be like a hundred and sixty years old. Impossible!"

"Bronson Preminger is one hundred sixty-four years old and his wife Catherine, one hundred sixty-two! I realize that it's crazy to contemplate, but hear me out and I'll be happy to prove that what I say is true."

Richard looked at Willow and for the first time, they appeared to be on the same side in their conclusion that Peter Nance suffered from dementia.

Peter continued, "As actors, you have played fanciful characters in impossible situations. Well, at least you have, Willow. Regardless of how impossible the story is, you play it as if it's real, to make the audience believe what the story depicts. I'm asking you to step out of your real perception of what possible is and allow your mind to believe the impossible. At this particular time, I'm the actor and you're the audience. It's my job to make you believe what I'm telling you. Can you do that?"

Willow, intrigued, said, "Yes, I can do that. After all, I played many characters of legend in stories of complete and utter fiction."

"You have my attention, sir," confirmed Richard.

"It all boils down to fate. We live our limited lives, we procreate, and then we die. Fate has its limitations and dictates that we grow old and wither away to make room for a new population. Ponce de León, the Spanish explorer, spent his entire life searching for the fountain of youth. Well, I'm here to tell you that I found it in the form of a mysterious island, well off the coast of Florida. Bronson and Catherine Preminger set sail in 2013 and they suffered through many storms trying to get back to Florida and their daughter Brooke. Their boat capsized and sank. They were able to get their lifeboat off and floating before the boat sank and, as you know by the book, they were very strong swimmers and easily swam to the lifeboat. They spent days on the boat until they came across an uninhabited island and encountered strange, deadly plants, dragons, and other dangers."

Richard held up his hand to ask a question. "Now you are asking us to believe in dragons?"

Peter thought for a second. "Well, yes, I am."

Willow also spoke up. "This is fascinating. Richard, don't interrupt. Remember, we're the audience and I, for one, am

intrigued as to where all this is going. A little more experience in the field and you will see what I'm seeing."

Richard listened intently as she spoke, because she did
not deliver the usual hateful statement or demand. She delivered a thoughtful, respectful critique designed to inspire
him to be the best actor he could be.

Peter continued. "I forgot where I stopped? Oh yes, the
island. After being on the island for a few years, they noticed
changes in their physical appearance and the disappearance
of Catherine's illness. They noticed, over time, that they were
getting a year younger for every year they were on the island. They arrived on the island in their elder years. They
spent the remainder of their lives trying to get off the island
before they age-regressed into infants, ill-equipped to take
care of each other."

Richard again interrupted and stated, "That's not in the
book or the script."

Peter looked at Richard. "That's right. Brooke Preminger
wanted to tell an honest account, but she didn't know what
happened after their boat left the dock. I altered the story to
make the readers believe that they lived the remainder of
their days on the island and died together. Brooke didn't
know about the island. She just knew they were lost at sea,
but I convinced her to add the part about the island to relieve her tension and never-ending nightmares about her lov
ing parents' plight. She wanted to believe that they found
land, and I convinced her that it could have happened. She
never had another nightmare after that."

Richard, getting exasperated at the long story, wanted
Peter to get to the point. "You said that Bronson and Catherine were still alive. Where are they?"

Peter sat back in his chair and smiled, then leaned forward. "I'm looking at them! You two are Bronson and Catherine Preminger!"

Willow and Richard's mouths hung wide open as they listen to the preposterous notion. From that statement, Richard
stood and challenged Peter's assertion angrily. "I sat here patiently and I listened, but now I find out that I'm listening to
the ramblings of a deranged mind. Peter, I knew my mother
and I have a picture of my father right here with me."

Equally angry, Willow stated, "You're a ridiculous old

man. My parents are my parents. How the hell can you assert something like that?"

Peter allowed them to rant and rave as they tried to convince him that he could not have known the original Bronson and Catherine. Peter did not listen to their attacks on his sanity, because he knew what he knew and they each had the proof in their pockets. After they screamed at him for a few minutes, he made a simple request.

Peter raised his hands and requested that each of them remove their coveted photos. "Please, each of you place the photo that you hold dear on the table."

They complied and, as they did, Richard noticed Willow's photo. It shocked him. "Why are you carrying a photo of my father?"

"Why do you have a photo of my mother?"

Peter stood up and remarked loudly, "Stop bickering. These photos do not depict your parents. These people are you! You are Bronson and Catherine Preminger!"

They noticed that the picture of the younger couple that Willow possessed looked exactly like Richard and her at that particular moment in the director's office. Willow had not noticed it prior to Peter bringing it to their attention, but the evidence clearly proved it. However, not convinced, Richard challenged Peter to explain how they'd gotten to where they were.

Peter took a drink of water as someone knocked on the door. Gary Norman asked if he could have his actors back; he wanted to continue going over the script. Peter stood. "You can have them back soon. Have everyone go to lunch on me. Gary, if they dine together, they will bond as actors."

Gary, looking at the two actors' strained faces, asked, "Is everything okay in here?"

Both Willow and Richard answered in unison, "We're fine!"

Gary closed the door and took the entire cast out to lunch as Willow and Richard stayed behind to hear the rest of the story.

Peter continued. "I see that I've got your attention, but I also see that you both are skeptical despite the photos and the realization that the people in the photos are strikingly identical to both of you. I don't blame you. If an old man such as myself came up to me and told me this story, I wouldn't believe it either. Thirty-one years ago, I chartered a boat to search for the island. At the same time, a bad traffic accident caused me to be hospitalized for months. The boat still went out and found the island. They were there a week, looking for two children running around naked. I mentioned a cave at the top of a mountain at the southern tip of the island. They investigated and found two infants sleeping in the grass. They found the infant girl malnourished and dying. The young male looked to be two years old, malnourished as well, but stronger. They removed the children and went back to search for their parents, but only found three graves. The graves they found were unmarked, so they assumed that they were the children's parents.

"I didn't talk when they returned because of my injuries. They gave the children to the local authorities, thinking that I'd lost interest because of my unresponsiveness to their many attempts to contact me. Child Welfare Services determined through DNA that the two children were not related to each other or to me, so they were put up for adoption. The crew gave the Child Welfare Services two photos that they found on the island and stressed to the service that the photos were probably of their parents and should go with the children if, sometime in the future, they should want to find out who they were. Richard, you were adopted by your mother. I can't say why she hid your past from you, but whatever the reason, I'm sure she loved you. A single woman, her wish to become a mother escaped her because she couldn't have children of her own. She committed suicide, and alcohol drove her to it. I only recently found you when you walked up to the lunch table on Rodeo Drive as I discussed the movie with Yaro and Willow.

"I've been researching your past ever since. Imagine the shock of knowing who you really were and spending years searching for you with nothing to show for it, and then you merely walk up to the table. You walking into my life convinced me that fate employed me to put an end to this story. Willow, you were adopted by two very high-profile show business people, so you were easy to track. I made sure that I knew where you were once I found out that both of you were adopted. Fate brought us all back together. I hoped for your reunion in my lifetime. Fate made you an actor, Richard, and fate made you want to be in this movie, Willow. You turned down how many opportunities to be here, right?"

Willow spoke up. "Ten!"

"That's right! So, here we are! All together again."

Richard scratched his head, still not wanting to believe the preposterous story. "We? If all this is true, how are you involved in this?"

The old man stood up, smiled, and said something that sparked them both. "I'm not Peter Nance. My name is C.K. Corker, or Charles, as you referred to me, Catherine—I mean, Willow."

Both Willow and Richard screamed in unison, "Charles? Oh my fucking God!"

Peter replied, "At your service. We all have tempted, conquered, and defied fate, and now I think it wants to correct it all by ending my life soon and allowing you and Willow to get another lifetime together. You must have really loved each other to be the recipients of such a gift. A barge rescued me at twelve years old. They removed me from that rickety raft. By that time, it was in bad shape with leaks everywhere. Remember? The boat we moored just off the island helped prevent me from getting any younger, but sometime during the night, the anchor rope broke and I woke up in open seas without a sign of the island. A week later, I languished on a leaking boat. They brought me back to Florida. I tried to explain the location of the island, but I couldn't remember enough for many years after."

All of them were part of an impossible, extraordinary story told through the heart of a distraught and loving daughter and an anonymous ghostwriter who added a glorious ending just to appease a heartbroken Brooke.

Despite the overwhelming preposterousness of the situation and the revelations revealed to them, the headaches persisted with both Richard and Willow. However, their pain was numbed by the mystical story coming full circle. The two long-lost lovers stared a deep soul-searching gaze into each other's eyes, which brought about a more meaningful kiss.

Peter smiled at the couple from his wheelchair at the end of the table, and as sudden as their serendipitous meeting, a glorious explosion of two lifetimes of memories, long forgotten, returned to them from the darkest recesses of their mind. With 150 years of memories flooding their thoughts, their painful headaches subsided like a dam breaking to ease the pressure.

They parted and gazed a stunned stare at each other, not knowing if their thoughts were real or a conglomeration of vivid dreams all muddled together to create a singular utopian existence.

Richard said, "I don't know how or why we were chosen to be fate's experiment, but I remember you as a younger women in a different era, place, and time when I asked you to be my wife. Do you remember?"

"Yes, I remember that day now and all the days afterward."

Richard asked, "Do you remember what I said?"

"You said that a lifetime was not enough time to spend with me, but if I became your wife, our life together would test the bounds of eternity."

"Yes, and what did you say?"

Willow cried openly and without fear of whoever was watching and stated in broken, emotional words, "I said 'I don't know about eternity, but I'll settle with forever. Yes, I deeply, desperately want to be your wife.' I remember it as if you said it yesterday."

"It sure seems as if I said it yesterday, but just in case we've been given our eternity, care to see where it takes us?"

"Are you asking me to marry you...again?"

"Yes, I want to continue this magical ride with you. It's always been you."

"Yes...yes...yes!"

In their euphoria, they barely heard Peter say, "Easy, you two. You have a movie to make."

They embraced and kissed so hard that they fell to the lushly carpeted floor. Still on the floor, they could not see Peter. Richard helped a still emotional Willow up and asked Peter, "My best friend Bronson was related to Brooke. He told me that she was his great grandmother. Does this mean he was actually my great-great-grandson?"

Peter responded, "Yes. He and Becky were your last heirs. I'm sorry to say that all of them have died outside of a few in-laws here and there."

"He was our last heir? Damn, with his death, our line is

broken!" Richard sadly acknowledged.

Peter said, "Well, it's a miracle that you two are still here. Perhaps other miracles are out there waiting to be observed."

Willow looked at Richard with newly opened eyes. "I believe! Do you, Bronson, my love?"

Richard said, "I do, but I think we've used up our miracles quota."

Their hands locked tightly together.

When Gary returned from lunch, he walked in and noticed a sudden change in the once tense atmosphere. "Are we ready to make a movie, people?" he asked as he noticed how close together Willow and Richard sat.

Willow stood and said, "Yes, I'm ready, but first there's going to be a wedding when we get to Tahiti. I've agreed to be Richard's wife and he's agreed to be my husband."

"Whoa, Peter, that must have been quite a pep talk. What did you say to them?" asked Gary as he opened the door for a smiling, crying couple who seemingly were deeply in love when, an hour earlier, they had been at each other's throats.

Peter smiled and said, "I just introduced them to each other. Now let's make the best picture that has ever been produced in the two hundred years plus of the movie industry."

Epilogue

Richard and Willow were married on the set of the movie on an uninhabited island near Tahiti a few months later. They vowed to refer to themselves as Richard Marlowe and Willow Barrett in public; however, in the privacy of their own minds, they were Bronson and Catherine Preminger. They were as happy a couple as anyone had ever seen. But Peter had another miracle to deliver to them.

Peter scheduled the movie's release for a week before Christmas in New York City. He delivered his final gift to the newlyweds during the festivities. The stars of the movie sat to sign promotional material for the movie. Peter stood behind them as, one by one, they greeted the fans, signed a complimentary photo of themselves, and gave it them.

Richard, seeing Peter standing behind him, said, "What do you think of my new car, Peter?"

"It's beautiful. I had one exactly like it before the plane crash. A 1956 Cadillac convertible. Where did you find such a beautiful car?"

"Oh, I found it in Florida. I had to borrow the money from Willow to get it, but I did." Richard looked at Willow with a broad grin on his face.

"What are you two conspiring about? I've seen those grins before," Peter asked.

Richard threw him the keys and they both said, "Merry Christmas, Peter."

"What? That car is mine? No shit! It's mine?"

"Yes, I looked up a certain explorer and saw a picture of a young man proudly standing next to it. So, we thought that you'd like to have it back," Richard explained as he greeted the fans and signed their photographs.

"Where did you find one of those? I haven't seen one in

decades and I've been looking," he confessed.

Richard again smiled at Willow as she handed a photo back to a fan.

Peter commented, "Again with the smiles?"

"Yes, we are smiling because that car out there is not some random 1956 Cadillac. That is the original one in the photo that you once owned," Richard relayed.

"I don't know what to say, guys. This is one of the kindest things anyone's ever done for me," Peter confessed.

Willow turned around and hugged Peter. "You are our most precious gift and we love you very much. You have given us the greatest gift we could ever ask for. A chance to re-live our lives together. We wanted to give back a little of your youth as well. We love you, Peter."

Peter, overwhelmed with emotion, cried, and he told Willow to sit because his Christmas present approached the table. Willow and Richard looked at each other and watched as a teenage girl nervously approached the table with a photo in her hand. Neither Willow nor Richard recognized the beautiful young girl. She tried to talk to them, but her nerves got the best of her and she could not speak.

Richard saw that the girl shook with excitement. "It's okay, honey. We're just people. Do you want us to sign that?"

The girl, still shaking, placed the photo in front of them, and Richard took his pen and looked at her. "What's your name, sweetheart?"

The girl said, "My name is Tess. Tess Walker."

Richard's hand started shaking when he heard the name. "You're Tess Walker? You don't remember me, do you?"

The girl did not remember meeting him, so Richard explained. "Willow, this young lady saw a withered and worn homeless man sitting in the rain in Connecticut and gave him a five-dollar bill. He hadn't seen that much money in one place in many months."

"How do you know all of this?" asked Willow.

"Because I'm that man and she's that girl," stated Richard.

Willow and Richard stopped what they were doing, stood up, and hugged Tess. They asked her to step to the side because they wanted her to be with them for the rest of the evening when the promotional event ended. Tess cried at the fact that her favorite actors were so interested in her, given that her life had been so hard of late.

She shared a little about her life as a young girl growing up homeless after her parents died in a traffic accident. The story broke his heart to hear that when he left for California, the sweet young girl who'd helped him numerous times during his destitute days had been placed with abusive foster parents. She had eventually left the house for a troublesome life on the streets. Richard told Willow of her kindness to him when he was at his lowest point and wanted to make sure that her life would forever be altered for the better.

Tess stood proudly beside Peter. Richard and Willow saw him talking to Tess, and they wanted to know what they were discussing.

"Go ahead, tell them," Peter said.

"Tell us what?" Willow asked as she signed autographs.

Tess nervously approached and confessed, "I've already seen the movie, and I loved it."

Peter interjected and said, "No, tell them the other thing."

Tess nervously brought out a weathered old photo of a soldier. "This is my great-grandfather. He deployed and died in the Iraq war in 1990. His friend took this photo. While he was away fighting the war, my great-grandmother, Peggy Preminger, was pregnant with my grandmother. My grandmother told me that he wanted to keep their marriage a secret from his parents until after he came back. He didn't know of Peggy's pregnancy and she wanted to deliver the news once he returned from war but he never returned. His parents were Bronson and Catherine Preminger."

Willow fainted when she heard another twist to the story, but mostly from shock at hearing that her son, Bradley, had a child whom even he did not know about.

Emergency personnel revived her and sat her back in her seat. Peter announced the postponement of the promotional event to the next day and apologized to the ones who had been in line for hours.

Richard, Willow, Tess, and Peter left for the stars' elaborate suite. The large room amazed Tess.

Willow asked, "Where do you live, sweetheart?"

"I don't have a home. I live on the streets of Mystic Harbor, Connecticut, where that man in the wheelchair approached me. I told him my story and he asked me to come see you. I told him that I had no money, so he gave me some. I remember giving Richard that five-dollar bill, but I did not recognize you."

Richard looked at her shabby clothes and said, "That's okay, no one recognized me back then. You will live with us for as long as you want."

Willow concurred. "You bet your ass she is. I mean, yes, you can, Tess, for as long as you want."

Tess smiled and all could tell how elated she was that she'd come that fateful day.

Willow leaned into Richard and whispered, "Bronson, can you believe it? Tess is our great-great-granddaughter. Our line is not broken! We have an heir!"

Richard whispered back as Tess talked to Peter, "Remember that miracle that Peter talked about?" asked Richard. He embraced his wife and wished her a merry Christmas.

"Yes, I think we've just experienced it. I can't wait to spoil her rotten."

"We have many years in front of us to make that happen."

"Oh, Bronson, we've come so far," Willow said as a single tear of joy streamed down her face.

Peter wheeled his chair to the happy couple and said, "Well, here is where we part ways."

Richard asked, "Part ways? What do you mean?"

"I think it's time for me to take a sail," he responded.

Willow asked, "Where to?"

"To a place that will give me a tomorrow. I'm an old crippled man. I need to stretch these useless legs and curl my toes in the sands of an island that will give me that tomorrow and hopefully, many more."

Richard and Willow looked at each other and smiled. Willow reached down and kissed him on the cheek and said, "I bet it's beautiful there."

"When time and age brings you to the brink of death, come visit. You two will be most welcome."

Peter's assistant wheeled him away and he held up a weathered aged hand to wave goodbye and was gone but certainly not forgotten.

Richard said, "What an amazing man."

Willow smiled and agreed.

Richard said, "We have a lifetime to live, Sweetheart and possibly more."

"We do and I can't wait to live it. I want the twenty odd years that we spent apart back."

Richard embraced her and said, "Yep, the past is in our wake, there's wind in our sails, and the horizon awaits."

About the Author

A prolific writer, Gary D. Henry is an award-winning author who has penned twenty novels and touts several works-in-progress. Specializing in the field of horror and mystery, Henry is not shy about blending other genres into the mix. Averaging two to four releases a year, Henry's first publication came in September 2009 with the release of *The Westward Journey of the Nebraskan Wind*. Since then, several of his books have gone on to win awards, such as: *Opulence Among Us*, Honorable Mention at the 2012 Los Angeles Book Festival—DIY award; *Legacy of the Unsung*, First Place in the 2011 Halloween Book Festival—Time Travel Category; *Falling Waters*, Honorable Mention in the both the 2012 Paris Book Festival Award—General Fiction Category and the 2012 Beach Book Festival Award in New York; and the *Abel Conspiracy*, Honorable Mention in both the 2012 San Francisco Book Festival Award—General Fiction Category and the 2012 The Halloween Book Festival Award—General Fiction Category. Recently, Henry has dipped his pen in the genre of short stories after being compelled to write a story about Alzheimer's Disease, which claimed the life of his father Ray Henry.

Previously, Henry's career spans twenty-three years in the environmental field and an additional twenty years as a government defense contractor, where he continues to work and is where he discovered his knack for writing. As a technical writer for many years, he has written countless reports regarding testing procedures and testing results presented to government agencies for review and acceptance.

Among Henry's writing habits is the playing of old movies in the background, which nudges his subconscious so the words can flow. He is single and lives in Sterling, Virginia, where he has lived most of his life. Visit Gary D. Henry's website at www.garydhenry.com